BLOCKBUSTER

Richard H. Smith

TWICE TOLD TALES

To
Sung Hee

CHAPTER ONE

A shark, its mouth open and baring rows of jagged teeth, shot upward and closed in on a naked female swimmer. Someone help her, I caught myself thinking, almost saying aloud. This felt strange because I was looking at a movie poster, just arrived in the mail. But what a fantastic poster it was, seizing me in the primal gut and curbing my wish for a beach trip.

The title read *Jaws* in bold, red letters.

I placed the poster in the first frame customers would see when they entered the main theater lobby, smoothed each corner, and snapped the frame shut. In the mid-1970s, summers were a slow time for movie theaters, including ours in Durham, North Carolina. But *Jaws* would change this when it started in two weeks. The buzz about the movie was everywhere, and sell-out crowds were guaranteed.

The stubby, rounded shape of Horace Bullock emerged from the door leading up to the manager's office.

"What do you think, Horace?" I asked.

Bullock hitched up his lime-colored polyester slacks. He studied the poster.

"Folks love getting scared, Nate."

"You know it," I said.

A hopeful look came over his scarred and vaguely piggish face. I knew what he was thinking. As theater manager he got a five percent cut of our concession profits, and for Bullock, movies amounted to how much popcorn, soda, and candy we sold. That was it, period. He'd told me this after he promoted me to assistant manager the previous year, the day after my high school graduation.

Did Bullock know *Jaws* was a movie version of a best-selling novel of the same name? Probably not. And anyway, seeing people with books irritated him, got him riled. "Who do you think you *is*?" he had once asked, when he had seen me reading a book, *Tarzan of the Apes*. I had smiled with fake embarrassment and said nothing, figuring his question hid an inferiority complex better left alone.

Milton Spicer, a high school kid scheduled to work that evening, strolled in with his usher jacket draped over a shoulder and a fluorescent green comb planted in one side of his Afro. He was twenty minutes late, and he pretended to ignore Bullock, who was standing near the entrance, coiled and fixing to pounce.

"*Boy*," Bullock said. "That's the last time you'll be late working for me."

Milton froze his lanky frame for a second and hurled his jacket in Bullock's direction.

"I ain't your boy!"

Ducking the jacket's flight path, Bullock pointed his finger at Milton's face.

"I'll call you boy any time I want. You're fired. Now git. Move your butt out of here before I throw you out!"

Milton, his eyes wide and flashing with anger, reached in his pocket, whipped out a folding knife, and flipped open the blade. He jabbed the knife at Bullock, who jumped back like a bloated cricket.

"Hey, put that away," Bullock said, his voice pitching higher.

"What makes you think I want to work for your white ass?" Milton punctuated his words with long jabs.

"Nate, call the police!" Bullock lurched back further. Milton advanced with stutter steps, reminding me of Muhammad Ali.

Ignoring Bullock's order, I raced around the concession counter and placed myself between Milton and Bullock. I kept light on my feet and watched the knife, ready to snatch Milton's wrist and twist it behind him.

"Milton, cool it, back off," I said, our eyes meeting.

I got along well with Milton, and I figured he wouldn't hurt me. He lowered the knife, closing it with a dramatic snap. Lifting a fisted right arm, the salute of Black power, he pushed past the entrance doors into the early evening air.

CHAPTER TWO

"Calling him 'boy' wasn't a very good idea, Horace," I said, thinking I had to say something.

"Don't give me that," he said.

There was no point in pushing it. I bit my tongue.

Maybe I should have called the police. The knife, and the way Milton used it, was a scary surprise. And I didn't want Milton working for us either. I'd been getting on him for cussing around customers. His militant streak worried me more. He resented that white students now attended Hillside, an all-Black high school before the court-ordered desegregation of the Durham city schools happened several years earlier. I'd overheard him say to a friend, "Cream in coffee weakens it. I hate white people."

I could understand why he felt this way, but I hoped he'd made an exception in my case. But now this knife. Where was it heading? His getting fired was for the best.

Bullock checked his watch, as it was getting close to starting time for the first show.

He said, "Where's Hogan? Cain't anybody get to work on time?"

Phil Hogan was our projectionist. Like Milton, he reveled in arriving late, probably to annoy Bullock. But since he headed the local projectionist union, he came and went as he pleased.

Hogan was full of puzzles. A large, middle-aged guy

with a bulky strength, yet he walked with a faint wave of his hips, reminding me of Norman Bates moving up the stairs to attend to his mother in *Psycho*. His head resembled a cube, highlighted by a crew cut. His natural habitat had once been a Klan rally, but now he could jive talk like Shaft on a Harlem street corner. Hogan was halfway through a transformation, and the life-form poking out from the larva was a wacko species.

Hogan's '57 Thunderbird glided into the parking lot and took a reserved space. He exited the car and ran a finger over a smudge on the front whitewall tire. He ambled his way into the theater and then toward the door leading to the projectionist booth of the main theater.

Bullock bolted toward Hogan like he might tackle him. "What makes you think you can just come in when you want?"

Hogan blew him a kiss, disappeared through the doorway, and snapped the door shut, locking it behind him.

Bullock grabbed the doorknob and twisted it hard.

"Hogan, you open this goddamn door."

He cussed one ugly word after another, ignoring the customers already in line for concessions. I'd had enough. I left the lobby and checked the projector in our second theater.

This second theater had been added three years before, with a state-of-the-art platter system for showing the movies. Mostly automated, it was a natural threat to Hogan, who only took care of our older, bigger theater with its traditional, change-over projection unit. Why hire a projectionist if you could train managers to run the automated platters? This was the view of the theater chain owners. Projectionists were going the way of the dodo bird.

The theater company trained Bullock in using the equipment, and he showed me the basics too. While the projectionists' union fought with the owners over who could run the new machine, Hogan refused to run it. Bullock sided with the owners and wanted Hogan fired. I didn't enjoy being caught in the middle, but there it was.

After checking the projector, I found space in my head to think again about Milton. For a kid of sixteen and the son of two high school teachers, he'd used the knife with disturbing ease. Yes, I was relieved to see him go. I knew combative tactics from my dad, who had learned them while serving in Korea. I kept in practice at the downtown YMCA, and I'd even found myself in a few unsought fights growing up in Hickory, one involving a knife. But taking that weapon away from Milton, with the natural way he handled it, might have ended badly. Bullock was a brain-dead racist, but I was happy Milton wouldn't be with us anymore.

When I returned to the lobby, Bullock had retreated to his office. Customers now clustered at the ticket window, a larger crowd than expected. But we'd manage without Milton if I pitched in where needed. Bullock could stay in his office for all I cared. We were set for the evening. Soon, I had started *Rollerball* while Hogan got *The Conversation II* going in the main theater. We entered the calm between the five o'clock and the busier seven o'clock shows.

CHAPTER THREE

Carrie Jenkins, our best concession employee, lifted her face from the book she was reading, her bright blue eyes reflecting hints of her auburn hair. A dusting of freckles spread across her upper cheeks and nose.

"Do you think Milton will come back after Mr. Bullock? That knife was alarming," Carrie said.

"It will blow over," I said, trying to avoid staring at her. "I think he'll stay clear of us."

"You were fleet of foot, getting in between them like you did." She was impressed with what I'd done, which caught me off guard. But it made me feel pretty darn good.

"I wasn't worried about Milton," I said.

"But that knife."

"Yeah, that surprised me as well," I admitted, still basking in her praise.

"And Mr. Bullock has such a temper. Can he fire Mr. Hogan too?"

"Phil does his job."

I was more worried than I let on. And more about Hogan than Milton. Hogan constantly aggravated Bullock, usually making him blow a gasket, like what had just happened. Bullock razzed Hogan about being a sissy, often calling him "Phyllis" instead of "Phil." Hogan's reactions confused me. Sometimes he shrugged it off, swaying his hips more. Other times, he turned red and agitated, as if he struggled with why Bullock would ride him in this way.

Interestingly, as I had come to know them better, they seemed more alike than different. They were the same age for starters, around fifty-five. Both came into the world in the back of some turnip truck in rural North Carolina and achieved little education beyond grade school. Only Bullock, however, took an in-your-face pride in his ignorance.

There was one other thing. Sex consumed them both. As far as I could tell, Bullock saw all women as burdened with hang-ups caused by abstinence, a problem best solved by him. He made the point more crudely when he shared this philosophy with me one slow evening. He kept a cot in the back room of his office for women he paid to prove his theory. As for Hogan, an unstoppable flirt, he came aglow like a firefly around every cute high school boy we employed.

In any case, they despised each other, and I hated the danger zone this created.

Carrie said, "You get along with Mr. Bullock. He likes you. I can tell."

"I don't use big words around him."

"That's the secret?"

"Actually, I think it's because I improved the way we make popcorn. He gets a cut in concession profits."

"That's why? Really?"

"That simple. Before I started here, he had the kernels popped in advance, stored in bags, and reheated. I convinced him and the district manager to let us make it fresh, and with better oil and seasoning."

"We do make exquisite popcorn," Carrie said.

"One whiff, instant craving," I said. "The popping sound helps too. Mr. Bullock noticed the difference in how much we sell. Kept me, keeps me, on his good side."

"And they require drinks and candy to go with it, right?" Carrie said.

"You're thinking like Mr. Bullock," I said, pleased by the unexpected back and forth.

"Uh-oh," she said, a hand covering her mouth in a teasing show of concern. We both laughed. This was fun. How could I keep the conversation going?

"Like the book?" It was *Fahrenheit 451*. I'd seen the Truffaut movie version on TV and had started the book, never finishing it.

"It's an easy read," Carrie said with a shrug.

"Watch out when Mr. Bullock comes down," I reminded her. He didn't like employees reading on the job, even during slow times, but I let it go.

I added, "I bet he'd love a book burning."

"You've read it?" Carrie gave me a puzzled look, which I think embarrassed her, because she blushed a little. Why should she assume I hadn't read the book and knew about the book burning in the Bradbury novel?

"Sure, a while back, well most of it." I didn't mention Truffaut. It was from the movie that I knew about the book burning.

One of our ushers, Billy Gossett, who had finished sweeping the main lobby, handed me a magazine across the concession counter.

"Mr. Burton, have you seen this?" he asked. It was the *Time* magazine article about *Jaws*. "During a pre-screening, it says here that some people were so scared they ran out of the theater and threw up."

"That's great," I said. "The scarier the better for us."

"Yeah, and they ran back in. This will be *dyn-o-mite*."

I figured Billy hoped to get Carrie's attention because he looked more at her than at me.

"Love at first fright," she said. I let out a spontaneous laugh, surprising myself in its intensity.

Carrie was so smart. She had taken classes at Duke University where her dad taught history. She'd be starting college in the fall and heading to the University of Chicago. This impressed me, even intimidated me, since I had about as good a shot of going there as flying to the moon.

Billy looked confused. Was I the only one who appreciated her clever comment? Maybe he craved her attention so much that, oddly, he missed it. Poor kid. No Casanova, he spoke in a squeaky voice when excited. Scrawny and cursed with acne, Billy had pimples on his pimples.

I didn't blame him for liking Carrie. She got cuter every day. But dream on. Perhaps a world existed in which he'd have a chance. Not likely, for him or me.

And she had a boyfriend, Owen Becker, whose VW van I now spotted entering the parking lot, with its side panels decorated with psychedelic flowers easily passing an Electric Kool-Aid Acid Test. Owen found a space, and I studied him as he exited and approached the theater in his smooth, carefree way, his hands half-slipped into the front pockets of his low-slung jeans. Slim and good looking, with shoulder-length hair parted in the middle, he could pass for Jackson Browne.

He entered the lobby, and I noticed flecks of bleached gold in his hair probably from early summer visits to the Outer Banks, where I'd heard his oceanographer dad studied marine life. Owen was one lucky bastard.

I thought about my own contrasting look in the cheap, black theater jacket and tie and the assistant manager pin I had to wear. The picture of *un*cool. At least I had an inch or two on him in height. But most people gave me curious stares when they first met me. I assumed it was the slight Asian slant to my eyes, which I got from my Korean mom. This jarred with my dad's light brown hair. What was I, the stares seemed to ask. And unlike Owen, my smile didn't enjoy the benefits of an orthodontist's straightening. His teeth were too perfect to conclude otherwise. Sadly, the few times we'd exchanged words, I'd found him self-assured and sophisticated, the boyfriend you'd expect Carrie would have. He was also starting college in the fall, at Northwestern. Had they picked schools near each other? I didn't like him.

I felt I was missing out, that theater work, or something close to it, was my lot in life. Carrie and Owen lived in a world of exotic advantages beyond my reach. Would I be watching from the dugout? Around Bullock, I wanted to sound ignorant. Easy enough. Around them, I had the opposite goal of sounding educated, for which there was no quick fix. But longing over other people's advantages was foolish, wishful wanting. A man in hell would want a drink of water too, as my dad had been fond of saying. I could hear his voice.

At nineteen, I wasn't much older than Owen and Carrie, a fact I didn't advertise. If everyone thought I was older, this probably helped me in my role as assistant manager. And anyway, events in my life had forced me to grow up fast, and so I acted older than my age. I had lost my mom when I was nine, and my dad four years later.

I moved to Durham to live with my uncle after my dad passed, but I was on my own by eighteen, finding a room in an elderly woman's place near downtown. It was in a neighborhood on the decline, and she liked my being around because she had suffered two break-ins. I kept watch over her property.

This was about the time I started at the movie theater since it gave me the days free for school. I kept the theater job after high school and was promoted to assistant manager. I had hoped to start college right away, but having no financial help, I waited.

Owen said as soon as he saw me. "Hate to tell you this, but you misspelled 'starting' on the marquee."

"I don't think so," I said, hiding my irritation at his cool and confident voice.

"Yeah, you did, man."

I couldn't see from where I stood, so I moved to the far side of the lobby to check. *Damn*. He was right. Earlier, I had added a line to the marquee announcing that *Jaws* would be "STRATING SOON." I had reversed the letters.

"That was stupid," I said under my breath. My face flushed, but I kept my back turned to everyone. I pushed through the nearest exit door.

The marquee stood on two thick polls about thirty yards from the theater. A narrow walkway with a waist-high railing wrapped around the lower part of the sign itself. I climbed the metal rungs running up one pole and squeezed through the entry door to the walkway. After fixing the letters, I glanced down to the lobby and saw Owen pointing toward the marquee as Billy laughed, Carrie too it seemed. Blood inflamed my face and neck.

CHAPTER FOUR

I needed time to steady myself. After climbing down from the marquee, I took a few minutes to collect stray cups and candy wrappers. Had Owen intended to embarrass me? I wasn't sure, but he had me rattled. But when I returned to the lobby, Carrie was back to reading her book. Where was Owen? Maybe he'd snuck into one of the theaters. Fine with me. The whole thing suddenly seemed unimportant and forgotten. I went to check the projector in theater two.

I heard a troubling sound coming from the top platter of the projector. What did this mean? With each revolution, and at the same point, the film slowed down along a feeder arm and scraped against the platter, almost freezing. It didn't sound right, didn't look right, not what the illustration in the machine manual recommended. Also, the print of *Rollerball* was old. We were the third theater to show it. I had noticed many splices in the film where it had broken and been repaired. Would it break again? Would the platter malfunction? A nightmare thought of having to deal with a frustrated crowd wanting refunds unnerved me, but I couldn't see fixing the problem. I made a mental note to call the main office first thing in the morning to request a service visit. I would need to check it more often too.

Returning to the lobby, I saw Bullock trying to start up a conversation with our cashier, Samantha Hicks. Good luck. I'd shown her the *Jaws* poster earlier, asking her opinion. All she'd said was, "That's sick," her thin lips narrowing even further as they parted. In the full three weeks she'd been working for us, I'd never seen her in a good mood. Why someone couldn't get just a little excited over this movie, and our getting it in particular, was beyond me. The movie had me stoked.

Samantha wore glasses tinted with gray, adding a flat, distant quality to her eyes, as if shaded in with pencil lead. She had just turned twenty-two, at least based on the date she put on her job application. Her hair was blonde and thick, like bristles on an exotic animal. And she carried a lot of pounds, her spreading flanks swallowing the seat of her swivel chair, challenging its strength. I felt sorry for her, but she always had a Coke and an open box of Peanut M&M's at her side.

Bullock asked her, "Got enough twenties?"

He stretched his hand over the cash drawer to examine a stack of bills, his elbow brushing up against her left breast. She flinched and jerked her body away from him.

"You gave me enough." She took an angry suck on the straw of her drink like it was an intravenous tube on which her life depended.

Bullock shrugged his shoulders and continued a quick thumb-through of the stack. He probably assumed his touching her would stir her interest. And I guess it was how he tested the waters because I think he liked her, I mean in an oversexed way, which seemed his only way. The test disgusted her, and I didn't blame her one bit. I'd have paid to see her deck him cold.

Two high school girls came in with soft drinks. They must have come from having a meal at the nearby Hardee's and were finishing their drinks. Bullock shot toward them like a mongrel terrier defending his front yard from intruders.

"Can't you girls read the sign? There's a trash can over there."

Bullock hated people sneaking in food or drinks. Those girls might as well be stealing from his wallet.

They rolled their eyes and threw the cups into the trash.

A middle-aged man wearing a U.S. Navy cap entered with a bag of chips partly hidden by a sports jacket. Here we go again. More trouble.

"Friend, you'll have to toss those chips. We don't allow food from outside," Bullock said, half-politely this time, I guessed because the man's wife tailed behind him. And Bullock was about five-five, with wedges added to his wingtips.

"None of your business, *friend*."

"Damn straight it is," Bullock fired back, instantly losing his cool. He reached to lift the man's jacket.

This wouldn't end well. The man swept Bullock's arm aside. Bullock lunged again, gripping the jacket and yanking it.

"Gimme that bag," Bullock said.

"Like hell I will," the man replied, swinging his other arm. His elbow connected with Bullock's nose. The bag went flying and hit the wall. It was already open, and chips scattered.

I again raced from behind the concession counter and pulled the now bleeding and stunned Bullock away from the man.

His wife also leaped into action. "Earl, Earl. Stop!" she said, grasping both his arms from the back.

I said to Bullock in a low voice, close to his ear, "Calm down. It was an accident. You're gonna get yourself into trouble."

Bullock tried to take a swing at the man, but I held him tight. I had a good six or seven inches on Bullock, and although I may not have looked it, I was wiry strong.

"Let's go, Wanda," the man said as he grabbed her hand. "This guy's a moron."

Releasing one of Bullock's arms, I snatched a few napkins with my free hand. He took them from me, holding them against his nose to catch the bleeding. His eyes looked vacant and unfocused. I guided him over to the door leading to the manager's office and steered him up the stairs, relieved that he then took my direction.

I called out to Samantha, "I need a ten and two passes."

She gave them to me, and I caught up with the couple before they reached their car. I apologized for Bullock's behavior and convinced them to see the movie for free.

"Who will make up the ten?" Samantha asked when I returned.

Her eyes, normally so dull, now sparked through her glasses, as if a match suddenly flamed inside her. Then, just as suddenly, the effect faded, the flame snuffed out. I wasn't sure I'd seen it.

"I'll take care of it. You won't come up short."

Why would she think I'd make her accountable for the ten when we compared the final take-in cash with the ticket numbers? It was the second complete sentence she had said all evening, leaving me irritated. When it came to Bullock, I was on her side, but she gave me no good reason to like her either.

CHAPTER FIVE

I took the stairs to Bullock's office and found him in bad shape, his nose swollen and purple, his eyes streaked with red. He already smelled of the whiskey from the Jack Daniels he kept in a desk drawer.

"Looks nasty. Think it's broken?" I asked.

"Naw, that's no problem. Sue Ellen, she found out about a woman I bring up here. She let me have it."

What could I say? He had told me about his female companions, but we weren't friends, and I preferred it this way.

"Damn if that woman didn't call Sue Ellen," Bullock continued, slurring his words. "Why'd she have to do that? I owed her cash, but I thought she liked me. Now, Sue Ellen says I cain't go home."

"I don't know, Horace," I said. "She is your wife."

"She knows I'm hot-blooded. She knows that. I've always had a lot of, you know, lead in my pencil. She *knows* that about me," Bullock said, as if he were the wronged party. That was one way of putting it, I thought.

He shook out a cigarette from a pack of Marlboros he kept in his shirt pocket and lit it with his Bic lighter. I saw the primitive wheels turning in his mind as he sucked in and funneled out the smoke.

I wondered what would happen to him. What a patch-work of scars he had on his face from a lifetime of idiotic

fights. His left ear was cauliflowered. I found it impossible
to feel bad for him. With all his glaring defects as a human
being, he went around acting superior to everyone, Black
people especially. It left a stench.

"I'll get you some coffee," I said, noticing the coffee
maker half full. The whiskey had loosened his tongue way
more than I was curious.

I poured coffee into a mug, one with a pink silhouette of
a Playboy rabbit on both sides, and placed it in front of
Bullock. He slurped it down, his lips extended and flapping
like a camel from the zoo.

"Nate," he said, hesitating. "There's another thing. I owe
money. A ton."

Now what? Several evenings ago, a man had confronted
Bullock outside the theater. His square jaw and forehead,
together with the close-fitting dark suit and tightly knotted
tie he wore, reminded me of the gangster played by Harvey
Keitel in *Mean Streets*. I had been unable to make out the
conversation, but the man had finger-pointed and yelled.
Uncharacteristically, Bullock hadn't fought back. Was this
the person Bullock owed money to?

"Hey, when *Jaws* gets here, things will pick up, Horace.
Concessions will go through the roof," I said.

"I need it more sooner than that."

He rubbed his eyes, now so full of worry, almost fear.
Most of the time his thoughts bounced around in a self-
congratulatory echo chamber. Circumstances had forced
him to do something rare, to reflect on the consequences of
his behavior.

What about his car? He drove a new Chrysler Cordoba. What was he doing driving a luxury car? A tacky, bright yellow, but he could sell it, easy. He had another car, an old Ford Falcon.

"How about selling your Cordoba? You could get a lot for it." I tried to find within me an ounce of pity.

He glared at me as if I'd recommended selling his daughter to the highest bidder. "I couldn't do that. Anyway, I owe too much on it. And I love that vehicle, more than anything."

He stumbled, slack-jawed, over each word, the coffee having no effect on the alcohol in his bloodstream. He mashed his cigarette in the desk ashtray. Then, his mind seemed to go blank. Or a voice inside told him to shut up.

I knew the car was special to him. He washed and waxed it every week and sprayed the tires with something that kept them shiny black. But his days enjoying the Cordoba were numbered. The bank would take it away.

Wild, evolving images of Bullock's future came to me. He was careening down a narrow mountain road in his Cordoba chased by some goons in a black sedan, one guy firing a gun from a side window. A woman in the passenger seat with poofed-up hair and thick makeup hammered his head with her fists. Sloshed with Jack Daniels, Bullock pumped the brakes, but the car gathered speed instead. The images seemed so real. Things were closing in on him, and it wouldn't be pretty.

I returned to the lobby. He could stew in his troubles.

Samantha had already taken off, leaving her cash drawers for me to bring up to Bullock. She sometimes got a ride from a small, bony man with a wedge-shaped face. He drove a pickup with an oversized Confederate flag decal on the back window. He had been leaning against the truck for a good half hour, smoking. What an odd pair, I thought. If they were a pair.

Owen, lucky him, was waiting for Carrie in his van. Maybe he hadn't snuck into a theater after all. As they drove away, I fought off a rush of jealousy.

I took both the ticket and concession drawers up to Bullock's office. He was open-mouthed and asleep, his head leaned back and his nose even more blue and puffy from the hit he'd taken. Perhaps his mother would have been moved to pity. Me, not so much.

Placing the drawers on the desk jolted him awake. Without looking up at me or saying a word, he licked his thumb and began counting. Money was filthy stuff, but he didn't care. He loved counting bills, wrapping them by denomination, and rolling the coins.

"A good haul," I said, although his routine never failed to disgust me.

He said, "Sweet-smelling cabbage."

The coffee might have started helping because he no longer slurred his words. Evidently so pleased over the profits from concessions, he suggested I leave early when *Rollerball* let out.

"Want me to make the deposit?" I said, secretly preferring not to do it. But I figured he might need to stay overnight at the theater and use his cot. Bullock usually handled the job of placing the deposit bags in our bank deposit box on the upper deck of a nearby mall. But, sometimes, I did it.

"I'll shack up later with my buddy, Wayne. I'll do it." Great. I was off the hook.

To make the deposit, all we had to do was unlock a chute by the side of the bank and insert the bags. The chute was just to the side of the main entrance at the end of a bridgeway stretching from the upper parking deck to the mall. A lamp above the entrance provided plenty of light, but the area was deserted at that time of night unless the cleaning crew was still working. I felt exposed and defenseless. The place got me jumpy.

"Swofford?" I said. He was Bullock's main gambling connection, I figured from things Bullock had told me.

"Yeah, Wayne Swofford's my buddy." Buddy? I wondered. Swofford was playing him for a fool. I was sure of it. But how much did I care? This was a bed he had made for himself.

I said, "Oh, the platter system is acting up. It doesn't look good."

"What? Damn," Bullock said, as if he suddenly remembered that he had other responsibilities. "I need to take a look at that daggum thing tomorrow." He grabbed a few antacids from a jar he kept on his desk and crunched down on them.

"We need to call the main office to have it checked out, Horace."

"How about you do that for me?"

"First thing in the morning," I said. Why didn't *I* get a cut of the concession profits?

CHAPTER SIX

On my way home, I made a long detour through the Duke University side of town. A full moon created a smoky brightness as if a late dusk or an early dawn was frozen in time. I had seen Carrie's address on her job application, and I knew her home was in the Duke Forest area. This was where the University sold lots for faculty to build homes. I had never driven through the area, even near it, since I lived on the other side of Durham. I hoped to see where Carrie lived.

The faculty houses were on streets intersecting with a two-lane highway that wound through the mostly pine-forested land. It didn't seem like a residential area at first because broad sections of trees lined both sides of the highway cloaking all but a few blurry outlines of homes. I turned onto the street where Carrie lived, slowed, and followed the street numbers on the mailboxes, looking for her address.

The lots were big, and each house had its own, unique design. The first, set on an upward slope, had a set of white columns florescent in the moonlight. Facing opposite was a single-story structure, spread out in sections, no section alike. Its driveway had two entrances circling to a front entry door.

I felt pricks of longing. These were homes likely built with the owner's preferences in mind and with the help of a well-paid architect. That would be fun. I had lived in small, simple homes, all looking much the same. Not that the owners of these faculty homes were wealthy. They probably weren't. Yet they had enough money to build homes reflecting their separate tastes. And I could only assume that what went on in these homes was as interesting as their exteriors suggested. I wondered whether one could guess the academic area of its owner by the details of each design. I wanted what these people had, and with each home I passed, I felt smaller and more trapped.

The road took a wide, sweeping curve, and then sloped downward. Each home continued to vary. But as the road shifted back and upward, crossing several other streets, the lots shrank and the homes less varied. Some fronts were more like what I was used to, such as split levels and ranch styles. These looked older too.

I saw Carrie's house number. My pulse raced. I didn't dare stop, but I was intensely curious to learn what I could about it. It was a two-story home, ordinary by the standards set by the first homes, and less distinctive than I expected for a historian owner. Perhaps historians were low on the faculty pay scale. Light shone from a second-floor window. I imagined it might be hers. Was she reading?

No. Owen's van was in the driveway. Anger surged through me. I felt betrayed. But what right did I have to feel this way? What should I have expected? A rush of competing emotions caused my heart to pound, scrambling my thoughts. I sped down the street and left the neighborhood, awash in ugly feelings, and even more angry that they surfaced in me so strongly. Never had I been so thrown off balance, so full of desires, so dissatisfied with myself, so full of frustration and bitterness. I slammed my palms against the steering wheel, causing them to sting.

Hoping to turn my thoughts away from what I'd just seen, I switched on the radio. After scanning a few stations, I heard someone refer to *Jaws*. It was the last part of an interview with Richard Zanuck, one of the producers of the movie.

The interviewer said, "Mr. Zanuck, it's interesting that you picked a director, Steven Spielberg, who's not well known. Are you trying to enhance his career?"

"No, just the opposite," Zanuck replied. "I'm trying to enhance *my* career. I know how good this guy is, how he can tell a story. I knew this kid will do something brilliant."

Shifting to another topic, the interviewer said, "Some time ago there was a story in *Time* magazine. It had a photo of the mechanical side of the shark."

Zanuck said, "Yes, the photo got out and wound up in *Time*. We all were worried about it. Steve thought that it might kill the picture. The curtain was pulled back, ruining the scare. But, like I said, it's not been a problem."

"Yeah, I've heard when some of the actors see the movie, even they get into the story and go with it. Like it's real."

"It's a great story," Zanuck said, ending the interview.

I got to thinking about how different it would be at the theater when this movie started. We had sold out the larger theater for *The Godfather II*, back during Christmas, but only the first weekend. We had run out of ice, and we wouldn't want that to happen again. Not during the summer.

I reached home and turned up my driveway. The kitchen light was on. Mrs. Roe, my landlady, didn't sleep well and often waited up for me. I cut the engine. She must have heard the tires on the gravel. By the time I'd exited the car and reached the rear of the house, she stood at the top of the back steps.

"Nate, let's come in, shall we? Join me for a cup of tea?" she said in her British accent, still strong although she had arrived from England with her husband in the early 1950s.

"You bet I would."

Her slender, bent shape was in partial shadow, but I could make out the outline of her smile. An angle of kitchen light gave a sparkle to her kindly eyes.

"Why the long face?" she asked, as she held the door open for me.

"I'm fine," I said, not expecting my sour mood to be so obvious.

Byron, her old Lab, wheezed out a greeting and dragged his arthritic body across the linoleum in my direction. Keats, her Siamese, roused himself from his cat bed and offered me a bored look.

I put the book I was carrying down on the kitchen table. It was *The Last of the Mohicans*. Mrs. Roe had encouraged me to try it a few days before.

"How do you like it?" Mrs. Roe asked as she moved over to the stove, a kettle of water already heating. A rerun of a

Columbo episode played on the small black-and-white TV she kept on her counter. She turned down the sound.

"I very much like it. It's just that, you know, I read so slowly. I like Hawkeye."

She seemed about to say something and reconsidered. Instead, she said, "Yes, yes, Hawkeye is a man's man, I dare say."

"He's good with that long rifle."

"Rather," she agreed with a laugh.

Several months back Mrs. Roe had suffered a mild heart attack, and her face had the pallor of someone with a weak heart. But with this laugh, color spread across both cheeks. She had such a good-natured face, although she thought herself ugly, claiming to have a long nose. She joked that she looked like the Wicked Witch of the West in *The Wizard of Oz*. It looked long if you only focused on it, but it fit her face so well it didn't seem so long after all. And she had an irrepressible good spirit, which, along with the trusting affection Byron gave me, fully defused the lingering effects of my drive through the Duke Forest.

I told her about the shark movie we'd be getting.

"I'm not terribly fond of sharks," she said with a frown, as she poured steaming water into a teapot.

"Me neither. But I want a good movie. This one will be great."

"Well, I'll tell you, my late sister lost her sweetheart at sea near Malaysia during the early part of the war, a frightful thing. From sharks, we found out later from one survivor. I shan't go into it. She never married."

"I'm sorry that happened, Mrs. Roe."

"My husband was lucky. He had a year of university training in chemistry before the war started. So, instead of combat they sent him to a research unit. Farnborough, it was. As fate would have it, one of his projects involved creating a shark repellent sailors could use if they found themselves 'in the drink.' The trick was to find something those beasts would dislike but wouldn't hurt the men if they swallowed it. Peter's team worked like Trojans but never mastered it."

"That's too bad."

I had not known this about her late husband.

"It was a pity, but they used a similar concoction for something else. They coated it on mines used to target Jerry U-boats. Otherwise, the meddlesome sharks would bump into the devices, setting them off prematurely."

Mrs. Roe put milk in two cups and filled each with tea. I added sugar to mine and stirred it with a teaspoon.

"Must have been heady times," I said.

"Yes, goodness knows." Her face clouded over, and the pallor returned.

"Anyway," she continued. "Bless 'em all, the long and the short and the tall. A dreadful war for soldier or sailor. As if the Jerrys and the Japs weren't enough, our men, and women, mind you, had to contend with those horrid creatures too. And that is that about that."

We were silent for a while. I tried to imagine being tossed into shark-infested waters, thanking the fates I'd come along at a different time and circumstances.

The *Columbo* episode ended as usual with someone arrested and taken away by the police and as Detective Columbo, wearing his disheveled trademark raincoat, looked on. The first credit appeared, the name of the director causing me a double-take. It was "Steven Spielberg." Did he cut his directorial teeth with TV dramas, I wondered?

I took my cup and said, "Tell you what, Mrs. Roe. You look tired. I'll take Byron out for a last round. I'll bring the tea out with me."

"I am feeling rather old and tired. I'm sure I do look a bit pale around the gills."

"You turn in, Mrs. Roe. I'll clean up."

"Thank you so much, Nate. To bed, to bed, sleepyhead. Good night, then."

She did seem much paler than usual. She left her tea untouched.

CHAPTER SEVEN

Around ten the next morning I came into work to do the weekly inventory. As I approached the theater from the main road, I saw an ambulance backed up near the entrance. Three police cars with lights flashing blocked access to the building and parking lot. Someone must have been hurt. Who was it and why next to the theater? Several clusters of onlookers stood close to a perimeter marked by yellow police tape.

I parked across the street and approached one of the police officers guarding the taped-off area. He wore mirrored sunglasses and a stiff, broad-brimmed hat, reminding me of the prison guard played by Morgan Woodward in *Cool Hand Luke*. The thought disturbed me. His name tag read, "Roy Slocum," which somehow added to the effect.

"Officer, what's going on? I'm the assistant manager here."

He didn't seem to believe me because he hesitated for a moment. I wasn't wearing my jacket and tie and must have looked too young for a manager. But why would I lie about this?

"Someone found a dead body by the side of your building."

"What?"

The air was already thick with muggy heat, but an icy current swept through me. I looked over to where three jacket pocket and wrote in it. He looked over the area and waved to the ambulance crew, the signal to collect the body.

Seeing the medics lift Bullock's body chilled and transfixed me. I'd expected it to be limp, but it was rigid and bent. He'd been dead for a while, I concluded, since around midnight, the usual time to make the deposit.

A dried, broad collar of blood stained the front of Bullock's shirt and suit. It came from his throat, cut from one side to the other. I retched at the sight. I was familiar with death, having endured both my mom and dad passing away. I'd seen a boy drowned at Lake Mickie, the memory of his pale blue, lifeless frame stretched out on the dock still vivid. But I'd never seen a murdered body, much less one butchered this way.

The paramedics placed Bullock's body on a stretcher and covered it with a sheet, lumpy because of the twisted way his body had stiffened. Soon, the ambulance headed away with a sobering lack of urgency. Horace Bullock was gone from this world.

"Like I said, stick around," Slocum said. "What's your name again?"

"Nate Burton. I'm not going anywhere."

I guess it wasn't this guy's job to make friends, but why did he have to be so unfriendly—as if I were a certain suspect? Again, I wondered whether I'd have to clarify where I had gone after I left the theater the previous night.

When would we be opening the theater? I didn't want to handle a busy Saturday managing on my own, not after this grisly murder. I needed to call Dan Drucker, the district manager.

When would they question me? How about Phil Hogan? They would learn about the hatred between him and Bullock. They would be talking with both of us soon. As bad as I felt for Bullock, I found myself more focused on figuring out what had happened and why. I wanted to watch the police do their jobs.

"Who found him?" I asked.

"The Black guy next to the mower," Slocum said, matter-of-fact.

It was Spence Reeves, standing off to the side, but within the taped-off area. He was the elderly man who did part-time cleaning and groundskeeping for us. He usually came in early on Saturday mornings to mow the grass and had probably discovered the body while mowing. The sun flared above and behind him. With his Stetson hat he was fond of wearing and the dignified way he carried himself, he reminded me of John Wayne in *The Searchers*, outlined by the sun. His right arm held his sickle, his favorite tool for trimming the grass. For a brief second the sharpened edge of the blade caught the sun.

When would Mr. Bullock have left to make the deposit?"

"Probably around eleven-thirty, after the second movie let out," I said, realizing that this was exactly a period during which I had no alibi. Bad luck for me, but I told myself to calm down. They'd have to catch the real person who did it.

"Mr. Reeves and Mr. Hogan would have left by then too?"

"Phil Hogan would have taken off after shutting down the projector in the main theater, about the same time Mr. Bullock did. Mr. Reeves would still be cleaning the theater, which likely took another half hour, no more than an hour."

Riggs continued to press, "Who, besides you, knew the procedure for making the deposit?"

He didn't ask these questions rapidly, but he didn't waste time either. He kept the relaxed drawl, each question following on the next as if he would be taking one sure step after another to figure it out. I had the image of someone needing to strip a wall covered with stained wallpaper and achieve clarity by doing so, piece by piece.

"Mr. Reeves and Mr. Hogan, and our cashier, Samantha Hicks."

I paused, now controlling my initial alarm and giving him time to write the names.

I said, "But we're careful about this. It's often a lot of cash. We always leave the theater with the bags hidden in something. At least I do. Don't like doing the deposit, to be honest. I feel defenseless. Someone might be out there watching me."

"A bullseye. I can see what you mean," Riggs said, surveying the entrance area. "I don't recall this place being robbed before."

"It's not leaving the theater that gets me most worried," I said, trying to make it clear I wanted to cooperate.

"How's that?"

"It's making the bank deposit at the mall. The place is empty at that time of night. That's where I thought we'd get robbed if it ever happened. Not here."

"I understand," Riggs said. "We've had trouble there before. Spent a long evening staking it out from the roof two summers ago." He took out his handkerchief to wipe again the sweat spotting his forehead.

"Mr. Burton," Riggs said. "Did you go directly home after leaving the theater last night?"

"Yes, well, pretty much," I said, jolted by his return focus on me. Already perspiring, now my upper lip and forehead seemed connected to a garden hose. Again, I had answered more quickly, less calmly than I wanted to. Had Riggs tricked me, not wanting me ready for the question? His eyes narrowed. Damn, he was gauging my reaction, and I hadn't handled it well.

"Pretty much?"

"I felt like taking a long way home." This sounded inadequate. I wiped a forearm over my upper lip.

"A long way?"

"I guess I wanted time to think."

Riggs paused for a moment, a corner of his mouth turning upward. He didn't seem convinced. But how could I tell him what I had done and why?

"So, when did you get home? Can you give me an exact time?"

"Close to twelve-thirty," I said. "I remember it was just when a radio interview was ending."

"Someone back you up on this?" he asked, now raising an eyebrow as if in accusation. Again, I wiped my upper lip.

"I was with Mrs. Roe, Hillary Roe. I rent a room in her house, near the YMCA, downtown. We had a cup of tea together last night when I got home. She'll remember this. I can give you her number."

Calm down, I scolded myself. *Wait, what if Mrs. Roe had a heart attack?* The thought scared me—then shamed me. I should be damned to hell, straight to hell, to first think of myself.

"That would be helpful. Can we get out of this sun? You look like you've sprung a few leaks."

"Definitely," I said, pulling the keys from my pocket and heading toward the entrance. Riggs seemed to regret his accusatory shift, his tone of voice changing back to its earlier, more friendly one. Maybe he sensed my sincerity. And that extra half hour—how could I have pulled off a gruesome killing? Also, did I look like, sound like, a brutal killer? He was just doing his job.

CHAPTER NINE

After we entered the lobby, I grabbed napkins from a dispenser on the concession counter and mopped every corner of my face. The lobby was warm, but it felt cool compared to the outside. I suggested we go to the office where I had the employees' numbers on a Rolodex. Riggs liked this idea, but he advised not touching anything unless he okayed it. Yes, he was trusting me.

I asked, "I'm guessing we won't be able to open the theater today? And tomorrow too? I'd like to call people about not coming in."

"Closed today. Maybe tomorrow—we'll see. Hold off on making calls."

Riggs asked for the office key. He retrieved the latex glove from his pocket and pulled it over his fingers, snapping the rubber against his wrist. I smelled the fresh latex. He inserted the key and opened the door by twisting the key rather than touching the knob. He lifted the light switch, barely touching its surface.

I noticed the closet door at the back of the office was ajar. Bullock's cot was unfolded like it had been recently used. Normally, he kept it tucked away in a corner. Had he been planning on sleeping there instead of at Swofford's? I detected something faint and floral in the air. Perfume or cologne. It was hard to tell. I had smelled something like it a few times before, usually on Saturday mornings. Had another one of Bullock's women visited?

Riggs took a quick look around. I pointed toward the Rolodex. He picked it up and said,

"Let's go down to the lobby. I've got more questions for you, but I need to tell my partner something first."

Riggs introduced me to Detective Dupree, who had been standing at the bottom of the stairs. I thought I recognized him. Or at least he reminded me of someone. I took him to be in his early thirties, his hair closely cropped and receding an inch or two. He was chewing gum, and, except for this and his plump cheeks, his wire-rimmed glasses gave him a scholarly appearance.

"Pleasure, Mr. Burton. My wife and I have enjoyed movies here on many occasions. We crave your popcorn, truly."

His voice enhanced the sense of the scholar in him, each word, resonant and mellow, leaving an imprint in the air. I detected the unmistakable aroma of Juicy Fruit. And yes, I remembered. I'd seen him before at the theater, indeed with a woman who must have been his wife.

"Mr. Burton, excuse us for a moment," said Riggs, as he peeled off his glove. They moved far enough away to talk in private, and then Dupree left, maybe to retrieve something from his car.

Riggs returned, and we sat on one of the lobby benches.

I said, "I'm glad we won't open tonight. Saturday is our busiest day, even though we're in a holding pattern until *Jaws* starts in two weeks. It would have been tough."

"Saw the poster," Riggs said. "Will you take over as

manager?"

"The main office will find someone from another local theater, I guess."

"Why not you?" Was he wondering what I had to gain from Bullock's murder?

"Too young?" he said before I could respond. "You look like you're still in high school."

I hadn't wanted Bullock's job, and I didn't want him thinking I did.

I said, "I told the district manager I might want to go college soon, law school eventually. They prefer people who want to make a career in the theater business. Didn't want to promote me." I adjusted my accent to be just a little less Southern.

"I see," Riggs said.

I added, "I mean, that was fine with me. Their reasoning made sense."

"Remind me to tell you about my first career as a lawyer when all this is over," Riggs said. I liked the turn in the conversation.

Dupree came back with a legal pad. He wrote all the employees names and numbers as I read them out from the Rolodex. He shifted his gum from one side of his mouth to the other, smiling as he wrote. What was so amusing?

"We understand Mr. Bullock was married," Riggs said.

"Yes, Sue Ellen. I was about to ask if anyone had contacted her. You'll need to check the phone book. I don't have her number."

"Lonnie, why don't you find it and give her a call? Better

yet, take a trip over to her home," Riggs said.

"Affirmative," Dupree said.

"Before you go," I said. "There's something I need to tell you. Sue Ellen ordered Horace not to come home last night. She was real angry with him about him being with another woman. And so I don't know how she will react."

I did wonder what her reaction would be. We'd only met a few times, and briefly. She'd stop by in their old Falcon. One time I'd seen her chewing Bullock out in the parking lot. It lasted a good five minutes. He managed two words somewhere in there. But I couldn't see her doing this murder, couldn't imagine it, not the way it happened. So brutal. She might have come at him with a rolling pin, not a knife, Wilma to his Fred Flintstone.

"Why was she angry?" asked Riggs.

I told them all I could about Bullock's women, which wasn't much.

"Noticed the cot," Riggs said.

"The scene of *his* crimes," Dupree said. Riggs seemed irritated.

"That's where he met them, the women. At least I assume he did. I never asked. Never wanted to ask."

"We can comprehend that. No need to put your oar in it," Dupree said. Riggs looked even more irritated.

"Naturally," Dupree added. "She didn't take well to his *phil*andering."

"I guess not," I said. "And yet I have to believe it wasn't the first time she'd kicked him out. I figured they'd patch things up."

"Your boss had a randy streak. Just a provisional stay in the doghouse?" Dupree said as he picked up the pace of his chewing.

"Lonnie, put a lid on the editorializing. Let the man tell us what he knows."

"Roger," Dupree said, his persistent grin turning into a laugh. He gave Riggs a salute and left.

Riggs got right back to it.

"You can't tell me who the woman was? Her name?"

"Sorry," I said, frustrated I was unable to tell him more.

"About how many women did he meet?"

"I have no idea. He was careful about it. Probably because of Sue Ellen being onto him." There was a reason he wanted me to leave early the previous night. Was *another* woman visiting him?

"You've seen no one?"

"I saw women visit him during the day. But he never introduced them to me. They'd be up in the office for a while, and then they'd leave. I never knew what was going on. Didn't want to."

It occurred to me that Friday was one of his favorite nights for meeting the women. Of course, this was why he'd offer to make the deposit. This gave him an excuse to stick around. I'd be out of the way. He didn't want me to know. And it came across like he was doing me a favor. Saturday mornings, that's when I'd smell the residue of the perfume.

"No names?" he said, sounding frustrated.

"I bet Spence Reeves can tell you more. Phil Hogan too."

Riggs switched gears and said, "Mr. Burton, reason it

through for me. Why did anyone want to kill Mr. Bullock? Do you have any idea what happened here?"

I blew out a breath and said, "Yes and no, Detective Riggs. I'm shocked. I expected nothing like this. But now it's happened, it makes sense. Well, not murder, but something bad was going to happen to Horace. I'd even been half imagining it."

"How so?"

"It's complicated."

I told Riggs about Bullock's gambling debts and about the men who had shown up earlier in the week. I told him about Swofford too and the scuffle with the Navy vet.

Riggs probed for details, sometimes holding up his hand for me to pause while he wrote.

"Horace was hot-tempered, so impulsive," I said, as I struggled to find the best way to describe the difficult, combustible person he was. "I figured he would get into a serious fight, one that would escalate into something terrible, but not this bad."

"Anyone truly hate him?

"I don't know for sure, but something happened last night involving one of our ushers, Milton Spicer. He's young, only sixteen, a student at Hillside High School. Horace fired him for coming in late."

"Bad blood?"

"Ah, yes," I said.

I wanted to be careful. I didn't want Milton to get into more trouble than he deserved. "But I doubt that Milton would have killed Horace. Both his parents are high school teachers. He's just a kid."

"So, what was the problem?" Riggs asked, with slight impatience.

"He pulled a knife on Mr. Bullock."

"A knife? What was the name again?"

"Milton Spicer."

Riggs listened intently as I gave the details of what had happened.

"I understand why being called 'boy' would upset him, make him mad, but what's a good kid doing with a knife?"

"It surprised me too. But again, I don't think Milton did this thing."

"Listen. I'll be right back."

Riggs strode to his car and contacted someone using his radio. Probably Dupree. I figured it was about Milton. The incident with the knife begged for further investigation, and I felt foolish for being slow to bring it up. At the same time, I worried that I'd put Milton in a worse situation than he deserved.

CHAPTER TEN

Riggs returned and continued probing. "So, how did Mr. Bullock get along with other employees? What about Mr. Hogan?"

I hesitated.

"Ah, they didn't like each other."

Again, I wanted to be careful. I described the dispute with the projectionist union but stopped short on other details.

"And tell me again," Riggs pressed. "When would he have left the theater?"

"Right after the last movie ended. About eleven-thirty. That would be my guess." I wondered again whether Spence had seen something. He wouldn't have finished the cleaning by then.

"We'll be sorting all this out," Riggs said.

"Honestly, it looks like a robbery to me," I said. "Except for the way he got killed. I don't see Phil doing it. He's smart. This would have been a dumb thing to do."

"How do I get to his projection booth?" He seemed eager to move on.

"There's the entrance door," I said, pointing across the lobby. "But I don't have a key. Horace did. On his key ring. Phil hardly ever let *anyone* in. Even Horace was scared of going up there."

"You've never seen it?"

"No. I know that's hard to believe." Not that I hadn't been curious and tempted.

"What is it, a Mormon temple? We'll need to take a look. From what you say, I'm wondering whether there was anyone who *didn't* have it in for Mr. Bullock. They spring up like mushrooms." Riggs said, shaking his head and running a hand through his hair. "And you keep defending every last one of them."

"Sorry, I don't mean to—"

"Don't worry about it. I'd want people to do the same for me," Riggs said.

I listed all the other people working the previous night and noted those who had seen the knife incident. Riggs seemed satisfied. And he had asked no questions about Spence.

He took a card from his wallet and gave it to me. "Call me if you think of something. We'll need this place closed another day. I'll keep the lobby and office keys until tomorrow."

I gladly found the two keys I needed off my key ring and handed the rest back to him.

"Another thing. I still need the number of your land-lady. I'll give her a call."

"I understand, believe me, I want you to call her," I said, forcing a smile. I told him Mrs. Roe's number, which he added to his notepad. His eyes bore down on me, taking in my reactions. Was he testing me again? Well, that *was* his job.

I said, shifting to practical matters, "I really would like

to talk with all the employees. When can I call them?"

"Hold off for a couple of hours."

We walked outside together, the heat engulfing us. Riggs asked me when employees would arrive, and I gave estimates. He was particularly interested in Hogan, whose Thunderbird I noticed had just come to a stop across from the theater. Here was an opportunity to end the conversation while I appeared in the clear.

"Phil Hogan's here," I said.

"The guy in the Thunderbird?"

"Yeah."

"We'll talk again."

Riggs was already making a beeline to where Hogan had parked.

I spent half a minute in my car watching them. Hogan looked surprised, but not as much as I thought he would be. Riggs led Hogan into the lobby. I figured that he would get the same treatment I received. And maybe Spence would be next.

Spence was talking with Officer Slocum, who had removed his sunglasses. Both had grins. That Spence could make friends with anybody. And, Spence, I reminded myself, could handle any situation. I recalled him telling me of his time in prison way back in the 1940s. I mean Spence was old. He had shot a man, one of a mob of hooded Klansmen. They didn't like Spence's union organizing and had tried to bully him by firing bullets into the living room of his farmhouse one evening. Spence had returned fire. Turned out the man he shot was a lawyer who went around in a suit and tie by day, Klan outfit by night. The man survived. Spence had only used birdshot. Otherwise, Spence might have been lynched or sent to the chair, even though he was defending himself and his property.

A news truck from Channel 5 showed up. Not wanting to do any interviews, I left for the Riverview Theater, where I could use a phone to call Dan Drucker.

CHAPTER ELEVEN

I found Kaywood Turrentine, the manager of the Riverview, in the back room heaving a sack of popcorn kernels onto a shelf next to a popper. Turrentine was a small man with wide hips, rounded shoulders, and a fleshy neck. As he'd lost all his hair and had yellowish skin, he closely resembled a summer squash.

"Nate Burton," he said, not missing a beat. "Take a look at this."

Behind the popper in the corner of the backroom, a short stem of growth, pale with a hint of green, had appeared from a single, unpopped kernel of corn.

"Ain't that the weirdest thing you ever saw?" he said. "Where did it find enough light and water? I mean it's just sitting on lin*ol*eum."

"Didn't even know they could sprout, Kaywood. Gives me the creeps. Like it'll turn into a triffid, or the blob, and do us in."

Turrentine said, "We'd better kill it while we have the chance."

"Probably indestructible," I said, with fake seriousness. "Steve McQueen used a fire extinguisher for the blob. Hey, plant it. Might be good luck."

"The humane thing to do, I guess. But, know what, I won't." Turrentine crushed it under his shoe.

"You killed a new life-form, Kaywood."

"At least it'll never become an old maid."

"What?"

"A kernel that never popped. At the bottom of the popcorn box."

"Is that what they're called?"

"Didn't you know that? Now, what brings you, Nate?"

Kaywood had been in the theater business for some thirty years and had seen it all. It had taken him a long time to become a manager, and he prized the position, giving him just enough power and respect he needed. That was my read. To Kaywood, nothing was new under the sun, but when I told him what had happened to Mr. Bullock, he raised an eyebrow of surprise and said, *"Jesus H. Christ."*

He cracked the knuckles on each hand as he digested the information.

"Horace, that poor bastard. Let's talk in my office."

Kaywood finished two cigarettes as I gave him the details.

"I'll say this. Owing Wayne Swofford money was plain stupid," Kaywood said. "But do you think Hogan might have done it? I know for a fact he hated Bullock with a purple passion. But, not like you tell it. I mean, his being butchered."

I said, "That detective, he'll be looking everyone over, even me."

"Come on, Nate. That's crazy."

"Well, he gave me the third degree."

"Nah, you don't look the part. Looks like robbery to me."

"I guess."

"Nate, glad you called. Hoping you would. Saw it on TV. Couldn't believe it. Horace, poor bastard."

"It was terrible," I said. "Watched them take his body away. Spence Reeves found him in the side bushes while he was mowing this morning."

Drucker said, "This is one screwed up world, just screwed up. I've been trying to reach you. No answer at the theater."

"Sorry, I couldn't answer the phone. I wasn't even able to use it. I'm over at the Riverview."

"I called your home too. Talked with a lady." Drucker tried imitating a British accent. "She'd heard about it too, by George. A detective called her."

I laughed for Drucker's benefit, but I was thinking, *that was quick.* I felt a surge of anxiety I'd hoped I wouldn't need to suffer again.

"Nate, how about the deposit? The bank told me this morning they didn't get it. Did the police find the bags?"

"They're gone, as far as they let me know."

"We're insured, but it's a pain to deal with. They have any idea who did it?"

"Not yet. I told them all I could think to tell them. Robbery, I'm guessing. But I don't know. If it was just robbery, why did whoever did it have to kill him? I mean in such a brutal way. His throat was cut."

"I bet Horace put up a fight."

"Yeah, but Mr. Drucker, you should have seen his throat. I think he was surprised from behind. It was ear-to-ear. I'm telling you."

"Poor son of a bitch. Hey, listen. I'll drive over from Raleigh. We need to talk. Gonna call Sue Ellen first. Does she know?"

"By now she does," I said.

"How about we meet at that Waffle House near the Yorktowne? Say, three o'clock?"

"I'll be there."

CHAPTER TWELVE

"Jeet yet?" asked Drucker as soon as we got our Waffle House menus. He seemed to have moved past Bullock's murder with ease.

"Missed lunch with all that's happened," I said.

"Order anything you want, smothered and covered. On me." Drucker scanned the options, his eyes barely visible past the puffy features of his face.

"Topped and diced?"

"You bet."

"Thanks, Mr. Drucker. Pancakes—hash browns too."

Drucker had played nose guard for North Carolina State in the early 1960s, but any muscle from those days was soft and saggy, his massive frame creating gravitational pull. He was the type of guy who had resented the Beatles and long hair when they burst onto the cultural scene. Maybe he viewed himself as a defender against the changes that had now overtaken the land. If he'd seen *Easy Rider*, he might have half-sided with the local men in the pickup who gunned down Wyatt and Billy, the hippie characters played by Dennis Hopper and Peter Fonda. What was it the guy said before he shot Billy off his motorcycle? *Why don't you get a haircut?*

I'd met Drucker a few times. He'd liked me at first because of our increase in concession sales from the tastier popcorn, for which Bullock had given me credit. Another thing that impressed him was the framed articles I'd placed on the walls. They described the health benefits of popcorn, which were true as long as you passed on the shots of imitation butter and extra salt. The article he liked best described popcorn being a kind of toothbrush. Make sure there's popcorn left after you finish those Whoppers. Your teeth will thank you.

But during one of his visits I'd made the mistake of being too frank about my ambitions. Drucker had taken me aside and asked in a buddy-buddy way,

"Nate, are you wanting a career in the movie theater business?"

I had replied, hesitantly, "I like it. Sure. I really do. But I'm planning on college, then law school." It was a goal half-formed in my mind, having only a vague notion of what being a lawyer entailed. What I meant, I suppose, was that I hoped to do something *different* from what I was doing. Theater work, good for the moment, had started me imagining alternative lives. It was not for me.

That wasn't the answer he'd wanted to hear. He preferred someone all in and for the long haul. The enthusiasm in his eyes faded, and he lost his cozy way of talking. He checked his watch, and the meeting ended. I never got another raise.

He wanted me now, though. After we ordered, he said, "Nate, I need you to take over as manager." He gave me a hopeful look. I sat there trying to hide my surprise.

"Hear me out," Drucker continued, bringing his face closer to mine. "From what I know, and, honestly, from what only a fool couldn't see, you've been doing most of the managing, anyways. Horace—I ain't going to lie to you — we should've fired him a long time ago. Almost did in Georgia before he came up here. But he was a vet, and we don't like firing vets. And he'd been with us for twenty years."

"All news to me," I said.

"Point is—it'll get ridiculous when that shark movie starts. It'll be doggone Christmas in July, and I need you. And you'll need an assistant too. Go for anyone you want. What yah say? Comes with a raise. Another hundred a week?"

I tried to take it all in. Sounded good. My body started expanding at the thought. I felt ready for it. Manager, at nineteen. Would Carrie view me differently? Probably not. Still, I liked it. Although theater work was not for me, I had no crystal ball to predict the future either. I had once met an undertaker who had never figured it would be his career. But an uncle had given him the opportunity for a good-paying job at a funeral home. He took it, expecting a short-term gig. A wife, two kids, and a few raises later, he was stuck. Something like this might happen to me. No disrespect to undertakers—or to theater work. The undertaker told me it was an interesting career and an important job. He met all kinds of people, and he liked helping families through their grief. Even dealing with dead bodies was fine after a while. There are few things you couldn't get used to.

I said, "What about Jimmy Reynolds over at the Center? Got much more time at this than I have."

This was a no go, even if Kaywood liked him. The Center was a wreck. The lobby carpet had dark stains from want of regular steam cleaning, and its air was more foul than fresh. The drinking fountains ran warm and tasted like bathwater. The restrooms, well, they were health hazards too. And whenever I visited, Jimmy acted like running a theater as a toxic dump was normal. Yet I didn't quite understand why Drucker would want me. There would have to be someone better out there.

"*Jimmy Reynolds*. His cheese, it done fell off his cracker."

"Ah, you mean—"

"Porch light's on, but he ain't home half the time."

"Appreciate the offer, Mr. Drucker, but like I told you before, I'll be wanting to go back to school."

"Want that hash brown?" Drucker asked, already extending his arm toward the remaining one I'd been ignoring on my plate.

"Has your name on it."

Drucker scooped it up and inserted it whole into his mouth. Down it went. When it was man against food, Drucker won every time.

"Nate, let me be as straight as I know how to be. I gave up on you last year. I realize that. It was *bid*ness. Know what I'm sayin'? Got to support guys wanting this line of work. Give you credit for being honest with me. But, listen. I need you. And tell you what. You'll get a cut on the concession profits. I did this for Horace, and I can do it for you. Two percent. That's something you'll notice. Guaran-damn-tee you. Just wait till *Jaws* comes."

I looked real thoughtful. Wouldn't he figure I knew about Bullock's deal of five percent?

"I wouldn't want to be out of line, but Horace told me he got five percent."

Drucker's face turned pink. He said, "Horace had those years working for us, two decades. Think he started out at five?"

"Three?"

"Deal." Drucker extended a hand. I shook it.

"Deal."

"Unless you're the one who put that hit on Horace," Drucker said, in a serious tone. "Gotcha," he added as he slapped me on the shoulder and gave out a belly laugh. He had moved on from Horace Bullock. I suspected he saw Bullock's passing as good for business. And he was probably right.

"Just don't tell no one, promise?" I said, laying on a hick accent and returning a laugh. So far, though, this was no joke. Until Riggs had cleared me a hundred percent, I wouldn't find much humor in it.

"Listen, gotta run," Drucker said, jumping up as if he didn't want to give me a chance to change my mind. "I'll be in touch tomorrow. If I don't get through, how about calling me?"

"Will do. And I'm going to visit Kenny Riley over at the Riverview about the assistant job."

"Go for who you want."

Drucker tossed two dollars on the table for a tip and

paid the bill. We headed out to our cars. My front seat was blistering hot, and I rolled down the side window to release the heat. I was about to turn the ignition key when I saw Drucker's two paws holding on to the base of the window. His face peered down at me, his jowls drooping.

"Nate, you know about our spotters, right?"

"Sure, they check that we're doing things right," I said, remembering how we had been slapped on the wrists for not saying the right phone greeting during Christmas. What was it this time? Had they caught Carrie reading?

"We had one stop by the Yorktowne last night. We've had complaints coming out of ears about Horace. The spotter saw the whole thing with that Navy guy. Real impressed with how you handled it. Horace really got into it. Could have been a lot worse. He saw you give the money back and those passes."

He slapped the top of the roof and headed off to his car.

I was spooked to realize how much I had been watched. But why argue with an unexpected pat on the back? I'd take it.

CHAPTER THIRTEEN

I headed back to the Riverview to talk with Kenny Riley about the assistant manager position. I first stopped at a bakery to pick up a few pastries Kaywood and Kenny liked. Two Long Johns with the custard cream filling, not the white, for Kaywood in one bag. For Kenny, a cream horn with the white filling *not* the custard, alongside a glazed doughnut in the other bag. Plenty of napkins for the powdered sugar on the cream horn. A Long John for me, custard filling, planned for later since I was full. But I polished it off in three bites.

I saw Kaywood first. He spotted the bakery bags.

"Back again? What yah bring me?"

"Long Johns," I said, tossing him the bag.

I filled him in on my landing the manager's position and my interest in hiring Kenny. The prospect of my taking Kenny off his hands excited him.

"He's yours. He's up in the projection booth. How many did I eat? Anything else for me?"

"For Kenny," I said.

"Get on up there before you start thinking straight and change your mind."

Excellent. Kaywood was right about Kenny getting distracted by the movies. But Kenny had skills and a knack for fixing equipment. He was at least thirty-five and had been working in theaters for over ten years. He'd helped us out two months back when Bullock was down with the flu. The Riverview used platters, and so Kenny knew the machine much better than I did. Plus, we got along well. I knew he'd like it better at the Yorktowne, a lot better. It was kind of perfect. Most of what Kaywood didn't appreciate about Kenny were things I liked.

Maybe because I was a slow reader, I loved movies, but Kenny, he was a movie fanatic. Ask him anything about the history of movies and chances were that he knew the answer. Whenever we met, I learned something.

Kenny's favorite director was Ingmar Bergman, and Kenny's frequent praise of Bergman had me curious about the director too. When our public TV station scheduled one of Bergman's movies called *Wild Strawberries*, Kenny had urged me to watch it. And I did, on Mrs. Roe's kitchen TV. Filmed in a dreamy black and white, I could barely read the subtitles on the small screen. A simple story about an old man reconnecting with his daughter, but I enjoyed it so much that it got under my skin, stuck to my ribs. Kenny was all right with me.

Kenny was in the projection booth splicing leader onto a reel of film.

"Just a second, almost done. There. Hi, Nate. Kaywood told me about Horace. Horn in there for me?"

"Doughnut too," I said. He seemed unmoved by the news.

"Hand 'em over, amigo. Gracias."

He eyed me through his thick, Coke-bottle glasses. Each lens resembled aged plexiglass and needed a good cleaning.

Man, he was as goofy looking a human being as I'd ever seen. Nothing he wore could handle the strange, impossible contours of his flesh, which hung loose and collected in ways that fought against how clothing is made. One shirttail usually flapped around his backside. His teeth, well, they were so jumbled and bucked, you had to doubt the cosmic wisdom of how humans evolve. They were hard to look at without staring.

But Kenny was comfortable with himself. If, say, he caught someone staring at his teeth, he'd come out with something like, "I know, but my grandma says they're handy when you need to eat corn through a picket fence." Yeah, I liked Kenny Riley. Respected him.

Kenny moved to an old couch set away from the splicing table. As messy as he was, he was careful enough around film. He knew better than to have sugar powder settling on the print.

As I gave him more details about Bullock's murder, he showed little reaction.

"Robbery. Expected it might happen to one of us someday," he said as he wedged the last section of cream horn in his mouth. Powder had dusted across the front of his shirt where his belly announced itself and where a single dollop of white filling rested from an earlier bite. He added,

"Heck, we didn't go into this business 'cause it was dangerous."

He took a finger and made a deft sweep to collect the cream from his shirt and sucked it down.

"It's sad," I said. Kenny gave me side glance, as if to say, you're lying, right?

"No, Kenny. Wouldn't wish what happened on anyone."

"I have a sneaky suspicion he reaped what he sowed. Sorry, I ain't shedding any tears over Horace Bullock. He was an ignorant SOB in my book. And I didn't like how he looked at me."

I said, "Keep talking that way, and you'll need an alibi. Hey, I understand. Anyhow, guess what, you're looking at the new manager of the Yorktowne."

"No way."

"Way. Any interest in being my assistant?"

"Nate, are you kidding me?"

"I'm serious."

"You bet I would. Hot damn. Ah, how about Kaywood?"

"He's cool."

"Figure he would be. Don't matter. I'm in. Dang."

He shifted right away to ideas about what we might do as a team. Could we convince management to have midnight shows on Fridays and Saturdays?

"I know a ton of killer low-budget films, good for just one showing. Heard of *Pink Flamingos*? Main character is a drag queen." I'd never seen him so juiced up.

"Ah, I dunno," I said.

"Some are so bad they're good. *The Texas Chain Saw Massacre*. I've been wanting to see that."

"I like the general idea, Kenny. How about something more tame?"

"But that's the point. Why go with vanilla? You get a

different crowd."

"Can you think of a movie less, ah, weird?"

"I'm talking about films that are group experiences. Happenings. There's another one coming out soon, *The Rocky Horror Picture Show*. The lead's a transvestite."

"Drag queen, transvestite?"

"They're just fun. Hoots. *The Rocky Horror* one is a takeoff on science fiction and horror movies. It's a musical."

"We'll have to think about it."

I would have to throw a rope around him, bridle him. But I appreciated him being a little wild. It *would* be fun. Didn't want him domesticated.

Kenny countered with, "How about *Night of the Living Dead*?"

"Let's run all this by Drucker. Anyway, we need to talk about other stuff. *Jaws*, for one thing."

"*Jaws*? I've been hearing about it since last year. Read the book too."

Kenny shifted a stack of newspapers, magazines, and food wrappers to the side to reveal a paperback version of the Benchley novel. It was a recent edition as the cover was the same as the movie poster.

"Here. Take it."

Kenny tossed it to me. Its cover felt sticky.

"Ah, Thanks."

"Nate, this will be movie history. It's already movie history. Did you see *Duel*?"

"No, can't say I have."

"That was Spielberg's first movie. It's a thriller set in the

Southwest. A crazy driver with an eight-wheeler truck terrorizes a random motorist. That's all it is, but it's great, a gut puncher. This guy knows what he's doing. I owe you. I'm telling you, Nate. I feel like a possum with a tray of honey buns. And, by the way, can I get one of those *Jaws* posters?"

"Good luck. You know Phil Hogan."

"Yeah, about Phil," Kenny said. "Do you think, I mean, being serious for a second, is there any chance Phil did it?"

"Don't think so," I said with more confidence than I felt. Hogan had twists and turns to him that made him unknowable. But I wasn't going to voice my concerns. Not yet. "Yeah, they hated each other. But, Phil? No, I don't see it. And, Kenny, if you'd seen what Horace looked like. God-awful."

"I agree," Kenny said. "Phil's a varmint, but we're good. He loves pulling my chain. It don't bother me. Just yank his harder. It'll be fine."

"Anyway, you'll be seeing a lot more of him. Why don't you come by tomorrow afternoon, and we both can talk more? It looks like we won't open again until Monday."

"Kaywood won't need me. It's so darn slow around here."

We walked through the lobby together, and I headed to my car with the copy of *Jaws* cemented to the palm of my hand.

It was past five o'clock when I got back to the Yorktowne. Officer Slocum was still on watch, but most of the police cars were gone. Someone had fetched him a burger, and he was working on it. I was eager to talk with Spence, but I couldn't locate his car, an old Buick Electra.

Slocum let me enter the theater lobby, where I noticed Riggs, who seemed to be brooding about something. When he saw me, he perked up.

"Greenlight on making those calls," he said.

A good sign, I thought.

Detective Dupree drove up. He and Riggs stood apart from me and talked in the lobby for a few minutes. Then Dupree left in a hurry. I figured things were breaking fast.

Riggs looked preoccupied, turning over something in his mind. As curious as I was to know more, I knew it wasn't my place to ask questions.

I suggested that I might head off home.

"Sure, but how about stopping by here tomorrow morning, around eleven?" Riggs said.

"Okay, I'll see you then."

It had already been a long day.

CHAPTER FOURTEEN

I entered Mrs. Roe's kitchen to the smell of something freshly baked.

"Hello, Nate. I saw what happened. It's all over the news. Simply horrible!"

"It was awful, Mrs. Roe."

"I've made some Yorkshire gingerbread for you. Let's have us some, shall we?" She cut two slices.

"This is so good," I said, taking a large bite.

"For he on honey-dew hath fed," she said, quoting a line of poetry from somewhere I assumed. "It's lovely, this, if I don't say so myself. And best when warm and sticky-like."

She put water in a kettle for tea, not bothering to ask whether I wanted a cup.

Shifting to a serious tone, she said, "I received a call from a detective. A pleasant fellow. Riggs, I believe he said his name was. We chatted a good while. His mother was English. And from near my hometown at that if you can believe it."

She must have sensed the extra gravity of Riggs calling her because she added,

"Don't worry, dear. I vouched for you. Just past midnight when you got home last night, was it not?"

I remembered again my selfish thoughts earlier in the day about Mrs. Roe and felt another rush of shame.

"Something near that." A little fudging couldn't hurt. I'd

come home closer to twelve-thirty. I tried to seem casual about the time. Mrs. Roe gave me a slight conspiratorial look. I hoped she didn't think I needed her help.

She fixed the tea as I filled her in on everything. She loved hearing it, all of it. And now that I was more in the clear, I enjoyed telling it.

"Robbery, yes," she said. "This is the most logical conclusion. Yet, too grisly? Do watch out for that Mr. Hogan."

"He's a wild card, but I hope he didn't do it. We need him with *Jaws* starting in two weeks. I mean it."

"A fitting prelude, I dare say," Mrs. Roe said, shaking her head.

I turned in early. I hadn't any idea who killed Bullock, but at least I felt better about my own well-being. This caused my thoughts to turn toward the coming of *Jaws*. That poster, it packed a raw, perfect punch. The title, everything, as a good a poster as I had seen. From what I knew about the movie, it would live up to the hype.

I reflected on my special link to the ocean. My mom had come from a long line of female divers from the Island of Jeju, off the southern tip of South Korea. These women were famous for being able to stay under the water for many minutes and to withstand the cold as they searched for abalone snails and conch. They knew how to work among the jellyfish and sharks.

I had the lanky build of my dad, but in some hidden ways I was a lot more like my mom. Growing up in Hickory, I had a few weeks of lifesaving training at the local YMCA. Part of the training involved swimming underwater laps as many times as you could in groups of about five or six boys. It was a small-sized pool, but I swam four laps before I stopped.

After the second lap the others had given up, which I'd only realized when muffled shouts filtered through the water. It occurred to me only then that I was doing something unusual. I was feeling the strain, but something gave me that second wind, and I had kept going for two more laps. When I came up for air, I saw the cheering faces of the other scouts.

"How many lungs do you have, Burton?" the instructor had said. I could have gone further.

CHAPTER FIFTEEN

When I arrived at the theater the next day, I saw Riggs leaning against his car and removing the remaining peel of a bruised banana.

"We're through, Mr. Burton." He pushed the last bit of the banana to the side of his mouth and sent the peel sailing into a nearby trash can.

So we could have opened after all. Yet, I was relieved because we needed the extra day. And, anyway, Sundays were slow. If I understood the overall economics of the business, the theater company might come out ahead, since payroll expenses would be less. I figured we'd be in a holding pattern until *Jaws* arrived.

Riggs continued, "We're making progress. I can share with you that Bullock died around two in the morning." He let this information hang in the air.

I couldn't think of what to say, but this was good news for me.

"Puts you in the clear," Riggs added.

"Like to assume I don't come across as a killer," I said, trying to make light of it.

"No, you don't. And you didn't. Talked with Hillary Roe. She confirmed what you told me. Lovely lady."

"Yes, she is."

I hoped Riggs might tell me more, and I said, "I saw Detective Dupree hustling off yesterday." But my indirect probing yielded nothing, and I pressed in a different direction. "Did you get into the projection booth?" In the back of my mind, I still wondered about Hogan. Would we need to be on our guard?

Riggs hesitated and said, "We did." What did he find? I wanted to ask but thought better of it. And Riggs didn't elaborate. What did Hogan want no one to see?

"It's about time that I examined that room too."

Riggs looked at me, puzzled.

"I'm the manager of this place now," I said.

"Really?" He didn't seem to believe me.

"Sure am. Just met with the district manager."

"But—"

"Take it up with him," I said, laughing. "It's the truth."

He fished out the keys I'd given him the previous day and gave them to me.

"You've got the keys now. Got to run," he said. "Oh, when you go up there, you'll find we forced the lock on the second door. I'll be in touch."

Riggs stopped, one hand resting on the exit door, and said,

"Another thing. Been meaning to follow up on this. What about Mr. Reeves? How did he and Mr. Bullock get along?"

Was Spence a suspect?

"They got along well, overall," I said, but I was recalling the most recent time Bullock had mistreated Spence, a few days before. I had been helping Spence clean the aisles in theater two. Bullock had stuck his dumb mug of a face in through an exit door and had said in a disrespectful way, "Spence, now you make sure you fix that urinal, hear? I don't want to come in tomorrow and see it broken. Don't make me have to bring in no plumber."

Spence had stopped his sweeping, and after straightening his back, had said, "We won't need a plumber, Mr. Bullock. I can get us a washer to fix it."

Spence had smiled in my direction. I guessed he sensed what I was feeling. Then, he had got back to sweeping. I had been offended for him and wanted to tell Bullock off. Spence, a thousand times the man Bullock was, deserved more respect. But Spence had been calm about it, like it didn't matter.

"Overall?" Riggs asked.

"It's complicated."

"How so?"

"Mr. Bullock didn't always treat Spence with respect. It happened a lot."

"He wasn't bothered by it?"

"Spence got along well with Horace, even though he had reason *not* to. It bothered *me*, not Spence. Honestly, Spence doesn't let stupid stuff get under his skin."

Spence had seen so much, been through so much—what was another slight from someone like Bullock? He understood things more than reacted to them. And, as he put it to me once, "There be times when its best to keep your tongue still."

"I'm running late. Need to go."

"Just one more thing, Detective Riggs. Do you realize

Spence was a Buffalo Soldier?" I said, curious what effect this information would have. Would Riggs know who the Buffalo Soldiers were?

"A Buffalo Soldier? How old is he?" Riggs said, losing his smooth, unflappable manner.

"At least eighty. And get this. He fought in the Battle of Carrizal in 1916, down in Mexico."

"1916?"

"That's right. In Chihuahua. He told me he joined the regiment at fifteen by faking his age."

Although Spence claimed to be past eighty, he didn't look it. He had the limber way of a man closer to forty. His gait was slow but efficient.

"Incredible," Riggs said.

"Take a look at his Buick. He repainted it black with gold trim, the colors of the 10th Cavalry."

"I noticed those silver buffalos on both fenders."

"Yep, he put those on too. And, come to think of it, one thing he said about his time as a Buffalo Soldier maybe helps explain why Horace never bothered him."

Riggs had been so intent on leaving, but all this new information about Spence caught his interest. He glanced at his watch and said,

"Tell me. Quick."

"Being a Buffalo Soldier was a huge achievement for a Black man. But you still had to suffer all kinds of indignities from many of the white soldiers, especially when there was no fighting going on. One time, his regiment was ordered by an officer to stand away from the wind, so that the other soldiers wouldn't have to smell them. But Spence said the men in the regiment took these slights in stride. You know why?"

"They had no choice?" Riggs said.

"Because they had come through in battle. As Spence told me, 'We were always there when they needed us.'"

"Interesting," Riggs said, as he seemed to imagine what it must have been like.

I said, "It really was a special honor to be a Buffalo Soldier for these guys, making it much easier to take those slights."

"I can understand. And I want to learn more about Mr. Reeves. And I will. I promise you," Riggs said. He stared again at his watch. "But, damn it, I need to go."

I was getting to like Riggs. As he drove away, I wondered why he had ended up being a detective instead of a lawyer. He'd never gotten around to telling me. Investigating murders did seem more interesting than legal work, in as much as I knew about each career.

Riggs was talking with someone on his police radio. I again sensed the case was moving fast.

CHAPTER SIXTEEN

If my first official act as manager had been to hire Kenny, my second was to check out Hogan's projection booth, so long off-limits to anyone but Hogan himself. I opened the entrance door, left unlocked by Riggs, and peered upward as I turned on the stairwell light. The flight of stairs was long and narrow, not reversing midway at a landing like the stairs leading to the booth for theater two. It felt eerie, as if the stairs led to another dimension. The door at the top filled the whole space, almost like an attic door, adding to this otherworldly sense. A sign on the door read "PRIVATE" in blood-red letters. Strangely, even though I was looking up, it seemed I was looking down.

"Creepy," I said aloud, as I headed up the stairs, closing the door behind me and hoping that Hogan wouldn't decide to show up right then. As manager now, I had every right to enter the room, but I felt like an intruder. Did the union rules gave him dominion? I'd look into that later.

The entrance door swung inward, and I felt for a light switch. Two shaded lamps at either end of the booth came to life, producing a warm, honey-yellow light, directed away from projector windows that overlooked the theater itself. The room smelled of stale cigarettes from an un-emptied ashtray. Something else too. A hint of Hogan's cologne. I recalled what I'd detected in Bullock's office. Was it the same smell? It was hard to tell. And, anyway, Hogan liked to change his cologne.

Hogan kept the room clean and orderly, so different from Kenny's messy, chaotic style. No stray slices of film or food wrappers lay about, and the splicing table was free of clutter. The film canisters for *The French Connection II* were neatly placed under the table.

Lining the back wall were three framed posters, each well placed. I had seen far-off glimpses of them through the projector window, but now I saw them up close. One looked like an original of *A Rebel without a Cause*, with James Dean standing, one leg crossed over the other, cigarette in hand.

The second I'd never heard of, *Crime in the Streets*. A young man, dressed like a thug, embraced a girl. Just above them, a phrase read: "How can you tell them to be good when their girlfriends like them better when they're bad!"

The third poster was smaller and had the title *Billy Budd*. Two sailors, their upper torsos exposed, fought on the deck of a boat. One had a knife. The main caption read: "The men, the mutiny, the might!"

Along the far wall was a couch with Western-style upholstery. I moved over to it and noticed a stack of magazines on a side table. On top was a copy of *Time* magazine, the issue that Billy Gossett had been reading several days before. Next were two muscle-building magazines, one called *Flex*, featuring a young Austrian muscle builder named Arnold Schwarzenegger. The second magazine was *Tomorrow's Man*, geared toward "The World's Finest Young Physiques." It also had the same man on the cover, an even younger version of him, probably taken when he was a teen. I could see the appeal of this guy.

Tiger Beat was the last one. I'd seen this issue in drugstores. Teen idol, David Cassidy, from the *Partridge Family* TV show was on the cover. I recalled the provocative, controversial almost nude photo of Cassidy on the cover of *Rolling Stone* a few years back.

I was reminded of something that had happened a few weeks earlier. A high school kid had applied for an usher position. He was a close replica of Cassidy, his long hair parted down the middle exactly as Cassidy's. We went over his application while sitting on one of the lobby benches. When Hogan entered the theater, his head whipped in the kid's direction like it might spin right off and I'd have to catch it. We didn't hire him because he couldn't provide a reference, which had miffed Hogan.

Poor Hogan. He must have had a splintered, painful upbringing. How could it lead to anything but heartache?

And Hogan hated Bullock. He had to. Was he capable of snapping? Killing? I hoped not, but this was more than I knew.

I heard the door open at the bottom of the stairs. My heart pounded against my chest like it might break through. Was it Hogan? The idea that Hogan had killed Bullock took sudden hold as if it were a certainty. I looked around for something to defend myself with. I reached for a film canister and got ready to use it as a weapon.

"Phil, are you up there?" It was Kenny. I put the canister down. I felt foolish. My pulse returned closer to normal.

"It's me. I'll be right down," I said in a loud voice. I didn't want Kenny coming up. I placed the magazines back in the same order I'd found them and hurried to the top of the stairwell.

"Phil up there too?" Kenny said, his distinctive frame filling the stair entrance.

"No. You scared the crap out of me. Thought you might be him. He lets no one up here," I cut the lights and made my way down the stairs. "He doesn't even know I'm the new manager. Heck, he might have killed me."

"Serious?"

"No, but I'm sure glad it was you not him. Come on, let's move. He might show up for real."

I closed and locked the door. How would Hogan react when he noticed the second door's broken lock?

Kenny asked with exaggerated timidity, "Are you the manager or him? Mind if I check out the other booth?"

"Shut up. It's open. And it's all yours. I'm going to clear Bullock's junk out of the manager's office."

Hogan's Thunderbird entered the parking lot just as Kenny left the lobby. A shiver went through me. That was cutting it close.

Hogan entered the lobby, and the rush of summer air funneled in the scent of his latest cologne, yet another new kind. A silver fertility symbol, new as well, hung on a thick chain around his neck.

I said, "Hi, Phil. Awful about Horace."

"Yeah, I guess," Hogan said, with little conviction.

"I couldn't believe it," I said.

"Listen, I ain't going to pretend I'm sorry about it."

"You and everybody else. But it was gruesome."

"You saw the body? I heard Spence found him."

"Got there just before they carried him away."

"Lucky you."

"What?"

"Okay, I admit it," Hogan said. "I hated that bastard. You saw how he talked to me."

"I know, I know," I said, and I thought again of the many times Bullock had humiliated Hogan, or tried to. I didn't blame him for despising Bullock. Not one bit. "Who do you think did it?"

"Like you say, I wasn't the only one who hated his guts. All I know is that he was still in his office when I took off around eleven forty-five. Saw the light on. And his stupid Cordoba was still out front." That sounded convincing, I thought. Was it true?

"My guess is robbery," I said. "But he was butchered. I'm telling you. Who does that for money?"

"Who knows? Who cares?"

"Man, you really hated him."

"That's what I said. He had a dead rat for a soul. I hope he's burning in hell. Is that clear enough for you?"

"Crystal. Well, how about Milton?"

"You saw him pull the knife. I didn't."

"Maybe. But, no, I doubt it. He's just a kid. Anyway, how did it go with Detective Riggs?"

"He got me mad. Maybe he thinks I did it. He wouldn't let me in the theater yesterday. Didn't like the way he questioned me. Had me squirming like a worm in hot ashes.

Went all over my T-Bird too."

Hogan glanced over toward the projection booth entrance. He looked worried. He knew Riggs had been up there.

"Got the same treatment," I said, trying to make it feel it was just Riggs doing his job. "He made me nervous too."

"Why should *you* be nervous?" Hogan said, giving me an extra close stare.

"Look. Neither of us need to be worried," I said, not wanting Hogan to think that I suspected him. "Detective Riggs told me they estimate the time of death around two. All of us were long gone."

"Two?" Hogan said, still looking anxious. "Did you talk about the bad blood between me and Horace?"

"Yeah," I said. "I had to, Phil." This was awkward. But what could I say?

"Sheeeit!"

"Phil, what was I supposed to do? Lie? Anyway, after he was through with me, he had to figure everyone couldn't stand Horace. Come on. It was going to come out."

"Yeah, yeah. I told him about it too. Well, most of it."

I liked the way the conversation was going. His comments felt real and honest. A small part of me still reserved judgment, but my earlier panic made me laugh inwardly.

Changing the subject, I announced, "Guess what, Drucker asked me to take over as manager. I took it."

"You?"

"Don't look so surprised," I said, though he had good

reason to be.

"Aren't you getting big britches."

"You have no idea how large my ambitions are."

"And Horace's body ain't in the ground."

"He wanted me bad, Phil."

Hogan stepped back and said, "You know I want you too."

Before I could think of a response, Kenny entered the theater.

"Kenny Riley," Hogan said. "What's your lazy ass doing over here?"

"I resent that remark," Kenny said, but with a smile.

"Kenny here is our new assistant manager," I said.

"Is that the best you can do?" Hogan said, "I guess he can't help he's ugly, but do we have to scare people too? Was his daddy a raccoon?"

"Look who fell out of a tree and hit every branch on the way down," Kenny shot back.

"At least my family tree has more than one branch. But, I don't know. He'll do," Hogan held out his hand so that Kenny could give him a high five. Kenny's right hand awkwardly connected with Hogan's.

"Phil, what do I have to do to get one of them *Jaws* posters?" Kenny asked.

"Bless your little heart," Hogan said. "Get in line."

CHAPTER SEVENTEEN

The manager's office was a mess and reeked of substances I preferred not to think about. I found two cardboard boxes for Bullock's personal items. They were a sad mix of things, such as a Norelco electric shaver, an imitation gold watch with a broken minute hand, a jar of Tums, and two bottles of Jack Daniels. I planned on bringing the items to Sue Ellen, if she wanted them.

Bullock had loved his Jack Daniels. The best-selling whiskey in the world for a reason, he would repeat, yet distilled in a dry county in Tennessee. The strangeness of that fact never failed to get him laughing and shaking his head as if it explained everything confusing in life.

Some items I was sure Sue Ellen wouldn't want were a stack of *Playboy*s and various personal care items linked with Bullock's women. Several I could not identify their function, and I found them difficult to touch, wishing I had a pair of those latex gloves I'd seen Detective Riggs using. I put these throwaway items in a heavy-duty plastic bag destined for the dumpster out back and the final anonymity of the county landfill. The cot, perhaps best summing up the man, Horace Bullock, was no longer in the back room. Riggs must have confiscated it.

Conflicting feelings about Bullock arose in me as the odors of a life snuffed out still haunted the air. Disgust won over pity, and I wanted the lingering stench gone. I fetched a bottle of Ajax from the supply room and used it to wipe every surface. Then I went outside to the back of the theater and tossed the bag into the dumpster. Out of a superstitious fear I couldn't shake, I said a prayer for the dead.

My thoughts turned to Spence. I had dreamed about him the previous night. In the dream we were both inmates on a prison farm like the one in *Cool Hand Luke*—perhaps Officer Slocum, and his resemblance to the prison guard in the movie, had affected me more than I realized. Curiously, in my dream, Spence had challenged the prison warden to a game of chess. With a white hat and a nasal twang to his voice, the warden looked and sounded like Strother Martin, the actor who played the character in the movie. It was a crazy setup, like a prizefight, with inmates and guards gathered around, yelling and clapping at every move. Spence kept a mask of cool mastery, even as beads of sweat merged and flowed down his skin and drenched his prison clothes. The warden, his uniform also soaked with sweat, concentrated like it was life or death. Along with the other inmates, I rooted for Spence. We whooped and hollered when Spence checkmated the warden. That's when something woke me up. I now reflected on the dream as if it had actually happened and felt disappointed that the dream had ended before I got to see the warden's reaction to losing.

What did Spence think about Bullock's murder? I called his number. He answered right away but said he was heading out to fix up some of his rental property. He suggested I meet him at one of his Massey Street houses, and then we might have a late lunch at a nearby restaurant. I jumped at the chance. Interesting, I thought. Spence had rental property.

I'd driven near Massey Street many times on the way to the airport. Most homes in the area were small and humble. Some were rundown, but there was a sizable middle-class community, especially around North Carolina Central University, the historically Black school in Durham. The largest Black-owned insurance company was head-quartered in Durham, as well as the Mechanics and Farmers Bank. There was a reason Durham had once been called the "Black Wall Street."

I drove down Fayetteville Street, past St. Joseph's Methodist Church, and took a left on Massey. I slowed to count street numbers and came to the address Spence had given me. It was a small, single-story house with whitewashed siding and a slither of a front porch, set on a narrow plot of land, like most of the houses on Massey. Spence's Buick filled the cramped driveway.

Spence was in the patch of backyard playing with his lab, Blackjack, who I'd encountered a few times on Saturdays when Spence brought him to the theater. They were pulling on either end of a stick. Blackjack let go when he saw me and gave me strong, croaky barks, until he seemed to recognize me and settled down, tail wagging. With his once jet-black fur graying in places, he struck me as the same age as Spence, in dog years. I scratched him behind the ears.

Blackjack stayed right at Spence's heels as we entered

the house through the back door. Drop cloths, anchored by cans of paint and a step ladder, covered the hallway and the living room. My nose stung from the smell of wet paint and turpentine.

"Be renting this out presently," Spence said. "Needs a little touch-up. Like my places looking fine when new folks move in."

How many places did Spence have?

"You rent out other homes?" I asked.

"Yes, sir. All on Massey, two on this side and three on the other. See the one yonder?"

He directed my gaze out the window at a house across the street.

"That's the one I want to get next. It's *his*toric. Want to fix it up as something special, a landmark."

"Landmark?" I said, showing my skepticism. Nothing about it suggested anything special. Two windows had plywood nailed over them.

"Blind Boy Fuller's home, till he died in '41. Doubt you know of him."

"Afraid not."

"Played masterful guitar and sang in these parts. Songs were powerful."

"He lived there?"

"When he passed. A historic site, that's what I have in mind to make it. First, need to buy it. 'I Want Some of Your Pie.' That was my *fav-or-ite*." He sang the title out loud.

I laughed. "That's a lot of property to manage."

"Naw, rent to good folks. Enjoy it. Always keep busy.

Don't need the theater job, but I like it too. Don't mind the work. Benefits, they good, enough to have put up with Horace Bullock, may he rest in peace, somewheres. These days, don't need much sleep. Three hours, I'm up."

"Three?"

"Putting two grandkids through college."

"Jeez."

I was learning many new facts.

"Thaddeus. He's at Central. Ricardo will be starting up the road at Chapel Hill come September. Now that Ricardo's going to be a lawyer. He's an apt a kid as you'll find. Put him at anything, he makes a success. He helps me the paper-work for the rentals."

"Spence, I'm just about desperate to learn what you think about all that's happened."

"Let's grab us some vittles."

"But, Spence, tell me, pah-*lease* tell me."

"Eyeballs is floating. Why don't you head out to the porch, and I'll join you."

I waited on the porch and thought hard. Spence Reeves, landlord. I looked over at the Blind Boy Fuller house. I sure hoped that Spence would get his wish. And it sure enough needed a historic marker next to it.

Spence came out onto the porch. Blackjack was still behind the screen door. Spence opened the door a crack and said to Blackjack in a quiet, eerie voice, "Now, Jack, you stay, stay watch here, until we get back. Hear?"

Jack looked straight at Spence, and I swear to God gave him a nod like he understood every word. Spence slipped

90

him a small dog biscuit too, which he'd been keeping in the palm of his hand, and closed the door.

We headed up Massey.

"Hadn't seen a thing like what happened to Mr. Bullock since Carrizal." Spence said, stopping in his tracks as if his recollection created a wall, right in front of us.

"Carrizal?" I asked, wondering aloud what Spence was talking about.

"Carrizal, M-eh-ee-co, Nate. We lost sixteen men that day. Most cut up worse than what I saw yesterday."

We were quiet for a few moments. I couldn't think of what to say.

"Let's get some grub," Spence said, and we started off again. My stomach rumbled.

I asked, "Did you know about Horace's women?"

"He was a rooster," Spence replied.

"He owed gambling money too."

"Knowed it, seed it, heard it," Spence said. "Those men came around *twiced*. They didn't pay me no mind. Mr. Bullock owed a big sum. Over thirty grand."

"No wonder he looked so worried," I said.

"That shell fired a while back and was sure to explode," Spence said.

"Yeah."

It took me a second to understand what he meant.

"They've arrested Milton," Spence said, without missing a beat.

"What?" I felt a rush of concern for Milton. He wouldn't have done this kind of thing.

"His daddy called me about it. Mom's taken sick over it," Spence said.

"He couldn't have. Could he?"

"Milton didn't do it," Spence said, as if the issue needed no discussion.

"But why did they arrest him?"

"He ran. That's why. Hiding in his aunt's farmhouse near Apex."

"He pulled a knife on Horace. I saw it."

"Hotheaded kid, true enough," Spence said. "You try figuring how to be a Black man in a white man's world. Would a son of yours kill a man like this?"

"Well, no."

"And you saw the body. No scrawny, sixteen-year-old kid would do this. This was planful. Milton's no premeditated killer. Anyway, his daddy helped Detective Dupree find him. Know each other from church. Had to do it. Word was out."

"Why would he run? And where was he Saturday night?" These things would need explaining.

"You ain't been Black, Nate," Spence said forcefully, suggesting slight disappointment in me.

"No, Spence, that I have not. That was stupid of me."

"Don't blame you. That would make me stupid. Anyway, they found him hiding and hungry in a shed next to an old tobacco barn."

"Poor Milton," I said.

"Reckon they had to arrest him, Milton running like he did. Got themselves a good lawyer, though. Won't stick."

I said, "That means the person who did it is still out there.

Spence chuckled.

"Could have been my sickle that killed Mr. Bullock. But here we are. Let's eat."

CHAPTER EIGHTEEN

I studied the modest outside of the restaurant from across Fayetteville Street as cars rushed by in both directions. The restaurant was a simple, narrow structure sided with brick veneer, extending back from the road about thirty yards.

"Let's go," Spence said, and I followed his lead through an opening in the traffic.

Spence held the door for me, and the smells and sounds of cooking made me ravenous. Although I heard talking and laughter, I could make out little as my eyes adjusted from being outside in the sun's glare. The further back I looked, the darker things appeared and in rough outline. Then, clusters of people sitting together emerged like images in a photographer's developing tray. On the right, I saw other customers on swivel stools along a counter in front of a grill area. Many gave Spence a greeting before I could see them clearly.

Two men stood up near a front table.

"We're finished, Spence. Let's clear this collateral damage," said one of the men, a barrel-chested, well-upholstered guy of advanced but indeterminable age, with as dark a complexion as I'd ever seen. He wore fine threads, neatly pressed. He collected the plates and brought them to the counter. The other man, wearing the overalls of a car mechanic, yet with no trace of oil, snatched up the empty glasses. He had light skin and was thin as a piece of plywood. After a chorus of see-you-laters, they both left in separate directions.

An olive-skinned woman with large rimmed spectacles, her frizzy hair gathered up in a loose bun, came from behind the counter. After introductions, she said,

"Lunch for you gentlemen?"

"Yes, ma'am," Spence said. "You okay with catfish and biscuits, Nate?"

"You bet."

"Coming right up." She placed two glasses of ice water on our table.

I chose a seat while Spence exchanged a few words with a huge man working on some fried chicken at the counter. After Spence settled into a chair, he completed the thoughts he started about ten minutes earlier.

"Point is, a heap of other folks could have wanted to do it—and done it easy. I could've done it easier than Milton—though I had no reason, no good reason."

"Does Milton have an alibi?" I asked.

"They're working on that. Parents think he's covering for somebody. Not someone who *did* it, but someone Milton was not supposed to *be* with."

"Girlfriend?"

"Might could be," Spence said with a grin and a wink.

"If Milton didn't do it, who did? Would robbery involve that kind of killing? Think they'll ever find the deposit bags?"

"See that man sitting on that stool?" Spence said in a low voice, as if I hadn't asked my question.

"The big guy, distinguished-looking?" I said, lowering my voice too. I knew it was useless to try controlling the direction of Spence's thinking.

"He is at that," Spence said. "Looks like a bear too, right?"

"I guess he does." He did.

"Well, he goes by the name of Carl 'the Bear' Easterling. He coaches basketball at Hillside High School. His '67 team averaged 107 points. Called it the 'Pony Express.' Now, you haven't heard of it, have you, Nate? Even though you live in these parts."

"No, I have not."

"But I'm thinking about that swivel stool he's sitting on."

"Just an old stool, Spence." Now where was he heading?

"Should be set up at the Smithsonian *In-sti-tute* in Washington, *DC*. Its own exhibit."

"Why, Spence?" I had no idea how he could make this claim.

"That stool is where Malcolm sat and drank soda pop when he visited Durham."

"Malcolm? Who? You don't mean Malcolm X?" Each hair on the back of my neck and down my arms stood on end.

"That's right."

"He came here? He actually sat there?"

"Truthful to God. Several times. They wouldn't serve him downtown. Back then, leastwise. Not that he wouldn't have preferred here anyway. Saw him with my own eyes. Black suit and bow tie. Soft-spoken, not like people think of him when he was giving speeches and confronting folks."

Spence looked misty-eyed. My body shivered. The sense of history here was overwhelming. I hurt inside. And I wasn't sure what to make of it, what to do about it. What did it all mean? The swivel stool—might it be preserved and placed as its own exhibit in the Smithsonian or somewhere? Blind Boy Fuller's music in the background. Would such dreams, so long delayed, ever happen? If they did, Spence's soul would sing. Yet I knew in my bones that this was a pipe dream. My hopes, one moment soaring, seemed to fizzle in mid-flight. History was a string of cruel turns, mostly forgotten.

But soon we each had us a plate of glistening, fried catfish, nestled in a bed of greens, along with coleslaw and a basket of cornbread muffins. I forked down a chunk of catfish, following it with slaw and cornbread.

"This is so excellent."

The taste and aroma brought back a memory of my dad's catfish stew. He had made it during a camping trip to Lake Mickie. One evening, we took our flat-bottomed boat and set trotlines in a little cove on the eastern part of the lake. In the morning as the sun rose, mist still hanging low over the water, we returned and found three catfish, hooked and ready for hauling in. This was the way to fish. No waiting with a pole when you could be doing something else. They caught themselves on the trotlines. They struggled when we pulled them up, as we avoided being speared by the barbed horns on their back and side fins. We knocked them out cold. Later, we pinioned their heads to a pine tree with a few rusty nails and peeled their skins with pliers. After filleting them with my hunting knife, we sliced up the flesh into good-sized wedges for stew. My dad used a special mix of other ingredients and seasonings he kept secret from everyone, even my mom.

"You okay, Nate?" Spence asked.

"In heaven," I said and told Spence about all the things Bullock had said that evening while drunk on Jack Daniels. I filled him in on everything I knew as I shoveled in the food between sentences. One by one, we went down the list of people who might have killed Bullock, starting with Sue Ellen.

We eliminated her right away. Physically, she couldn't have pulled it off. And, anyway, it turned out her sister had been staying with her that evening, visiting from Atlanta, maybe helping her deal with Bullock's latest fooling around.

As for Hogan, I was glad to learn that Spence had seen him moving about in the projection booth until at least twelve-thirty and had then seen him leave. This was way before two o'clock when Riggs told me Bullock was likely killed. And we reminded ourselves that even if Hogan had wanted to do it, he wouldn't have been dumb enough to do it right in front of the theater.

No one except Riggs or Dupree had talked with Samantha about it. Well, we assumed. Spence had a funny feeling about Samantha.

"She's got Freon flowing in her veins," Spence said.

"Mixed with lighter fluid, Spence. I've seen her angry

too."

However, I didn't believe she had cared about Bullock one way or the other. She was from another planet. And she'd left just before ten o'clock. Except for the men Bullock owed money to, including Wayne Swofford, we couldn't think of anyone else. We figured Riggs would be looking into these possibilities too. Spence seemed to be holding back his thoughts.

We finished lunch, and I needed to get going because I wanted to attend Bullock's midafternoon burial service.

As he paid for both of us, he glanced in my direction and said, "They be putting Mr. Bullock in the ground quick."

"My guess is that Sue Ellen had no reason to wait on it," I said. But it had seemed mighty quick.

I tried to leave a tip, but Spence covered that too.

CHAPTER NINETEEN

Sue Ellen, her sister Alma, and Kaywood Turrentine were the only people attending the burial. Several minutes into the service, Bullock's gambling buddy, Wayne Swofford, also showed up. I had never seen him up close. A tall and bony guy, his droopy assemblage of body parts hung downward as if he were pinned to a wall. He stood, fidgeting and shifting his weight from one leg to another.

The second the service ended, Swofford lit a cigarette and handed something to the minister. Two cemetery employees appeared out of nowhere to lower the casket into the ground.

The service saddened me more than I expected. I reminded myself that Bullock had recommended me for the assistant manager position. I appreciated this. An ignorant man, proud of his crude passions and prejudices, and yet his appetite for life impressed me in its own way. A guilty part of me had enjoyed watching him lose his temper and say things that others wouldn't say. I half saluted him for this raw, if lame-brained brand of honesty.

And, sometimes, he'd tried to give me advice, usually based on lessons he'd learned from his time in the army.

One bit of wisdom I remembered well. He had said, "In the army, you had to put up with a lot of crap. But, Nate, I don't care how bad things were. If you'd look around, you'd see some poor knucklehead who had it worse, a lot worse.

That always made me feel better. You know what I'm saying?" I had to give him this because sometimes I'd found it true, Bullock's own demise a case in point.

And I think he had loved Sue Ellen—a flawed love, but real enough, and mutual if Sue Ellen's tears told a story.

The minister, sweaty and uncomfortable in his dark suit, had seemed impatient to speed to the end. Not that I didn't share the impatience. The service itself felt like a rush job, happening so soon after Bullock's death. The minister couldn't go fast enough through his worn-out phrases, such as Bullock being in a better place. Maybe he was, maybe he wasn't. Given what I knew about Bullock, it amounted to pious baloney.

After Bullock's pinewood casket had been lowered into the ground, no one stuck around to watch the cemetery workers cover it with dirt. I accompanied Sue Ellen to her car while her sister talked with Kaywood.

"Horace had a mess of demons," she said, as she fetched a pack of Lucky Strikes from her purse. "I guess you knew about the gambling. And all the money Horace owed?"

"Some of it," I said. "He told me he was in big trouble. You know who he owed the money to?"

She placed a cigarette between her lips and lit it with the weak flame of a lighter, low on fluid. Her first inhaling was hungry and deep, and as smoke funneled from her nostrils, she replied, "That snake over yonder, Wayne Swofford. He was a bad influence on Horace."

"He does look a little shady."

"He's feeling guilty about something," Sue Ellen said,

"He told me he'd pay the minister for the service, which won't no good, in my opinion."

"I've heard better," I said.

"I don't know. I don't know," she said. "I had a mind to leave Horace many times. I'd pitch a fit and then never do it. Can't explain it. We go so far back. Horace's brother married Alma. She's my twin. We had houses next to each other in Atlanta. But he passed last year of lung cancer."

"These things are hard to understand. That much I do know," I said, hoping this would help.

Sue Ellen said, "I near about left him for real before moving here. But let me tell you, Nate. Mr. Drucker knows this too. And I figured he'd be here. Horace was accused of assaulting a girl at the theater he managed down in Macon. He told me nothing happened, but I don't know. She, well, claimed he raped her. It never went to trial because the judge said there wasn't enough evidence."

"Horace never mentioned it," I said. Why would he? This got me thinking. Bullock had probably been guilty. That was my read, which pulled the final plug on the remaining good feelings I'd mustered for him moments earlier.

"That's why we moved up here," Sue Ellen continued. "The theater company almost fired him. They didn't, long as we moved somewhere else. So they let him come here and manage the Yorktowne. Dan Drucker set it up. Four years ago, this month."

"I knew none of this. Did you meet the girl?"

"Saw her in court. Just a once. They kept her name out

of the papers. It was, Lucy, no, Lucille. Don't remember her last name. She was young, like seventeen, from a messed-up home. I hear tell she didn't have a good reputation. Don't like bad-mouthing people, but she was a slut. She'd accused two other men of the same thing. Trailer trash, if you ask me."

"What happened to her?"

"Don't know. She was real mad though. Like she meant it."

"Did you tell Detective Riggs?"

"Yes. Well, not at first. Later, after I got to thinking about it. She made threats."

I wondered whether this girl might have hired someone to track Bullock down and kill him. No. That seemed far-fetched. Sue Ellen stared at the ground, and then a smile came over her face.

"You know," she said. "Horace liked my fried chicken."

For a moment, she seemed to forget all about him that she hated. Her face lost its angry and complicated lines.

"He told me it saved his life," I said.

"So he told you?"

"Yeah."

Years back, before the theater job, Horace's old army buddies had wanted him to go to an Elvis concert. He passed on it because Sue Ellen was making fried chicken that night. Heading to the concert, they got hit and killed by a drunk driver. What a wacky twist of fate.

We stood, saying nothing, each of us thinking our private thoughts. I broke the silence.

"Mrs. Bullock, I've got Horace's things from the theater packed in two boxes in my trunk. How about I set them in your car?"

"Thank you, Nate. Bless your heart."

I retrieved the boxes containing the sad fragments left from Bullock's life and placed them in the back seat of her old Falcon, its exterior oxidized by the sun and from the lack of waxing.

We parted, and I figured this would be last I'd ever see of her.

CHAPTER TWENTY

We reopened on Monday. I liked being manager, if only because I didn't have to wear the tacky assistant manager jacket, just a coat and tie of my choice instead. Mrs. Roe had given me several of her husband's blazers. They fit me well. The change took away the clownish feeling that came with wearing the company getup. Maybe the feeling had been a foolish one of my own making, but I was glad to lose it all the same. In this small section of the wide universe called the Yorktowne Theater, I was boss.

All of us worried about Milton, but his arrest and the publicity surrounding it was welcome in at least one respect. We stopped scaring off employees and probably moviegoers too. Those who agreed to stay took on extra hours until we hired replacements. Bullock's murder had been a grim event, and yet what could we do about it? Anticipating *Jaws* helped. There was so much media attention, and the full realization we would get this movie had us jazzed.

Hogan and I got along well. He was off the hook as the murderer, so I assumed. Also, he now seemed proud to show off his projection booth, especially after I went out of my way to praise his choice of posters.

Kenny had started right away and was already proving to be a great help. As I'd expected, he was much better than me at maintaining the platter system. The vibes between him and Hogan were cool too.

I had also decided to evaluate all of our employees because some I suspected of stealing. Mindy Hawkins, who mostly did concessions, was my main worry. I'd seen her pocket Reese's Cups more than once, and as far as I could tell, she hadn't paid for them. Ever since she was hired, we had been coming up short after the weekly inventory. I needed to solve this problem.

But I thought about Carrie Jenkins the most. Not because she needed evaluating. She was on mind constantly. Even when we were in separate parts of the theater, I was aware of her presence, as if my thoughts worked like radar, always operating and locked in on her. When I couldn't see her, I saw her.

Had she noticed the change in my appearance? I hoped so. Did my being manager impress her? Why did I keep entertaining such stupid ideas? Pure fantasy. I felt like Pluto, circling the sun, out in the cold.

Carrie must have spent time outside, because her complexion seemed more coppery, bringing out a deeper blue glow to her eyes. I could hardly stand it.

After the first shows started, I found a chance to start a conversation with her.

"I guess you finished *Fahrenheit*? Did you think about what book you'd be?"

I liked Bradbury's idea in the book, set in a Nazi-like dictatorship, of having people who resist the regime each be responsible for preserving an important book through memorization, a living library.

"Good question. There're so many I love. Emily Dickinson," she said, showing me the cover of the book she was now reading, *The Collected Poems of Emily Dickinson*.

"Didn't she write one about a bird eating a worm?" I asked, as I tried to remember a line from high school English.

"He bit an angle-worm in halves and ate the fellow, raw," Carrie said, reciting the line with instant recall.

"That's the one," I said, glancing over at the *Jaws* poster.

"Well, how about you? What book would you be, Mr. Burton?"

I'd considered the question in advance, hoping she would ask me. At first, I had decided on *Robinson Crusoe*, but as I thought about it again, I figured she might not consider it great enough literature. Because she'd mentioned a poet, I instead said, almost without thinking, "I'd go with Robert Frost, his collected poems."

"Frost? Oh," she said. Evidently, not an inspiring choice. Strike one, I figured.

Owen entered the lobby. Damn him. I hadn't seen him drive up. He wore a tie-dyed shirt with a hallucinatory pattern and low-slung pants with a thick rope for a belt. Leather sandals completed the picture of coolness. Once again, I felt like a clown. Strike two.

Carrie filled him in on our conversation.

"Robert Frost, really?" Owen said. "That reactionary?"

What's wrong with Robert Frost, I wondered? Reactionary? I wasn't sure what Owen meant. This shook me. And Owen realized my uncertainty as he followed up by saying,

"I mean, hasn't he had his day? And kind of right-wing?" That's what I had thought he'd meant.

"At least with Frost, we still want to learn his poems by heart," Carrie said, offering me support. I liked her point.

"You mean in middle school?" Owen said with a laugh.

Carrie gave Owen an irritated look. But why couldn't I defend myself? I hated looking weak.

"Hey, Frost is great," Owen continued. "And he needs preserving. No question. But, who's your favorite painter, Norman Rockwell?"

"Owen, don't be such a snob," Carrie said. Now, she gave him a serious frown.

"I kind of like Norman Rockwell," I said, mostly because Mrs. Roe had framed a centerfold Rockwell had painted for *Look* Magazine and had placed it in her living room.

"He's not an artist. He's a good illustrator. And another reactionary," Owen said.

I felt confused, unable to counter Owen's claims. The Rockwell centerfold had been painted in the mid-1960s during the desegregation crisis. It depicted an actual event from 1960 in which a young Black girl had been led to her New Orleans elementary school by federal marshals needed for her protection. How reactionary could he have been? And *just* an illustrator? I wasn't trying to claim he was Leonardo da Vinci.

"Owen, cut it out," Carrie said.

"Sorry, sorry," Owen said.

"I need a drink of water," Carrie said. She headed across the lobby.

Owen trailed behind her and said, "What did I do? He *is* just an illustrator."

I should have defended myself better. Yes, Rockwell was probably best described as an illustrator. But the content of the magazine cover was hardly reactionary. And I was sure Frost was a good choice, a *great* poet. I didn't know more than a couple poems, the "Two Roads" one best, which I indeed had memorized in middle school. I should have picked a contemporary poet, except that I couldn't think of any. So what? Frost had been given the honor of reading a poem at Kennedy's inauguration. I remembered seeing a photo of him taken on that freezing day in 1961. Yet he had looked about a hundred years old. All this amounted to strike three.

CHAPTER TWENTY-ONE

I made an excuse to end the conversation, claiming I needed to check on something outside. The grand, bulky shape of Spence's old Buick eased into the parking lot. It was so long and wide it floated along with its delta wings, more barge than automobile. Spence parked halfway down the lot and soon his tall, lean frame appeared out of the darkness. He wore his Stetson hat, with its distinctive pinched look across its top. He shuffled over to where I stood next to one of the *Jaws* posters near the lobby entrance.

Spence tilted the brow of his hat upward and inspected the poster, the whites of his eyes contrasting with his creamy dark skin. There was a ton of living in those eyes. He seemed to be thinking hard.

"Scary, don't you think?" I said.

"Reckon so," he said, his thoughts elsewhere it seemed.

A bottle of Coke came from around his back, where he had been holding it with his left hand, the long sway of his arm allowing a wide motion. He lifted the bottle to the same side of his mouth and took a slow swallow, the bottle angling off even further to the left as well, as I had often seen him do. I stared at the way he held the bottle. Spence noticed my staring because he said,

"A woman, she hit me upside my face with a two-by-four." He pointed to his right side and continued, "Had a rusty nail on it. Stuck in my jaw. Yanked it out, but this side swelled up like a squirrel planning for winter. Lasted about three months. Got used to drinking from this here other side."

"She must have been real mad at you, Spence," I said, curious why she would do this.

"Love bite was all," Spence said, with a smile spreading across his face. He liked talking in riddles. I wouldn't be finding out any more about that woman, at least not now.

He changed the topic and said,

"What's eating you, Nate?"

"Nothing," I said.

"Hum, you look like, like you in love," Spence said. "Yes, you in *luv*." He elongated the word as if he were blowing a low note on a saxophone.

"What are you talking about, Spence? It's nothing."

Spence persisted, smiling, "It's a lot of nothing. Yes, you've got yourself a heartthrob."

I had to admit that his joking about it ended my bad mood. And was there anything he didn't notice? Fool that I was, I had fallen for Carrie from the first day I met her when she had walked into the lobby seeking a summer job.

I had been changing a Coke syrup canister on a slow Saturday afternoon in early May. From a distance she seemed about fifteen or sixteen because she was so small and slender. She was dressed in faded jeans and a plain blouse, both a size too big for her. But as she got closer, her striking blue eyes, so full of keen energy and intelligence, stunned me, transforming my impression of her. And she spoke with a voice so mature, like a woman of twenty-five, already full of achievements.

"Can I help you?" I asked.

"Carrie Jenkins." She held out her hand and gave me a strong handshake. "I saw the sign outside that you're hiring. I'd like a job for the summer." I detected the scent of something. Not perfume. More like a bar of soap.

She pronounced each word with such confidence, matching the rich energy in her eyes. The effect was unnerving.

I stuttered out a reply. "I'm the assistant manager. I'll get you an application."

My hands fumbled, and I accidentally released the pressure on the cable attached to the new canister. A spray of amber Coke syrup hissed upwards, splattering the upper part of my shirt and the counter before I could close the line.

"Damn," I said under my breath, my face reddening with embarrassment. "How about taking a seat over there?"

She grabbed a handful of napkins from a dispenser and offered them to me.

"Thanks. They're old cables. We need new ones."

"My fault, I distracted you."

I appreciated her kind explanation, hoping she believed it. I got her an application and had her working for us by the weekend.

And so there was no fooling Spence. He had too many years experiencing the ways of people, and he had kept piling up wisdom along the way.

Later, after everyone else had left for the evening, I helped Spence with the cleaning. With each row, he swept up the trash as I followed with the mop. He had a Coke, which he set down in the aisle. After finishing a row, he scooped it up and took a swallow from that one side of his mouth. I thought again about the woman who had hit him with the two-by-four years ago. I swept the mop from side to side to finish the row and asked,

"Spence, if you don't mind my asking, if you're so smart about love, why did that woman hit you with that two-by-four?"

He didn't answer. Not right away. He started another row. When all the cups and popcorn boxes from the row were in the trash container and I had finished the mopping, he straightened his back and said, "Married to her for thirty years, until she got the cancer."

"Oh," I said. "I'm sorry."

"Long time ago."

We did another row in silence.

"Nate, I'm going to tell you something," Spence said. "A while after I first married and I'd be working in the field, before I got my own patch of land, there was a woman who lived in a house overlooking it. Sometimes, I'd walk across that field, all the way over to her house. And I'd get into bed with her. Later, I'd swear I'd never walk across that field again. And, do you know, the next day I might walk right back over there. Ain't that the darndest thing?"

"I guess so," I said, after his words penetrated my

thinking for a moment. "Is that why, well, your wife used the two-by-four?"

"I love the loving. Don't you, Nate?"

"Of course. But, Spence, did you love your wife?"

"Love my wife?" he said, with an intense expression on his face, its meaning I could not label. Then, the look in his eyes softened. "Not one day passes I don't pray her alive, *un*dead."

This threw me off balance. We finished the last few rows in silence.

CHAPTER TWENTY-TWO

I spent most of the next day wrapped up in my own troubles. I caught myself looking in the restroom mirror, self-conscious over the Asian cast to my eyes and irritated by my irregular row of lower teeth. I avoided conver-sations, pretending to be absorbed with preparations for *Jaws*, even though Carrie dominated my thoughts.

After the last show started and most of the employees had already taken off, I noticed that the "S" in *Jaws* on the north face of the marquee had slipped. It was at a slant, creating a sloppy impression. I went outside to fix it.

After straightening the letter, I sat for a while with my legs dangling over the marquee entranceway. The night air was thick with moisture, but a cooling breeze felt good. A mosquito landed on my forearm, and I swatted it away before it could bite. I took a few moments to survey the property with fresh eyes.

At this height and in the darkness, I might as well have been in a space capsule on its way to Jupiter, as in *2001, a Space Odyssey*. I summoned up strains from the theme music, enhancing this sense. The cars swished by the main road in both directions, like streaking comets. The light from the theater lobby shone just enough for me to notice a squirrel zigzag about near the base of the marquee. It found something worth gripping in its mouth and shot across the grass and up a pine tree. Sitting in this position, looking

115

down on the world, partly cleansed me of resentments. I felt hungry and remembered an almost empty box of Junior Mints I had in my jacket pocket. I ate them, one by one, savoring each.

I studied the theater building. The vast size of our main theater struck me anew, and I reminded myself that it was by far the biggest in the area. It stretched down a natural slope that had probably made the grading easy when constructed about twenty years earlier. Just a simple structure, red brick with no frills, and yet it had a grandeur to it. Sitting there, sturdy and sphinxlike in the night, it was a functioning monument to the movie theater business.

It fit over 750 people. With rocking-chair seating, full stereophonic sound, and a super widescreen, it was the obvious choice for *Jaws* over other theaters. We rarely filled it, but when we did, it was exhilarating. True, the headaches caused by foul-ups magnified as the crowds got bigger. The law of averages resulted in more people complaining, getting sick, stealing, defiling property, you name it. But there was no denying the energy that the crowds produced. A sold-out crowd meant that the movie was good and people were enjoying themselves. If someone was on a diet, to heck with that. Time to have a tub of popcorn, maybe with butter, a box of Raisinets, and Coke to wash it all down. What was life for if you couldn't indulge at the movies? Some of us completed our romantic dreams at the movies, lost it at the movies, and in more ways than one. *Jaws*, by all indications, would be spectacular. My shoulders made a slight shake in anticipation.

Owen's van entered the parking lot and took a place near the marquee. He had the windows down, and I heard his 8-track tape player belting out a Led Zeppelin guitar solo. Owen, instead of coming inside, waited for the solo to end and killed the engine. He got out and stood by the driver's side of the van. He didn't notice me, and I stayed quiet. Then it seemed I had to stay quiet, as if I were secretly hiding within a dark corner of someone's room. I stopped the swaying of my legs and drew them up, slowly.

Owen glanced left and right, reached into his shirt pocket, and took out a cigarette. He lit it and inhaled. It was a joint. The distinctive smell of pot wafted past me seconds later.

Carrie came out to meet him, and she said,

"Don't do that here!"

"Hey, it's good stuff."

"You'll get caught."

"There're never any cops around here."

"But Mr. Burton's out here."

"I'm scared," Owen said, with a mock expression of terror. "I mean, he's such a Boy Scout. Kind of naive. Don't you think?"

My head spun. *Boy Scout. Naive.* So that was what he thought of me.

"You didn't need to make him feel ignorant."

"Sorry, I can't help it. He makes it so easy."

Carrie, although she had defended me, seemed to agree with him too. My face felt hot. Had they *both* been just humoring me? Was I even someone they took seriously? Was

Carrie only being polite?

Owen leaned over to give Carrie a kiss, but she drew her face away.

"Come on," Carrie said. "Let's go. Throw that away."

They got inside the van, and Owen took the remaining drags from the joint. He tossed what was left of it out the window onto the asphalt, and they drove off.

I felt like a dated figure in a Norman Rockwell magazine cover. I recalled a scene from *The Incredible Shrinking Man*, the science fiction movie from the 1950s. The main character, trapped in the basement of his house and terrorized by spiders, realizes he has shrunk so small that his cries for help go unheard. Owen had me nailed. I was way out of my depth, a twenty-four karat fool. There was no sugar-coating it. And I was close to hating him for it.

CHAPTER TWENTY-THREE

When I came up Mrs. Roe's driveway, I was disappointed to see the kitchen light on. Mrs. Roe was still awake. She would be full of good cheer, and I was in no mood for matching effort.

I exited the car and saw her at the top of the back steps.

"Ah, creeping murmur and the poring dark fills the wide vessel of the universe," she said with a hushed, theatrical voice.

"Mrs. Roe, you always have a good one for me."

"Prince Hal, before the Battle of Agincourt, come from visiting his troops by their campfires."

"With *Jaws* coming, a battle *is* about to start," I said, sidestepping my ignorance of who Prince Hal was.

"Where's the smile I like to see you wear?" she asked.

"Oh, I'm fine."

I needed to put up a better front. Even in the shadows, my face told a tale.

I gave Byron a couple treats and took him out in the backyard for a few minutes. He looked so happy that, for a brief second, I wanted to trade places with him. A cup of tea awaited me when I returned to the kitchen.

"Tea for two?"

"Yeah, two for tea."

Mrs. Roe had placed the cup in a small, cleared space on the wide kitchen table among a spread of jigsaw pieces. She was halfway through completing the starting edges of what was probably a thousand-piece puzzle.

"What's the puzzle about?" I looked around for the box lid.

"Haven't the faintest idea. I found the pieces in a paper bag in a trunk down in the basement. The trunk still had the Cunard Line label on it from when my husband and I shipped over to the States in 1946. My late sister gave it to us. Makes it more fun, not knowing."

"This hits the spot," I said, after taking a careful sip of tea.

"Nate, what's on your mind?"

"Getting ready for *Jaws* is all."

"I've heard the radio ads with the haunting music," Mrs. Roe said with an exaggerated shake of her shoulders.

"They're good. They're all over the place," I said. "People are imitating the music around the theater all the time. There's something about it. Something deep and primitive."

"Yes, yes. And do you know, even my neighbor, Marion Lester—you've met her—is planning on taking her grandkids. But, Nate, dear, I see from your bookmarker that you still have a way to go with the book."

I had been carrying my copy of *The Last of the Mohicans* with me. I'd set it on the kitchen counter as I came in. The bookmark's place hadn't changed for several days. She paused for a moment and gave me a steady gaze.

"What is it, Mrs. Roe? What's making you stare?"

"A cat can look at a king," she said, laughing. "I daresay you remind me of several boys I had when I was teaching, and I have an idea. They were bright, but they had something, a condition of a sort, that held them back. I suspect you have the visual form."

"A condition?" I didn't like having a condition.

"I say condition, but the important thing about it is that it is something that interferes with the normal thinking of an *otherwise capable* person. And so, a very bright person can seem, and only seem mind you, limited, and unfairly so. Dyslexia is the name for it. This, Nate, I believe, is why you say you are a slow reader."

"Dyslexia?" I felt defensive, though she wouldn't want me to feel this way.

"Nate, dear, let me show you an example. Sometimes, you transpose letters. Look, I've saved one of your written notes."

She showed me a slip of paper upon which I'd written a note a week earlier. She must have had it handy for a while, waiting for the right moment to show me.

"Here, you spelled 'cat' as 'act', reversing the order of letters."

"I did that?" I said, hardly believing it.

"You must realize that these are *easy* words, words you know. I've seen you do it at Scrabble too. That's one clue, when someone does it for *simple* words, ones that anyone would know, really."

"Even the easy ones," I said with a sense of revelation. Yes, this was the key point. I recalled the mistake I'd made with the marquee letters and revisited the embarrassment.

"I know you don't think badly of your abilities, but, still,

I don't want you selling yourself short. You're a bright lad with a nimble mind."

Mrs. Roe told me more. She pointed out other things I did that were giveaway signs. My case was mild, which made it seem like I was just a slow reader. She said she could help me if I were interested. There were professionals she knew from her days as a teacher who could do a more complete diagnosis. There were things that could be done to overcome it, even for an adult like myself.

This excited me. I had been taken aback at first. Who wants to be diagnosed with dyslexia? Sounded like a disease. And yet, I liked this kind of explanation for why I was such a slow reader. I never thought I had a slow mind. Actually, I thought I had a quick mind. But I must have feared I was slow, maybe even partly believed it.

"I guess my reading has bothered me. But this fits," I said. I remembered when I was in fifth grade. The school placed me in the slower class because my reading scores were low. Doubts had burrowed their way into my young self. But soon they moved me up to the top class because of what I had said in class. Also, I had a good memory. Testing, timed testing with reading, was the problem, not me.

I added, "So, this can be corrected?"

"Especially now we're understanding it better. Big bowls take a long time to fill. Oh, and there's one more thing. Let's have a look at your tea leaves, shall we?"

"Tea leaves?"

She pulled my teacup toward her. A few leaves had risen to the surface, forming a slow, circling pattern.

"I will discover to yourself, that of yourself, which you yet know not of."

Another line I couldn't place.

"Ah, yes," she continued. "This looks good, very good indeed. I can't say what will happen. And it won't happen right away. But, as I say, marvelous things are in your future."

I gave her a skeptical look but went along for the fun of it.

She slipped a ring off her finger and let me hold it, examine it.

"It belonged to my dear mum. She ran a spiritualist church in Manchester. She ran seances, connected with the dead, and looked into the future. Reading tea leaves was one of her talents. She had the gift. I like to think I have the power too. Her ring might help?"

"Stop pulling my leg, Mrs. Roe." Though I wanted to believe it.

"Heavens no. Whatever do you mean? I wouldn't think of it, not over a serious matter such as this, gracious me," she said, a twinkle in her eye as she took the ring back and replaced it on her finger.

She added, "And of course, the roe is the best part of the fish."

I laughed, my bad mood now faded.

I asked Mrs. Roe whether she had a book of Robert Frost's poems. I hoped to learn more about Frost. What would a larger sample of his poems be like? I wanted to be impressed, to prove I was right choosing him. As I figured, she quickly found her volume of his collected works and placed it in my hands with much satisfaction and pleasure.

Before turning in, I also asked her, "Was Frost a reactionary?"

"Reactionary?" she said. "No, I think that would be going too far. Conservative, yes—reactionary no—in so far any label fits such a man."

"Afterall," I said. "Why would President Kennedy, a Democrat, ask him to read a poem at his inaugural?"

"Indeed."

"Would you call him old-fashioned?"

Mrs. Roe laughed. "Well, he would be over 100 if he were alive today. Some would call him so. In some ways. Yet his best poems are for all time. Let me pick one for you to read before you go to sleep. Ask yourself if it seems old-fashioned." She thumbed through the pages and came to one she had earmarked at another time. "Design" was its title.

Once in bed, I read the poem. I liked it from the first lines:

I found a dimpled spider, fat and white,
On a white heal-all, holding up a moth
Like a white piece of rigid satin cloth —
I had one foot dangling a little over the edge of the bed,
and I pulled it in quickly.

Assorted characters of death and blight
Mixed ready to begin the morning right,
Like the ingredients of a witches' broth —
A snow-drop spider, a flower like a froth,
And dead wings carried like a paper kite.

Richard H. Smith

These lines were bone-chilling and got me thinking about the *Jaws* poster yet again. Suddenly, a pride welled up within me over my choice of Frost. Hardly mere stuff for middle school. Hardly old-fashioned. And the rest of the poem was good too:

> What had that flower to do with being white,
> The wayside blued and innocent heal-all?
> What brought the kindred spider to that height,
> Then steered the white moth thither in the night?
> What but design of darkness to appall? —
> If design govern in a thing so small.

The poem left me pondering the mysteries of life. *Thither in the night*, I repeated to myself. What a great phrase. I wondered how much control I would have over my fate, but I glimpsed signs of a reinvented life and a brightening future.

CHAPTER TWENTY-FOUR

Friday marked a week since Bullock's murder and a week before *Jaws* would start. *Rollerball* and *The Conversation II* had both played themselves out. Kenny and I figured that even the start of the weekend would be slow. We figured wrong.

Possibly it was curiosity about the theater because of Bullock's murder, or interest generated by the coming of *Jaws*. In any event, we had good-sized crowds for the first two shows, which made me anxious. The platter machine still needed servicing in theater two. This wouldn't happen until Monday when a new system would be installed in the main theater. And with every showing we had detected yet another strange sound coming from the projector or one of the platters.

I didn't want to deal with a lot of refunds if the projector malfunctioned, and we couldn't fix it. The company required that we only give money back to people who still had their ticket stubs, but some would lose them or throw them away. We could offer passes, but tempers would flare. For me, this was the worst part of the theater business.

I stuck my head in the projection booth to check on the platter rotation. The film had broken and was spewing onto the floor in a pile already a foot high.

"Damn that machine." I stared at the lower take-up platter that spun with the one end of film flapping like a snake's tongue. The machine was supposed to cut off if the film broke. *Don't panic. Keep calm.* Kenny was over in the theater one. Until someone told him about it, this would be up to me to fix.

Maybe, just maybe, after stopping the machine, I could pull out the broken end of the film without creating a snarl or knot and splice both ends together. It might take only two minutes. Then I could feed the film onto the platter. The pile, though scary big, seemed free of tangles. Could I do it? I was about to find out.

I mashed the shutdown button on the machine. The sprocket wheels clattered to a stop, and both platters froze. The projector bulb faded.

Someone in the crowd called out, "Hey, the bulb blew!"

More shouts followed, but I blocked them out as I knelt to examine the pyramid of film. Careful to avoid movement in the pile, as if I were playing a high stakes game of pick-up sticks, I parted the film at a place where the broken end might be. No luck. I tried another section. Still no luck. The air in the booth was thick and warm, and sweat broke out across my forehead and upper lip.

I heard light footsteps racing up the stairs. It was Carrie. "Mr. Burton, the projector. Oh, Jee-*sus*."

"I'm trying to fix it," I said, now extra worried whether I could handle it in front of her. A drop of sweat fell from the tip of my nose against the film.

"This looks—impossible," Carrie said.

"You can help. If I can just find the end. There, got it."

I gently pulled the broken end out from under the pile

and extended it a few feet, watching for any knotting as I pulled. I extended it further so that the end reached the splicing table.

"Carrie, see the other broken end, on the lower platter. Unwind enough so I can splice it. Bring it over here."

She moved over to the platter. "The crowd's freaking out!"

"I know, I know. Ignore 'em. We've got time before they go completely berserk. Let's do this."

"Pull it?"

"Yeah, it'll unwind. Quick."

As she unwound it, I placed my end on the splicer and cut off the frame where the film had broken. She handed me the other end, and I grabbed her end. But my hand was slick from sweat, and it slipped from my grasp.

"Damn!" I said.

Carrie reached and caught it in midair.

"Good catch," I said. And I meant it.

I held the film extra tight this time and snapped the end sprocket hole into the splicer, making a clean cut. I brought the two ends together and applied the splicing tape.

"Good. That does it. Now let's see if we can wind it onto the platter. This is where we'll need some real luck," I said, praying to myself. "You turn the platter and I'll feed it. Take it slow. I need to watch for twists."

"Got it."

It went smoothly at first, but a knot appeared halfway through the pile.

"Hold, hold. Wait a second," I said, shaking the film,

praying that the knot would free itself. It loosened and straightened itself.

"Great, no tangle. Go. A little slower, slower." Another half minute and all the film was safely wound onto the platter.

"There is a god," I said. "Let me get her started again." I did a fast inspection of the film for proper looping at each sprocket wheel. Good to go. I hit the start button, and we were back in business. Cheers erupted from the crowd. We'd fixed it in less than two minutes.

"Carrie, you were stellar."

"I guess so. You too."

I wanted to hug her, do something. But I felt myself soaked with perspiration. With a brush of my sleeve, I wiped the sweat from my forehead and upper lip.

We stood looking at each other for an awkward second.

"Tell you what," I said. "How about you checking everything's cool downstairs?"

Carrie left with a bounce in her step. Owen was one lucky guy. And the world was not a fair place.

I took another close look at the machine. It seemed to be operating normally, with only a slight, uneven tension in the film on the lower platter. We'd be fine until Monday, I hoped.

CHAPTER TWENTY-FIVE

When I returned to the lobby, Carrie was excitedly telling Kenny how we'd fixed the break in the film. But everyone soon got distracted by a rush on concessions just before the nine o'clock showing of *The Conversation II* in the theater one. I wanted to keep a closer watch on *Rollerball* because the print had felt brittle while I was splicing it, but the crowd caused me and Kenny to help wherever we were needed, tearing tickets, fixing drinks, or popping corn.

The Conversation II had already started, and I saw a couple rushing up to the ticket window. The man was tall and stiff, like a store mannequin come to life. He had a full head of silver hair and long sideburns flanking tanned cheeks. I'd seen him somewhere before but couldn't place him.

Samantha took her time, deliberately I thought. As soon as she pushed the change through the ticket window, along with the two tickets, he snatched them up, handed one to his companion, probably his wife, and bolted into the lobby. She was attractive, slender, also well-tanned, and expensively dressed in a flower-patterned dress. I guessed she was at least fifteen years younger than him. She had a stressed, distorted expression on her face.

I recognized him. He was a Duke Hospital heart doctor named Halderman. I'd seen him on TV several months back because the family of a patient was suing him and Duke

Hospital for malpractice. He was known for some controversial, experimental treatments, and this one turned out badly. But what I most remembered about him was something Mrs. Roe had told me. In the late fifties, her husband had been his patient at Halderman's private clinic, before Halderman had been hired by Duke. He had changed doctors when he had discovered that Halderman required his Black patients use another entrance and waiting room. Now this was a long time ago, and times were different. Halderman too, presumably. But you had to wonder what kind of man this Halderman was.

He took long strides toward where I had moved over to the box we used for ticket stubs. His wife headed to the concession counter. He shot past me without giving me as much as a glance, handing me his ticket but showing no interest in his stub after I had torn it. I held it in his direction as he sped across the carpet to the theater entrance. A guilty wish arose in me. Perhaps someone would accidentally extend a leg in the theater aisle and trip him. I tossed the stub into the ticket box. His wife was nicer. Despite carrying two drinks and two popcorn boxes, she showed me her ticket, wedged in between two fingers, and let me squeeze her stub back between the same fingers. I led her to the theater door entrance and opened it for her. Poor woman.

At least ten minutes passed before Kenny and I checked on the projector.

"Do you hear that?" I said as we entered the projection booth.

"Uh-oh," Kenny said, his eyes bulging wider than I thought possible.

We saw another pyramid of film piling on the floor next to the projector. The safety arm had failed to shut down the projector once again. I felt like the sorcerer's apprentice in Disney's *Fantasia*. The brooms were multiplying out of control, but dumping spirals of film onto the floor rather than water. Something else must also have failed because the upper sprocket wheels now chewed a section of film that had backed up into the projector bulb area. Blackish smoke curled upward, the air increasingly thick with the distinctive smell of burning celluloid.

"Holy crap!" Kenny said.

Kenny punched the projector stop button, shutting the machine down. A small blue flame blossomed from where the film had backed up and was pressed against the projector bulb. I slapped it out with a dust cloth. The sprockets were caked with bubbling, melted film.

"Refunds," I said, with a full sense of the mayhem this promised.

I glanced through the observation window. We'd sold just over fifty tickets, but it seemed like a hundred. Shouts had already started.

"You deal with this. I'll handle the refunds," I said, as Kenny nodded his agreement. He got right to it, and I hustled downstairs. We knew the drill, but that wouldn't make it much easier.

Several people had already exited the theater.

"Sorry, folks," I said. "The projector broke down."

They groaned.

"We'll be giving refunds or passes. Just line up by the concession counter. Give us your stubs if you still have them."

I went into the theater and made a general announcement. More groans. Soon the concession area was a mass of frustrated people, jostling for position, wanting their money back. We set up two areas, one for refunds, which Samantha would handle, and one for passes, which I would handle. Carrie helped me with passes.

I kept a watch over Samantha. Her sour attitude might set people off. But she took care of business, collecting stubs when she could, otherwise directing people to me and Carrie.

Halderman and his wife were at the back at first. But Halderman elbowed himself toward Samantha while his wife headed outside. People gave him fierce looks. He plowed right through.

I was about to ask him to wait his turn, but he was already at the counter holding up two fingers for two refunds. He had no stubs. How would Samantha handle this? Curiosity got the better of me, and I held off saying anything.

Samantha kept her attention on a woman and her son who she had been about to serve.

Halderman said, "Two. I'm a doctor. I need to leave."

Samantha gave him a withering stare and said,

"I don't care if you're Elvis. You can get your uppity ass to the back and wait your turn like everybody else. And make sure you have your stubs." She turned away from him like he didn't exist and asked the woman, "One adult and one child?"

Halderman's face turned red and veins in his neck and forehead expanded like he was blowing on a trumpet.

"Give me the damn refunds," he said.

"Wait your turn," someone in the crowd said.

"What does being a doctor have to do with it?" someone else said.

Halderman finally seemed to realize how outnumbered he was. Two beefy men in the crowd came forward, forming a barrier. Halderman appeared to shrink.

One of the men, short but wide, decorated with snake tattoos on each exposed bicep, said in a squeaky drawl that belied his appearance, "Why don't you turn around and apologize to that nice lady. Then we'll let you get behind us."

"Like hell I will," Halderman said, but with weak bluster. He made a move to exit through an opening, in a direction away from the two men. But a hefty woman blocked his path, apparently emboldened by the others.

"I don't think so," she said.

The fun was over. At the back of where Halderman stood, and just to the right of Samantha, was an entrance door to the concession area. I swung it open and said,

"Follow me."

I grabbed his closest elbow and pulled him toward me and closed the door. He drew his elbow away, but he followed me even so.

"Hey, what's going on?" someone yelled.

"That's not fair. He should wait like everyone else," another person said.

The other side of the concession area faced the smaller lobby of the second theater. It was empty. I led Halderman through to a corner hidden from the crowd.

"Sir, why don't you take these two passes. And, here, you can have two extra passes for your trouble. That should square us."

He said nothing, but I detected a shift in his thinking, possibly a hint of embarrassment.

"I'll just take the two," he said, giving me back two of the passes. He exited the theater to join his wife, and they took off together, exchanging angry words.

I returned to giving out more passes while Samantha continued to handle the remaining refunds.

"Good riddance," someone said.

There were a few more complaints, but soon everyone seemed content to get on home.

When we'd finished with the last person, I thanked Samantha.

"I liked the way you handle that doctor."

"His crap's the same as mine," Samantha spit out each word, causing me to back away slightly.

I found nothing to say in response, concluding that the nasty side of Samantha was the larger part of her core. If someone crossed her, they'd regret it. I wasn't going to be that person. I turned and walked away.

Carrie had seen everything. She asked, "Mr. Burton—"

"How about Nate?" I said, without thinking. This felt right. Carrie must have felt it too because she shifted without missing a beat.

"Yeah, Nate. Why did you offer him the extra passes? Did he deserve them?"

I thought for a moment about how to respond, thrilled she'd used my first name so smoothly.

"I didn't plan that out. I guess I didn't want him to leave us thinking he had a legitimate complaint."

"I see. The customer's always right? But twice over?"

"I don't know. It felt like the thing to do."

"Anyway, his behavior was awful." Carrie narrowed her eyes, their blue sparkle focused and challenging me to give her a better reason.

I thought for a few seconds. I liked this. I liked that she felt comfortable pressing me. And I very much liked standing next to her. Her soapy, fresh fragrance just about made me dizzy. I considered the question more, and an idea came to me.

"Let me put it this way," I said, warming to the challenge. "I remember hearing about a pro baseball player named Baker. He'd gotten into big trouble over cheating on his wife. The tabloids had fun with it, and rival fans ribbed him from the bleachers."

I stopped for a second. I could tell she was wondering hard where I was heading. I continued, giving her a confident smile. "Hold on. There's a point coming."

"I'm listening," she said, with a doubtful but intrigued look.

"There was a particular fan who had it in for Baker. This guy heckled him every time his team visited, yelling out the name of the woman. Ronda, I think it was. You get this kind of junk at baseball games, usually from the bleachers, but this guy seemed to make it his mission in life to ridicule Baker. Have you been to a pro game?"

"No, but what does this have to do—"

"I'm getting to it," I said. I was enjoying elongating the point, how I'd seen Spence do it.

"You see, this guy spewed out vulgar stuff like it was his only passion. Even as the players left the stadium after games, the guy waited outside the exit to yell at Baker. After one game, sure enough, there he was, at it again. Baker usually tried to ignore him, but his time he didn't. Baker happened to be carrying a baseball, and he—"

"He threw it at him?" Carrie said, anticipating what I would say, but seeming to realize that this couldn't be what he did. Not considering how I'd handled Halderman.

"This is the thing. He stopped right in front of the guy, extended his hand, and gave him the baseball. He *gave* him the baseball."

"Really?"

"Yeah, the guy was so surprised that he accepted it and shut up. And, you know what? He never heckled Baker again."

"Come on. Did this really happen?"

"As far as I know."

She looked at me in a curious way I couldn't quite figure.

CHAPTER TWENTY-SIX

We lucked out with the projector. After Kenny cleaned it of dried celluloid, he started it up for a test. All the sprocket wheels ran smoothly, and film fed through the whole system as it should.

Later, Hogan corralled me in the lobby to gloat, "Those platters work, but only when they work. Otherwise, they're junk."

"Phil," I said. "I don't disagree with you. But what can I do about it?"

A woman who looked familiar came out of the main theater. It was the wife of the man who had hammered Mr. Bullock a week before. Maybe she and her husband had returned to use those passes I'd given them.

She staggered against the wall, letting her pocketbook fall to the carpet. Hogan, closest to her, sprang in her direction and held her steady.

"You okay, ma'am?" Hogan asked, as he eased her toward a nearby lobby bench. I grabbed her pocketbook. She gave both of us confused stares. Was she having a heart attack? What if she collapsed and stopped breathing? I'd seen someone administer CPR, but could I do it?

Sweat dotted her forehead. Her pupils were enlarged. She slurred a word I couldn't understand. I felt one of her wrists, the pulse erratic, thumping. Others had gathered, all seeming to look at me to do something.

I recognized the medical bracelet on her wrist. It was similar to one I'd seen worn by someone with diabetes. I led her over to a lobby bench.

"Are you a diabetic? You need some sugar?"

She didn't answer, but I looked at Hogan and said, "Phil, get me a Coke. Make it quick. Straw too."

I went with the odds and figured it couldn't hurt to give her the drink. Hogan had Carrie fix a Coke, and she rushed it over to us. I pressed the straw past the woman's lips, which were now clammy and limp.

"Here's some Coke," I said.

As if by muscle memory, she started sucking, almost like a baby.

"That's right. You'll be fine," I said, hoping this was true.

She continued sucking for half a minute while we all watched. It was helping too. She looked up at me and said, "My head hurts. Where am I? Who are you?"

"You're at the Yorktowne Theater," I said, pressing my hand again her wrist. "You have diabetes, don't you? Your sugar was low, but you're getting better now."

"Yes, yes, I do. I must have had a reaction."

"You look okay now."

"It was mild, just mild. I'm fine, really. I need my tablets. Where's my pocketbook?"

By this time her husband had exited the theater.

"Oh, honey. There you go again," he said, as he came over to us, not looking too concerned. He knelt and reached for her pocketbook, which I had placed near her feet, and found a medicine bottle. He shook out two pink tablets and popped them into his wife's expectant mouth.

"Here, honey," he said.

She crunched them and took another suck of Coke.

"Wanda, right?" I remembered the name from before.

"Yes, it's Wanda, Wanda Mallard. I'm so sorry to have caused a problem. I'm fine now. Thank you all so much."

"Why don't you and your husband both get back to the movie."

Mr. Mallard stood and glanced down at his wife. Then he took my arm and led me off to the side. He said, "About last week, I want to apologize."

"Hey, all's forgotten."

"And I'm sorry about what happened to your manager. I wouldn't wish that on nobody."

I said, "Listen. I appreciate your saying this. But you both go enjoy the movie. No need to miss any more of it."

Mrs. Mallard was now standing, and her husband led them both back into the theater.

Carrie asked me, "Nate, how did you know what was wrong with her?"

"The medical bracelet she had on her wrist."

"She was lucky you figured it out."

"Pin a medal on his chest," Hogan said with a strange purring sound.

"Her husband would have taken care of things soon enough," I said.

"I suppose so," Carrie said. I liked the sound of her using my first name.

CHAPTER TWENTY-SEVEN

The following afternoon Spence came by early to introduce me to his great-grandson, Ricardo. With the same creamy dark skin and long-limbed build, he favored Spence. He also had a similar wise cast to his eyes, like he'd already figured out how the world worked. They were twins, born sixty some years apart. We decided that Ricardo would do both concessions and ushering as needed and help with the cleaning when *Jaws* started. Ricardo's mom would pick him up soon, and he moved to a lobby bench to wait for her.

"Spence," I said, once we were by ourselves. "Any word about Milton?"

"There will be directly." This got me going.

"What's up? Tell me."

"I will, presently."

"Tell me, Spence."

"Not yet, Nate. Can't yet. You plant your seed in April, and you harvest it in October."

I should have known I couldn't rush Spence. It occurred to me that this was how he worked too. When he did the landscaping, he never hurried. He took his time. The effect seemed fast, though. If you left him alone, when you came back, the job was done. He was on to something else.

Owen and Carrie came into the lobby. This shifted my attention. Usually, they walked close to each other, sometimes touching. But this time they came in separately,

Carrie first, looking unhappy about something. She headed to the restroom.

Owen said, "Guess I gave you a hard time yesterday. Sorry."

His eyes were streaked with red. I detected the smell of pot on his clothes. He was high. From his pocket he pulled out a small metal object, placing it in front of me on the counter. He said, "You say you like Norman Rockwell. That's cool. What's your expert opinion on this, this piece of sculpture."

"I'm not sure," I said. What was he up to?

It was small for a sculpture, but it had some interesting shaping. I suppose it showed creativity. Was he testing me? I didn't think much of it, but I didn't want to offend him—on the chance that he had made it. Mindy Hawkins and Billy Gossett were watching, and I said something positive.

"I like the material it's made of."

Carrie returned and saw the object. Her face flashed with anger.

"Owen, what are you doing with that?"

"I'm just asking Norman, our art expert, what he thinks of this sculpture."

She grabbed it off the counter and thrust it back at him.

"Put it away," she said, glaring at Owen. "It's *not* sculpture."

"What is it?" I asked. No one said anything, though Carrie and Mindy exchanged glances.

"It's a specula or something," Mindy said, blushing slightly.

"What?" I said.

Carrie gave Owen another irritated look and said, "It's a speculum."

I understood. It was an obstetrical instrument. He'd been pulling a trick on me.

"Just wanted to make a point about art," explained Owen, with an innocent expression.

"Stop equivocating," Carrie said.

"Aww, come on. He knew it wasn't a real sculpture," Owen said, though he didn't seem to be swaying Carrie.

Owen continued, "I got the idea from reading about Thomas Hoving, you know, the art curator at the Met. How was I to know he'd never seen one before?"

"You are so very clever," Carrie said.

I wanted to grab him by his tie-dyed shirt and send him bouncing across the carpet, right out the front entrance.

Directing his attention back to me, Owen said, "My point is that art is subjective. If you like Norman Rockwell, I'm cool with that. Frost, he's hip too."

I wasn't sure how his demonstration helped make this point, but I said, "We agree on one thing. I don't need your approval to like something. I didn't think it was a real piece of sculpture."

"Owen, you've lost all credibility. That's what Nate gets from trying to be *nice* to you," Carrie said as she shook her head.

"Oh, 'Nate' is it?" Owen said in quick reply, shifting his focus back to Carrie.

I ignored this shift in focus—although I very much liked

Carrie using my first name—and said, "But now you bring up Frost, you're wrong about him, Owen. He's the equal of any poet I've come across."

"How many poets do you know much about? Hey, Mindy, hand me a box of popcorn. Put it on my tab."

Mindy ignored him.

"You make Nate out to be a Caliban. You're so pretentious," Carrie said, as if she and Owen were having a separate conversation, out of my earshot, one I might not understand. But who was Caliban, I wondered?

"Okay, okay," Owen said. Then he turned to me and said, "You stick by your man, Frost. He's a great poet."

"I'll do that," I said.

"Like Nate said, he *doesn't* need your approval," Mindy said.

I gave her a secret glance as if to say I'd handle it.

"So, Owen," I said. "Have you actually read many of Frost's poems?" I had settled down, and I wasn't sure why. Maybe, it was because I had been so impressed by Frost's poem about the spider. Frost was better than Owen realized. Anyway, now I was curious.

"Sure. I mean, everyone knows the two roads one. And, honestly, that was in middle school. *Elementary* school more likely."

"Everyone? Can you recite it?" Carrie asked, crossing her arms like an English teacher.

"Come on. Who can do that?" Owen said. But then he took the bait. After clearing his throat, he began reciting it,

"Two roads diverged in a yellow wood ..."

He paused.

"Don't tell me, don't tell me."

Carrie tapped her right foot. But Owen couldn't remember what came next. She helped him.

> *"And sorry I could not travel both*
> *And be one traveler.*

Owen reddened. Carrie continued,

> *"And long I stood*
> *And looked down one as far as I could*
> *To where it bent in the undergrowth.*
> *Then took the other, as just as fair,*
> *And having perhaps the better claim,*
> *Because it was grassy and wanted wear;"*

Carrie paused again. Owen frowned and rolled his eyes. He said, "Just because you know it—"

"Owen," Carrie continued. "I'm afraid we must give you a failing grade."

"You flunked, Owen," Mindy said, laughing.

"Yeah, you choked," Billy said. "And no wonder. You're stoned."

Owen looked straight at Mindy. "*You* don't laugh at me." And turning to Billy, he said, "I'm not stoned, airhead."

"You're not only a pothead, you're a jerk too," said Billy.

"This is so lame," Owen said. "Carrie knows it, but she doesn't count. Nobody else can do it."

I knew I couldn't. Only the famous ending lines.

"Anybody?" said Owen, looking smug.

Billy opened his mouth slightly. For a high school kid, I had found him well-read. He seemed to be mouthing the lines with Carrie. But he stayed silent.

Carrie came to the rescue and began reciting it again, repeating the last line she'd already spoken.

> *"Because it was grassy and wanted wear;*
> *Though as for that the passing there*
> *Had worn them really about the same.*
> *And both that morning equally lay*
> *In leaves no step had trodden black.*
> *'Oh, I kept the first for another day!*
> *Yet knowing how way lead on to way,*
> *I doubted if I should ever come back."*

She paused, looking around at everyone. No one knew them.

Carrie continued,

> *"I shall be telling this with a sigh*
> *Somewhere ages and ages hence:"*

Suddenly, I heard the more familiar last lines in my head. Billy too, because we said them together with Carrie in a loud chorus,

"Two roads diverged in a wood, and I
—I took the road less traveled by
And that has made all the difference."

Carrie said, "A poem worth remembering and remembered because it is good."

Owen broke the spell by saying triumphantly, *"But,* by going with Frost, you are taking the road *more* traveled by, are you not? Anyway, it's trite stuff."

"Always the last word. It seems trite because it *is* so well known. If it were inherently trite, it would not be so well known," Carrie said sharply.

"She got you, Owen," I said.

Mindy's face brightened. Owen had hurt her feelings with his earlier insult.

"Listen, friends, Romans, ushers," I continued, using a turn of phrase that surprised even myself, and made me feel I was inhabiting Mrs. Roe's skin. "We've got work to do."

CHAPTER TWENTY-EIGHT

"Did you hear all that?" I asked Spence in a low voice.

Spence had been sitting on a lobby bench, as he often did, biding his time before starting with the cleaning.

"Sure enough did. Follow me outside."

We went outside toward Spence's car. I think he wanted to make it seem like there was a reason for our going out together, beyond just chatting. He opened his trunk and grabbed something, a replacement rubber belt for our main vacuum cleaner.

"I'm going to need to show you something later after everyone's gone," he said.

"What?"

"Just wait."

"Spence, come on."

"Not yet. But, yes sir, I did. That young man can razzle-dazzle, but he thinks the sun rises to hear the cock crow. Needs to grow more knowledge."

"Yeah," I agreed, though I needed to think through what Spence meant exactly.

"A tin can makes a racket with a few pebbles in it. He set you up with a lie." Spence closed the trunk hard to emphasize his point.

"He sure did."

"Needed bringing down a peg. Anyway, I need to change the belt and tighten the pin in that vacuum."

"Come on, Spence. Tell me what you know."

"I need Samantha gone first," Spence insisted.

"Samantha? Spence, you've got my mind racing."

Samantha came out from the office door as we entered the lobby. I called out, "Good night."

She gave me a stiff nod and made her way past us. When she was outside, I said, "Spence, please put me out of my misery."

"Hold your water. How about fetching me a flashlight?" The expression across his face brimmed over with mischief.

"How come?"

"You'll see."

I retrieved a flashlight from the office. As soon as Samantha had driven off, he led me outside the building again and over to the side where he'd found Bullock's body. The area was dark, concealed from street lights or the marquee. I was about bursting with curiosity.

"What are you doing, Spence?"

"Turn that flashlight on and shine over at that juniper bush, the one where I found Mr. Bullock."

"Spence, what the—"

"Just do it, Nate."

Spence moved into the juniper bushes, parting their prickly branches until he got close to the brick. I gave an involuntary shudder as I remembered the sight of Bullock's body.

"Over here," he said.

He reached down, tore off something, and made his way back. In his hand was a leaf of poison ivy.

"Spence, don't play around with that stuff. That's poison ivy."

He folded it into his mouth and chewed.

"Are you out of your ever-lovin' mind?" I almost screamed.

He continued to chew for a few moments as I stood waiting for an explanation. Spence had to know what he was doing. He always did. He spat the resulting wad onto the asphalt in a long, practiced arc like it was spent chewing tobacco.

"It don't bother me. I work around it all the time. Early spring, I start eating it. Get mune to it. A trick my daddy taught me. Would make a salad with it—if I liked the way it taste."

He watched me thinking. He gave another spit, a smaller one this time. Suddenly, I understood where he was heading.

"Spence, you're a genius."

My mind shifted into overdrive. Chances were that the person who killed Bullock had a breakout of poison ivy.

"Them junipers, choked with it toward the back. Been meaning to do something about it. It's been almost a week since Mr. Bullock was killed. I'm thinking. Now it can take a while for blisters to show. Next day mostly. But a week, maybe longer, if the first time."

"Have you told Detective Riggs about this?" I asked.

"Naw," he said with a chuckle.

"We need to tell him. We've got to tell him."

"It ain't hard evidence. Don't want to make too much of

it. Just something gets you wondering a different way."

"Detective Riggs could use it."

"Likely not. But, in my observing, don't see no one with no blisters. Like I say, can take a while."

"I haven't either—though I haven't been looking," I said.

"It ain't much," Spence said. "Anyway, I've got a funny feeling about what happened to poor Mr. Bullock. Let's be watchful. Not me so much. I move about and nobody see me, pay me no mind. Maybe you."

"Me?"

"Nate, I *know* Milton didn't do it."

"Why would anyone want to harm me?"

"Whoever killed Mr. Bullock won't right in the head. Crazy. This worries my thinking—you making the deposit now."

"So, who did it, Spence? We've come up with blanks. We've been through all the possibilities."

"Sometimes, it's the dogs that don't bark will bite you bad. I've seen this to be true."

"Who?"

"How about Miss. Hicks?"

"Samantha?"

"Don't know we can rule her out."

"She's hard to figure. Tell you the truth, she is kind of creepy. Dead to the world," I said.

"She might be big enough to bring Mr. Bullock down," Spence noted.

"I guess she does have a nasty temper. I've seen it flash once or twice, and it was scary. Wouldn't want to get on her bad side, as I think about it."

"If she wanted, she could flatten you like she was laying asphalt like you was a week-old grape," Spence said.

"True enough," I admitted, recalling again one of the cold looks she had given me.

"She and Mr. Bullock didn't get along. Am I right?" Spence said.

"She ignored him, mostly, Spence. I don't think she liked his dirty talk. Did it upset her? Not enough to kill him. There's fire in her. I see that now, though I used to think she was more a block of ice. But she left early that evening, about ten o'clock."

"She's a snake," Spence added, scratching his chin in thought.

"Snake?"

"Lot of creatures come to my mind. Take the sow me and my daddy tangled with on the farm. She was just a regular sow, peaceful, her piglets sucking on their mammy's teats. But one day she ate one of them and ran off, crazy. Me and my daddy hit the woods to go kill her. Had to. She had the froth in her mouth. Rabies. So we killed her. Burned her. Buried her deep."

"Jeez, Spence."

"I'm not saying the woman's bad for sure. Can't say that. Want to be fair to her. Don't know the true facts. Facts are what you have to obey. Just saying she gets me thinking this way."

"I don't know."

"Two plus two ain't five. Let's be watching. You be

watching," Spence said, looking straight at me, as serious as I'd ever seen him.

Was there really something for me to worry about? I saw no basic harm in her. But Spence's concerns couldn't be discounted.

"There's another possibility, Spence. Horace got into trouble a few years back when he was living in Georgia. A woman accused him of rape. Did you know about this?"

"Nope. No surprise though."

"Sue Ellen told me about it after the funeral. Detective Riggs knows about it too. It never went to trial because a judge ruled there wasn't enough evidence. She harassed him afterward, even threatened to kill him."

"Kill him?" Spence said.

"Yeah. And the theater company transferred him up here because of all the bad publicity. Maybe she hired someone to do this."

"We're trying to figure which way tumbleweed gonna roll," Spence said.

"I hear you, Spence."

All the speculating about Bullock's murder left me in a weird, agitated mood. Spence's warning hit home. Should I be checking people for blisters? I would have a closer look at Samantha's hands. And, come to think of it, she'd been wearing long sleeves. But wasn't this her usual habit?

My uneasy mood continued through the rest of the evening. And an odd thing happened later. When I left the theater for home and as I approached my car, I noticed something stuck to the front grill. What was it? I looked more closely and shivered. It was a small bird, its body shattered against the steel. When had that happened? I found a paper shopping bag from the back seat of the car and used to extract the remains. They came loose after a brief tug. The spindly feel and jumbled state of these tiny bones produced in me another, deeper shiver, disturbing me as much as Bullock's death. I placed the bag in the dumpster and headed home.

CHAPTER TWENTY-NINE

As I started up the back steps of Mrs. Roe's house, I heard a whimper and a scratching at the door. My heart raced. Where was Mrs. Roe? I fumbled for the door key and finally got the door open.

Byron shot past me and down the steps as I hit the kitchen light switch. A pool of urine spread across a section of the linoleum.

"Mrs. Roe?" I called.

No answer. I moved through the kitchen, calling her name a second time, louder. Again, no answer.

I found Mrs. Roe sitting in her reading chair in the living room with a newspaper folded on her lap, a half-completed crossword puzzle on the page facing her. Her head was back, her eyes open and still.

"No, please no," I said, as if there were a power that could reverse what I feared had happened.

I knelt down and felt her wrist. It was cold. No pulse. She wasn't breathing. I whispered her name and held both her hands as if by doing so I could create warmth. Her poor, weak heart had given out. Tears welled up in my eyes, blurring the letters she had written in the squares of the puzzle.

I left Mrs. Roe as she was and returned to the kitchen. I called 911 and remained standing next to the phone for half a minute, shaken and bewildered. Byron barked weakly from outside. Keats meowed. I cleaned up the wet spot on the kitchen floor and let Byron in. He looked hungry, and I poured dry food into his bowl. I gave Keats half a can of cat food.

For the next couple of hours, I moved about in a numbed state. It seemed impossible to comprehend that this warm, wonderful woman was no longer living. Emergency personnel arrived and performed a perfunctory confirmation of her death. A police officer soon followed and took down an account of how I found her. A coroner arrived and also examined her. It was all a gut-wrenching set of things to endure.

I could not provide next of kin. Mrs. Roe had mentioned a sister but long ago deceased. She had no children. Marion Lester came over from next door when the ambulance arrived. She took it hard. We cried together for several minutes.

About three-thirty, just after the coroner's van took Mrs. Roe's body away, there was a knock on the front screen door. It was Detective Riggs.

I greeted him with surprise and pushed open the screen door.

"Working a homicide case tonight," he said. "I was just a few blocks over near the ABC store. I heard over the police chatter about Mrs. Roe."

"This is a tough blow," I said as I joined him on the porch.

"I understand. I liked her too. After only a short conversation over the phone."

"Want to come in?"

"No, thanks. Can't stay. Long day." He paused, his expressive eyes full of sorrow. "They've taken her?"

I nodded.

We stood for a minute without talking. The air felt heavy and thick with the scent of honeysuckle. Suddenly, as if responding to a conductor, the harsh, percussion sound of crickets came to life. Maybe I had failed to notice them until that moment.

"She had a weak heart," I said.

"My mother came from England too. North of London," Riggs said. "A place called Welwyn Garden City. Turns out Mrs. Roe knew it well. Shopped there. A planned city. The first of its kind."

"She took me in like I was kin," I said.

"Had my mother's accent exactly," Riggs said. "Spot on."

After another stretch of silence, I said, "It means a lot, your stopping by."

We shook hands, and he disappeared into the night.

Riggs seemed so different to me now. I had viewed him as someone filling a role and doing it well, a category of person. I would thank him again and in a better way.

I returned to where Mrs. Lester sat at the kitchen table, her head down and her eyes tearing again. In our different ways, we were fully stricken with grief. I stared at the jigsaw puzzle and tried to guess the content of the picture. Mrs. Roe had only completed the four edges.

"Hillary and I were the best of friends," said Mrs. Lester. "We taught together in the same high school. Nate, I want you to stay here and keep watch over the house until the estate gets settled. I'm sure she would want this. I'll look after Byron and Keats while you're at work and take care of what needs to be done."

I thanked her. This was very kind. She was about to return home, but paused for a moment and said,

"Let me find you something from Hillary's books."

We went into Mrs. Roe's library. While she examined the shelves, I picked up the newspaper Mrs. Roe had been using for the crossword puzzle and tucked it under my arm. I wanted to keep it safe. Mrs. Lester found what she was looking for, the collected poems of Alfred Lord Tennyson. She located a particular poem. In fact, it was bookmarked.

"Hillary loved Tennyson," she said. "This one she loved especially. She knew she might go soon. I think it will help."

Once I was lying in bed, I turned to the bookmarked page. The title read, "Crossing the Bar." Mrs. Lester's instincts proved right. I liked it from the first stanza. It allowed my sorrow to mix with something uplifting, the last lines especially:

> *Sunset and evening star,*
> *And one clear call for me!*
> *And may there be no moaning of the bar,*
> *When I put out to sea.*

CHAPTER THIRTY

Mrs. Lester must have entered the house early in the morning to attend to Byron and Keats. I woke up to see the clock hands close to eight-thirty and all tasks completed. I'd heard nothing. A note resting on the kitchen table described what she would do to handle Mrs. Roe's affairs.

Mrs. Roe's sudden passing would take a long time to get over, and knowing she would no longer be there, with her encouraging, cheerful manner, weighed on me. The world felt a much darker place.

I read the Tennyson poem several more times, and this again helped fight off constant waves of sadness. After an early morning rain shower, the clouds cleared, and the day promised to be full of sunshine, the air fresh and clean. I opened the curtains and blinds, letting sunlight find every corner of the house.

I had much to do to help keep my mind distracted. I made stops at two wholesale dealers where we got most of our supplies of candy, popcorn kernels, cups, and popcorn boxes, arranging a double delivery of these staple items. With *Jaws*, I figured we were about to experience something so unprecedented that ordinary preparations would prove foolish. I didn't want to miscalculate the category of hurricane likely to hit us.

The new popcorn machine arrived late morning. Kenny and I jumped into the task of getting it operational by breaking it in a few times.

"You're looking blue, Burton," Kenny said. We hadn't engaged in our usual banter. I told him about Mrs. Roe.

"Let's keep working," I said. "That's what I need."

We were both relieved to get the new machine. We couldn't see handling the numbers expected with *Jaws* without it, especially on the weekends where we could have five sold-out shows in succession each day, if we'd read the signals right.

Later, Dan Drucker came by as we were about to open and employees were arriving. He was heading back home to Raleigh after a long day of checking on theaters in his district. He asked about the new popper and tried a fresh batch along with a Dr Pepper and Milk Duds.

"You see, this is the only time I get to eat this good stuff. My wife won't let me—"

Drucker was about to say more, but he had stopped in mid-sentence. Carrie had just arrived, and he rubber-necked in her direction. Whatever he had intended to say seemed to vanish from his mind.

She wore a white skirt of a soft cotton material and a light-blue blouse, which gave an even greater blue charge to her eyes. One side of her hair was held back by a brooch containing a small yellow flower. She smiled, and the sum total effect of her presence was jolting—that someone so radiant and fresh could walk into the Yorktowne Theater in Durham, North Carolina and, what's more, work for us.

Drucker seemed to forget that high school for him was twenty years ago—and that he was married with kids. As for me, she took my breath away. I'd heard this could happen, but I thought it was just an expression. Now, I knew it to be true. My bad mood disappeared.

"How's my favorite Yorktowne girl?" he said, a swelling of milk chocolate bubbling at both corners of his mouth from the handful of Milk Duds he was already working on. I doubted Carrie liked being called "girl," but she was a good sport about it.

"Fine and dandy, sir," she said without a hint of irritation.

He may have realized how uncool he looked with his mouth chipmunked with candy because he said,

"Oh, I'm trying out some Milk Duds. Quality control. See with Milk Duds, you need to eat at least five or six at a time. This way they make a nice ball of caramel to roll around in your cheeks. You get the flavor and then, you know, the hunk to chew on."

Carrie said, "I like my caramel the Milky Way."

"How's that?" Drucker said, slow on the uptake, as I burst out an involuntary laugh.

"You both are too smart for me," Drucker said. "Anyway, how's my new manager doing? You know he's just a kid. What are you, Nate? Ain't you still nineteen?

"That's right," I admitted. I didn't feel like a kid though.

Carrie stared at me, her eyes wide and unconvinced. Others who were in hearing distance said, all together,

"Nineteen?"

Even Samantha, who hadn't bothered to place the book she was reading to the side when Drucker came in, gave me a fresh inspection. The straight line crease of her lips parted.

"Mr. Burton, I can't believe you're only nineteen?" Mindy Hawkins said, as if I needed to prove it.

"Guilty as charged," I said, this attention to my age making me uncomfortable.

I led Drucker to the back of the concession area to show him features of the new popper.

"Jeez, Mr. Drucker, why did you tell them that? They're looking at me like my voice changed last week."

"Didn't mean to undermine your authority," Drucker said, slapping my back. "Figured they knew."

"Anyway, thanks for this new machine. It'll pop a lot more than the old one. It works great."

"Well, you needed it, and you will need it. Listen, gotta hit the road. Two more stops to make. If there're any problems, just holler."

"Mr. Drucker," I said in a quiet voice. "Sorry about Samantha doing that reading. She gets her job done."

"No problem, Nate. Unless it becomes one. I saw her reading it. *Valley of the Dolls*. My wife loved it. *The Love Machine* too. And, by the way, that girl, what's her name, Carrie—she's cute as a button—like a scoop of butter melting on a stack of blueberry pancakes."

"I wouldn't disagree with you there."

Soon, he was on his way out, using his expansive, pillowy rear to push through one of the lobby doors as he poured the last portion of Milk Duds into his mouth. He tossed the empty box my way. I caught it and relayed it to

Mindy, who flipped it behind her back into the trash can. Mindy, she was all right, but I still needed to talk with her about the stealing.

Carrie turned to me.

"I'm stunned. You're only nineteen."

"How old did you think I was?"

She studied me for a moment and said, "Honestly, I assumed you had to be at least twenty-three or twenty-four. Maybe because you're the manager." She said the word manager with a playful emphasis, smiling at the same time. "But I did think you looked a lot younger than your actual age—well, what I thought your age was."

"Yeah, you look young," Billy Gossett said.

"Well, because he *is* young," said Mindy.

CHAPTER THIRTY-ONE

By Wednesday we were getting constant phone calls about *Jaws*. Ads blitzed all three TV networks.

Owen was the only one unmoved, and whenever he stopped by, he let us know. The more I saw of him, the less respect he created in me, and I now viewed myself at least his equal. I was pretty sure he had been sneaking in to watch movies. Why did Carrie like him?

Later, like a sore that never healed, Owen showed up again.

"Nate," he said as he came into the lobby and examined one of the *Jaws* posters. "You realize this movie's an abomination."

"How's that?" I asked.

"Ichthyologists would object to its basic premise."

"What's an ich—?"

"Ichthyologist, from the Greek words, 'ikhthus' meaning 'fish' and 'logos' meaning 'study.' Ichthyologists are marine biologists who study sharks, or any fish, for a living."

"Got it," I said, barely hiding my annoyance.

He stood with his arms folded, unable to hide his cocky attitude, which came to him naturally, I had been con- cluding.

"Shark attacks happen, sure. We've all heard about the famous cases. They're far from typical. Not even close. The odds are ridiculously low. Sharks aren't interested in attacking people. It's a myth. Ergo, an abomination."

He made sense, but only half sense. It was just a movie. Who uses the word ergo? I think he assumed I didn't know what it meant.

I said, "What you say may be true, but—"

"Listen, man, it *is* true."

"I'd like to hear you tell this to Navy guys who lost buddies to these *myths* in the Pacific during WWII," I said, now getting openly irritated despite myself. Plus, I knew a diver who had suffered an unprovoked shark attack near Ocracoke Island, and his telling of this terrifying experience had left a chilling imprint on my memory.

"Get real," Owen said. "Those were obviously freakish circumstances."

"Freakish?" I said, raising my voice. "It was a major, huge problem."

"Hey, take a chill pill, man. I feel sorry for those guys. But this shark thing's overblown."

"I'd like to see what *you* would have done in those shark-infested waters." He'd really got to me, and I was letting it show more than I wanted to.

Owen said, "I've met people who swim around sharks all the time. Never been attacked."

"That's different," I said.

"Okay. I'm not saying it wasn't a bad scene for those sailors. It has nothing to do with the risks of swimming at any beach. The poster is pure misleading bunk. The movie too. And more to the point, sharks have a valuable place in the ecosystem."

"I'm not saying we should kill all the sharks," I said, retrieving a calmer tone. "The poster is exaggerated, but what do you expect from a movie poster? Anyway, why don't you hold your opinion until you've seen the movie?"

"It's all about the green stuff. Hollywood, that's where the sharks are infested. I won't waste my time."

I thought that Carrie had been out earshot at first, but she must have heard most of our argument. She moved closer and said, "The poster is obviously over the top, but it's also brilliant. It's calculated to scare, and it succeeds. It's a movie poster like Nate said. In most waters, fear of sharks is unwarranted, clearly. But swimming among sharks is foolish."

"Carrie Jenkins, always the sensible one," Owen said.

"Owen Becker, always the provocateur," said Carrie.

I said, "It's going to be a great movie. I know it will. Have you seen the TV spots that started yesterday? The soundtrack alone is scary."

"Oh, I'm scared," Owen said, with fake exaggeration on his face.

"You are irredeemable," Carrie said.

I said, "The print's coming tonight. We'll preview it tomorrow afternoon. I, for one, am excited to see it."

"Count me out," Owen said. "Last time I checked, my brain had not been surgically removed."

Owen motioned over toward Samantha, who was fixing the cash drawers to take upstairs. He said in an indiscreet, audible whisper, "Does she ever say anything?"

"Don't bother her," Carrie said, mouthing her words so Samantha couldn't see her face.

Please don't feed the animals, I thought. Too late.

"Hey, what do you think of the poster?" Owen asked loudly in Samantha's direction. He didn't even know her name.

Samantha must have heard it all because she swiveled a half a turn in her chair. Removing her glasses, she tossed them aside and narrowed her eyes at Owen, the glint in her pupils resembling the points of two ice picks. Her body no longer seemed fleshy, but steel, transformed, like a bear trap, ready to close violently if you touched her. She eased her frame off the chair, the floor almost shaking underneath her, and unbuttoned the long left sleeve of her blouse. With angry twists of her right hand, she rolled up the sleeve and marched toward Owen. The concession counter separated them, but he stepped back a few feet.

"Sorry, sorry, I didn't mean anything," Owen said, his voice shrill, almost squeaking.

Owen's tan faded, and he backed away further. Samantha reached the edge of the counter. Her arm was bare, and she extended it toward him. Spread out along the inside of her bicep was a long, uneven scar, with flesh missing. Shark bite? It had to be.

She held her arm out for a few seconds.

"Take a look, smart-ass."

She rolled her sleeve back down and returned to her chair.

Owen looked as if a dump truck had come within an

167

inch of flattening him, applying its brakes just in time. Carrie had moved back too and seemed shaken. But I had barely focused on the scar. I felt a prickling along my spine and neck. I saw, speckled over both her wrist and forearm, smothered in calamine lotion, rashes and blisters from poison ivy.

CHAPTER THIRTY-TWO

If fear carried its own scent, I detected it in Owen. I jerked my right thumb toward the door. He took the hint and hightailed it out of the theater to wait in his van. Carrie grabbed a bottle of Windex and busied herself with helping Mindy clean the concession counters. I pitched in, exchanging glances with Carrie as we took in what had happened. So many of my assumptions about Samantha were now shaken, the apparent facts altered and scrambled.

Despite Spence's suspicions, I had never seriously considered Samantha as Bullock's killer. Why would she do it? She seemed so bored by the world, as if she didn't belong in it, her existence a weird mistake. True, she showed flashes of temper. But I had questioned whether she cared enough about people to like or hate them. Except for the natural disgust she had displayed when Bullock brushed against her, she had seemed unmoved by his crude behavior. Might she snuff out another person's life for little reason—for *no* reason? Did she have buried stores of anger making her capable of murder? Maybe being attacked by a shark had damaged and twisted her nature. Somewhere inside her was a simmering volcano, and maybe it was more active than we could see. And like Spence said, she could have dragged Bullock's undersized body into the juniper bushes.

But as I thought it through, the idea of her being Bullock's killer didn't take hold. The rashes were flimsy evidence, as even Spence had emphasized. Poison ivy was everywhere. And I still figured she needed *some* kind of good reason to kill him. She left the theater way before the murder—at least that's how it appeared. Although she might have returned and waited for the opportunity, this didn't seem likely. When Detective Riggs questioned her, he would have covered all the possibilities. Jesse Hooker, her friend, would have provided an alibi. Then again, had they pulled it off together? I felt my thoughts were being sent through a pinball machine.

Samantha finished with the cash drawer. She didn't bother handing it to me but just placed it to the side of the cashier's window and left without a word. I acted as I would normally, although my whole system had jack rabbited into a higher gear. My thoughts kept shifting about, ricocheting against each other. She was scary, but unraveling her motivations was impossible.

Could I encourage Samantha to quit? What a sour presence she was. She seemed unhappy enough in her job that a mutual parting made sense. Would suggesting this set her off? Spence would arrive soon, and I would get his opinion. Deep down, I didn't believe she had killed Bullock, but what if I became her next victim?

I was about to take the cash drawer to the office when Carrie stopped me and asked,

"Can we talk in a few minutes?"

"Of course, I'll be upstairs," I said. My mind hummed as my thoughts shifted away from Samantha. I was eager for a chance to be alone with Carrie. What was this about?

I found Kenny in the office ready to total the deposit. He was finishing the last wedge of a pecan pie.

"Can you keep a watch downstairs for a while?" I said, placing the cash drawer on the desk. "Carrie wants to talk about something. I think it's private."

"Sure, boss," Kenny said and gathered up the pan, which contained a few strips of crust and filling.

"I'll get this started," I said, pointing to the cash drawer.

"Want some?" Kenny held the pan in my direction as he headed out the door.

"You lick the platter clean."

"She need a chaperone?"

"Beat it." Had he figured it out too?

Kenny scooted away, ducking as I threw an eraser at him.

I moved an extra chair and placed it in front of the desk for Carrie to sit in. I settled in my own chair and stared past the paper bills and change filling the slots of the cash drawer. In the blur this stare created, I imagined what Carrie wanted to tell me. Did this involve Owen? He had crossed the line with Samantha, and this had irritated her. Did she have some insights about Samantha?

When I heard her light steps on the stairs, I sat back in my chair and tried to look relaxed and in control, despite my racing pulse.

Carrie peered in through the doorway. The office lit up from the energy in her eyes.

"You got me real curious," I said.

She pulled the door closed and took a seat. She appeared to collect her thoughts, unsure of what to say.

I broke the silence and said, "Owen got it handed to him by Samantha."

We both laughed.

"She was frightening," Carrie said.

"The counter saved him."

"He was shaking."

I felt at ease and composed.

I said, "Did you see his face? Pale, creamy, like the blood had drained out. I've never seen that happen."

"Like, say, before a shark attack?" Carrie suggested.

"Not unlike one," I said, grinning. "Owen needs some scuba diving instruction. I've read that the way to confront a shark is to wait until it gets right on you—then bare your teeth and strike its snout."

Carrie said, "We'd be writing his obituary. Anyway, I want to apologize for Owen's behavior. That's the first thing. The way he treated Samantha—so rude."

"I guess he didn't mean to insult her?" I suggested, wanting to sound like I gave him the benefit of the doubt.

"But he's been rude to you too," Carrie said, resisting my forgiving assessment.

"Oh, that was no big deal," I said.

"There was no excuse for it," Carrie said.

"He has been pretty tactless, even to Mindy."

"Unkind."

"Yeah, unkind," I said, boosted by the harmony in our thinking.

"I think the appropriate colloquial term is, as I am sadly

coming to conclude, is—jerk," Carrie said.

"That too," I said, nodding my head and laughing. She had a way of nailing things.

"And he smokes too much pot. You've probably smelled it on him." Carrie said.

"All the time, actually."

"I figured you must have. It's changed him," Carrie said. "And do you realize he's selling it too?"

"What? How could he be so stupid?" This shocked me—concerned me. I had no problem with pot, but I didn't want Carrie getting into trouble.

"His dad has stopped giving him money. It has me scared."

I wanted to ask her why she put up with Owen, but I said instead,

"I don't blame you. I hope he knows what he's doing. Right?"

"I just don't know anymore," Carrie said, shaking her head.

"Should I tell him not to hang around while you're working?" I asked. This was taking a serious turn. "I can tell him tonight."

Carrie said, "That won't be necessary. I broke up with him."

"Oh, I'm sorry to hear that," I said, lying through my teeth.

"Don't be," Carrie said. "I don't respect him, the person he is turning into. Overdoing the pot—and now the selling it. Everything. It's degraded him. And I don't want any part of it. I'm going to call my dad for a ride home."

It was all I could do to suppress a donkey grin.

CHAPTER THIRTY-THREE

Carrie's breaking up with Owen had my thoughts going down new paths. Fantasies of her taking a liking to me, tossed aside as ridiculous before, now returned fresh and almost possible.

"There's something else," Carrie said. "It's about Mindy."

"Stealing?" I said quickly—a guess, but I went with it, hoping to show I was on top of things.

"How did you know?" Carrie looked surprised.

"I've seen her take candy. Been figuring what to do about it."

"She takes money too."

"Money? I was worried about this."

"Twice that I've seen. Once it was a dollar. Another time a ten."

"No wonder we're coming up short," I said.

"Short?"

"We total all the candy, the cups, and the popcorn boxes we've used every week to check if it matches our take. We're always short, but much more lately."

"Can't have little hands in the cookie jar," Carrie said smiling. She turned serious. "You won't fire her, will you?"

"Doubt we'll need to. She's a good kid—don't you think?

"I like her," Carrie said, after a moment's reflection. "And I will say she's had a tough time at home. Her dad drinks. Gets abusive. That's what she told me."

"I'll go easy on her. Give her a second chance."

Our easy conversation gave me an extra adrenaline rush. I wanted to keep it going. It occurred to me that Carrie might help with Samantha.

I said, "Tell me what you think of Samantha. Owen had it coming, but she looked mean as hell. Has she done anything, or said anything, that would make you worry?"

Carrie said, "I've never had a long conversation with her, honestly. She's aloof to where she seems missing a human quality. She keeps to herself."

"She's kind of frozen over," I said.

"But she got so incensed, so furious."

"She reminds me of the alien monster in *The Thing*. Have you seen it?" I asked.

"On TV," Carrie said, scrunching up her face. Her eyes then widened. "I see what you mean. The monster was frozen when the scientists found it, but when it thawed, it tried to kill everyone."

"It needed their blood to survive and reproduce," I added.

We both laughed. This was crazy thinking, but damn it was fun. How quick she had been to anticipate where I was heading with the monster.

Carrie said, "Poor woman."

"Poor *thing*," I said.

Carrie laughed again and added, "She's no monster, of course. The shark attack probably did this to her. Changed her."

"There's more to it than we know," I said.

"The only other 'thing' is that friend she has."

"The one with the pickup—with the pointed face?"

"Like a hatchet."

"Exactly. Perfect," I said, with emphasis.

"Owen says he's a drug dealer. They've talked a few times while waiting outside. He tried to sell Owen cocaine. And he often seems high on something."

"Cocaine?" The word shook me. "We don't want that going on in the parking lot. Man, this is not good."

"No, it is not."

I needed to be much more watchful and ready. This was more than serious. Carrie had disconnected with Owen just in time. And maybe Bullock's murder was somehow linked. Detective Riggs needed to know about all this, though I suspected he was already on to it.

"And Jesse and Samantha—what an odd pair," I said, wondering what they were up to.

"Perhaps you thought the same about me and Owen," Carrie said, rolling her eyes.

"Owen's fine. He'll grow up." It was easy to be generous about him now. But I resented that he'd more than likely mature out of his cocky ways and be no worse for it. So much for karma. Some people were given a wider strike zone from the get-go in life. I added, "I wouldn't mind going to a school like Northwestern."

"Why don't you, Nate? You're just as smart as Owen. Smarter. And I mean it," Carrie said.

"I don't know about that," I said, embarrassed that my

intelligence even needed defending. But knowing that Carrie believed I was smarter than Owen sent a buzz right through me. I shifted to a different topic.

"Anything else about Jesse?"

"He uses the N word. That Confederate flag decal is not just for decoration."

"Right out of central casting," I said. Yet another reason for concern. I resolved to myself to tell Detective Riggs what I knew.

Carrie started to speak and hesitated.

"Go ahead," I said.

"Well, I just wanted to say, wanted to make it clear what I thought about that stunt Owen pulled with the fake sculpture. It was juvenile." Carrie's neck flushed slightly.

"Don't worry about that," I said. Was she concerned that I might assume they were sleeping together?

"It's just that I didn't want you do think—"

"It was a stupid joke." I tried to play dumb. I couldn't think of what else to say and blurted out awkwardly, "How about if I go check on Kenny. You can call your dad using this phone. Come on around."

I got up quickly from the chair so that Carrie could take mine. She got up at the same time and the edge of my right elbow grazed her shoulder, causing a sharp jolt of static electricity. We both flinched.

"Press line three," I said. "Phil must be using line two. Line one is for people calling in about show times. Just close the door when you're through."

I may have tripped over every other word.

CHAPTER THIRTY-FOUR

"You look like a tomato. What happened up there?" Kenny said when I entered the lobby.

"Shut your pie hole," I replied, but with a smile. Owen was out of the picture. Now I had a chance. The effects of the static electricity lingered. I'd seen a blue spark as well.

"Touché," Kenny said. "Hey, there's Gooch."

A van had just stopped outside the main entrance.

"The delivery guy?" I asked.

"Yeah, Lester Gooch."

I'd never seen him. We left the old film canisters next to the cashier window late on Thursday evenings. They were picked up way after we closed and replaced with the canisters for new movies. Amazingly, no one ever stole them. Then again, how many people had 35 mm movie projectors in their living rooms?

"What's he doing here so early?" I asked.

"You got me."

Gooch exited his van. He was a string bean of a man with weathered skin stretched over a bony face, a cigarette wedged between his lips. He loped in long strides to the back of his van, swung open the doors, and lifted out two canisters, one in each arm.

"They wanted these delivered special," Gooch said.

"Drop them here," Kenny said.

"Heard about your new gig," Gooch said to Kenny, his

cigarette keeping time with each word as he placed both canisters next to the curb.

"It's good."

"Turrentine's tickled."

"He would be."

I glanced at the label on one of the canisters. It read, "*Jaws*. Paramount Pictures."

"Awesome," Kenny said, giving me a fired-up look.

"To the max," I said, my pulse jacking up a notch.

"Somebody needs to sign this," Gooch said, squinting from the cigarette smoke as he retrieved a clipboard from the front seat of the van.

"I'll do it," I said.

Gooch added, "Too bad about Horace. Nobody's safe no more. Hogan around?"

"I'll get him," Kenny said.

I signed the delivery form while Kenny went to get Hogan, who was already entering the lobby and heading our way.

"Hot damn, Gooch. *Jaws*! Special delivery?" Hogan said.

"Yeah, they want to make sure theaters supposed to get, get it."

"Got it," Hogan said.

Gooch flicked the butt of his cigarette to the curb, announced he had other deliveries to make, and sped away in his van. Hogan lifted both canisters and carried them upstairs. Kenny followed him like an eager puppy. The *actual* fact of our showing the movie hit home. *This movie was really going to happen.*

But my excitement receded when the reach of the entrance lights revealed Owen leaning against the side of his van, parked in a space right across from the lobby entrance. The reach of the entrance lights revealed his body and face. He moved toward the lobby entrance. What did he want? Carrie noticed him too when she came back down to the lobby. Owen spread his arms, palms outward, indicating he wanted to talk. She ignored him, as I hoped she would.

"Want to wait up in my office?" I said to Carrie. "I can come get you when your dad arrives." We had moved into different territory. All my senses had shifted gears.

"I think I shall." She headed back upstairs.

Owen shook the lobby entrance doors, which were now locked, only allowing exit. Spence had also arrived, and as he unlocked the door, Owen pushed past him and into the lobby. Carrie was already up the stairs.

Owen rushed toward the door leading to the office. I reached it first and blocked his way.

"Get out my way," he said, his face wild.

"She doesn't want to talk to you," I said.

"How would you know?" He lunged for the doorknob, but I placed my hand flat against the door, preventing him from opening it. He tried to push away my arm. He couldn't move it, and so he swung his right elbow. I deflected it and grabbed his arm at the wrist, twisting it behind his back, pinning him face-first against the wall.

"You're breaking my arm!"

"No more swinging at me."

I twisted even harder. His biceps felt soft.

"Okay, okay. Let me go."

I let him loose. He took a few steps away from me and rubbed his shoulder and elbow, his cheeks red, his eyes flashing with indignation.

"I'm going to sue your ass. And this whole stinking, stupid place." Owen seemed to think he had regained an advantage. He said these words as if I were pauper and he was king, his upper lip curling with contempt.

"You do that," I said, with all the show of unconcern I could muster. "Mr. Reeves here will back me up."

"Who?"

Spence had been ambling closer to us.

"Him?"

Spence now stood, ramrod straight, next to Owen. He was at least four inches taller than Owen, but it seemed like ten.

Spence said, "You run along home. Have your daddy give Mr. Burton a call. Or do you want me to go outside and get me a switch."

Owen paused, confused, his swagger gone. Spence towered over him, powerful and intimidating. Owen opened his mouth to say something but appeared to think better of it, like the previous day, the flush in his cheeks going pink to pale. He turned, sped away, and slammed through an exit door.

"I'm glad you were here to see all that, Spence."

"Put some chili powder on the day," Spence said.

"You know, that felt *good*." And I meant it. We returned broad grins.

"He was fearful and jumpy," Spence said. "Like a frog on a freeway."

Mindy and Ricardo appeared out of the shadows near the exit to the main theater.

"Owen tried to hit you with his elbow. We saw it," Mindy said.

"Pass the popcorn," said Ricardo, grinning.

Carrie stuck her head out the door. She asked, "Has he gone?"

"Like a wounded rabbit," Ricardo said.

"What happened?" Carrie asked.

"Everything's fine," I said.

Mindy grabbed Carrie by the elbow and guided her toward the exit to wait for Carrie's dad. Carrie whispered to me as they passed by, "Girl talk."

They chattered away excitedly. Just before exiting, Carrie stopped, looked back at Spence and me, and said,

"See you gentlemen tomorrow. Thanks for everything, Nate."

CHAPTER THIRTY-FIVE

"Nate," Spence said in a soft, sweet voice.

"Give me a break, Spence."

"She's a sweetie pie. That's a fact. And easy on the eyes."

"Come on, Spence. But listen, listen. You won't believe what happened tonight. Let's talk in my office. Seriously, Spence. It's about Samantha. She's got blisters. They're all over her right arm. You called it."

"Can't say it surprises me," Spence said.

"But there's more. She got mad too. I'm telling you. She looked mean."

I pulled my desk chair around to the front of the desk and offered it to Spence while I took a folding chair. He settled into the chair, and I told him what had happened.

Spence said, "So where were the rashes *zactly*?"

"All over her wrist and forearm. She didn't roll up the sleeve of her other arm. But I could see lotion on both. Some were large, about peanut-sized."

"Always wear the long sleeves?"

"Usually down to her elbows. Maybe to hide the scar."

"Nothing on her hands?"

"No. Could have worn gloves while she was doing it. Well, assuming she did this thing."

"And the bite. A shark you say?"

"That's why she got so mad at Owen."

"He got her chewing on some bumblebees."

"She's so full of hate, Spence. I can see that now."

"Nate, let me tell you something." Spence stared into space, his eyes recreating a memory.

I sat back in my chair in anticipation.

"One time, when I still had my farm, we was hassled by a particular raccoons. We knew he was big from his tracks and, well, the size of his turds. Killing chickens and eating tomatoes. Got me a metal trap and set it one night. Used a chunk of sweet watermelon. Caught him. This critter was huge, barely fit in the trap. I could see he'd tried mightily to get out. All around the cage, the ground was scraped and bare from his scratching and clawing through the wire. And darn it, he had just managed to get out when I showed up. Figured he'd run. But he turned on me and gave out a growl. Rocked me flat backwards. All teeth and eyeballs too. Glad I'd brought my shotgun, because I was going to need it. Well, I raised my gun to the ready."

Spence stood up and lifted his long arms and extended them as if he held that shotgun. His left index finger about touched my nose.

"Now, this was the real scary part. Like I said, he was a big critter. He commenced to run right straight at me, in long, and I mean long, loping gallops. He covered a lot of ground in a short second, beelining straight at me. Shot that varmint in midair."

Spence pulled an imaginary trigger and jerked his shoulder back to simulate the shotgun's kick.

"That thing defied what I understood to be natural laws. Being in that cage made him crazy. And if I didn't have my gun, the fur would've been flying and goodbye Spence Reeves. I don't never, nohow, underestimate nobody and no creature. Now, I'm not saying Samantha did it. But why play poker with the devil?"

"Spence, should I call Detective Riggs?"

After reflecting for a moment, Spence said, "I wouldn't bother him. Unless he comes calling on his own. This is all speculation. Just us having some fun. Except I do want us be on the watch. Another thing about that raccoon. His claws, well, they were more like fingers. More human than creature."

"Samantha, I don't know. She seems more creature than human," I said, almost believing it.

"Reckon you right, to an extent," Spence said, still looking thoughtful. "But I needs to get to work. Faucet in the men's room leaking again. Found the right washer this time." Spence extended one of his arms, grabbed the office doorknob, and left the office, a man on a mission.

I was struck again by the remarkable length of his arms. They were like something a comic book hero would have, the Elongated Man, in the flesh. I remembered the previous summer when I'd first noticed this about Spence. He had finished mowing around the theater and was trimming with a sickle. He had spun the sickle in his right hand and had moved near the marquee. A rectangular brick casing surrounded the two thick poles supporting the marquee. With a few deft strokes, blending economy of motion with elbow grease, he trimmed about six yards of grass.

"How the heck did you do that without hitting the brick,

Spence?"

He had just grinned.

Spence used his own sickle. He had shown me where he kept it, hidden and wrapped in an oilcloth under the front seat of his Buick. He removed the sickle from its hiding place, laid it on the hood of the engine, and opened the folds of the cloth. There the glorious thing lay. It stirred something deep in me. The handle, shaped over the years to fit Spence's right hand, was stained with grime and sweat. The metal, although it had the classic crescent moon shape on one side, was thicker than other sickles I had seen. It widened at the end, coming to a second tip, like a spear, doubling as a gardening tool and weapon. The inside blade had been sharpened, and its silvery edge shimmered in the sunlight.

"Spence, this is no ordinary tool. I've seen nothing like it," I had said.

"That's because it ain't no ordinary tool. I use it for trimming, but it once belonged to an African warrior. A true fact. It's a better throwing weapon than a garden sickle. I like thinking in my mind about the man who made it, owned it, used it. I feel right safe with it too."

It was still early morning, and we were alone.

Spence said, "See that pine yonder?"

A thick pine tree stood over by the side of the theater, about thirty yards away. Spence looked around and set his feet in that smooth, efficient way of his. With an overarm swing of his right arm, he sent the tool arcing and somersaulting through the air. He let out a grunt, closer to a yell. The sickle lodged itself in the trunk, chest high and centered, sending back a "thunk" sound. Spence rubbed his shoulder.

"Spence, I mean. Did you just do that?" I wasn't sure I had seen what I had seen.

"Moving targets, they might get the better of me now," he said with emphasis and another grin, as he fetched the sickle. Was he kidding? I didn't know.

CHAPTER THIRTY-SIX

I followed Spence down the office stairs and then headed to the main theater for a quick check. *The French Connection II* had about a half-hour left. The Gene Hackman character, Detective Jimmy "Popeye" Doyle, was still battling the effects of heroin addiction, but soon would be hunting down Charnier, the elusive drug dealer. After grabbing a box of popcorn, freshly popped, and a cup of ice water, I sat in the back row to watch it for a while. I needed a break.

Mindy and Ricardo came in together from the opposite back entrance of the theater. I thought they both had left. Good. Later, I'd get a chance to confront Mindy about the stealing.

They immediately started kissing. This didn't surprise me. Everything Mindy did came with a sexy undercurrent. She wore thick make-up, too much for a girl her age. Lipstick exaggerated the fullness of her lips, plenty full as they were. She wore her clothes tight, the buttons on her blouse threatening to pop. Mindy was sixteen, going on twenty-one. She flirted with the ushers, and sometimes I thought she flirted with me. Once, when she had stopped by the office for her paycheck, she leaned over guaranteeing a peek at her bra. I finished up the popcorn and slipped out unnoticed. I felt a stab of envy over the fun they were having.

I hung around the concession area, applying and re-applying Windex to countertops. Mindy and Ricardo finally came out. They looked good together, like salt and pepper. They saw me. Mindy started giggling. Ricardo grinned and covered his mouth.

"Ricardo, Spence might need you. He's fixing to do theater two."

"Right on it, Mr. Burton."

Ricardo strolled toward the other theater in an exaggerated, silky smooth manner. I gave him a nod as if to say everything was cool with me too.

"Mindy, do you have a sec?"

"For sure, Mr. Burton," she said as she smoothed out her skirt. "I need to use the restroom first." I'd caught her by surprise, and she probably wanted to check her appearance.

"I'll be upstairs."

Soon, Mindy bounced into the office, took a seat, and looked at me with an innocent, expectant expression, the smell of a breath mint freshly dissolving in her mouth. I took an indirect approach to the stealing.

"Mindy, I've been asking everyone how they're doing, you know, one on one, after what happened with Mr. Bullock."

"It was terrible an all. But I like you being manager." She seemed relieved I hadn't mentioned Ricardo.

"Thanks, Mindy. You do a good job. How long have you been working with us? Almost a year?"

"Yeah, I like it here."

It occurred to me that one way to handle the situation was to reward her, maybe inspire her to change. I said, "I'm thinking we can give you a raise now, an extra fifty cents an hour. How does that sound?"

She straightened up and said, "That's awesome, Mr. Burton. Thank you, I mean it." For her, still in high school, this would be a significant increase. She was good at the job—when she wasn't stealing.

"Another thing. I'll be expecting more from you. You're already a leader, but I'd like you to do more."

"Sure, Mr. Burton."

"We've hired a few kids from the Riverview. I want you to teach them the way we do things.

"Of course."

"It's not just serving the customers, but also stuff like not taking candy and money from the cash drawer. You know how some kids are." As best I could, I avoided giving her any sense that I suspected her of doing such things.

"I can do it."

It was hard to tell for sure, but I sensed a slight tug on her conscience.

"And so, it will also be your responsibility to handle the concession drawers at the end of each show. Give them to me or Kenny."

"You can count on me, Mr. Burton."

"Kenny and I trust you, Mindy."

Now I could tell she was feeling guilty. She seemed too insistent about how she could be trusted. Anyway, this approach seemed worth a try. I'd wait and see.

"And, Mr. Burton, you asked about how I'm doing after what happened. Well, Mr. Bullock was kind of weird with the girls. He put his hands on me, and I mean where he shouldn't. That's not right. I wasn't the only one either."

"Mindy, I'm sorry to hear that," I said, shaking my head. My opinion about Bullock, already low, hit rock bottom.

"So, to be honest and all, I'm not too sad about him not being around anymore. I didn't want him killed like that. But—"

"I understand, Mindy. You're not the only person who feels this way." I considered what next to say. "I wonder, did Mr. Bullock ever treat Samantha the way he treated you? As far as you know?"

Mindy laughed.

"Samantha? He was scared of her. Just like we all are. I don't know if I should say this, but she gives me the creeps. But I liked what she did in front of Owen. I kind of wanted her, you know, to teach him a lesson. I mean, he's such a—such a—I don't know."

"Smart-ass?"

"Yeah. He treats me like I'm a ditz."

"He has no call to think that, Mindy. You're no ditz."

I told Mindy I'd talk with her again soon about the raise. Needed to clear it with Mr. Drucker. I had a good feeling about how the conversation went. Would it work? I'd have to wait and see. And a more complete picture of both Horace and Samantha was coming into shape. We both returned to the lobby, and she headed off home.

I joined Kenny, Spence, and Ricardo, and we all finished the cleaning together. After reminding Spence that we would be screening *Jaws* around noon the next day, I left to make the deposit at the mall.

CHAPTER THIRTY-SEVEN

I met with Marion Lester the next morning before heading to the theater. She filled me in on how plans were progressing with the funeral service for Mrs. Roe. She would help with Byron and Keats and adopt them when the time came. In their own way, they missed Mrs. Roe too. We all did.

I got to the theater around nine. The phone rang. It was Riggs.

"We need to talk. Stop by the theater in about two hours?"

"We might be previewing *Jaws*, but I'll be on the lookout for you. What's up?"

"Fill you in when I see you."

The case seemed to have taken a turn. What did he need to talk about? And why would he need to talk with me? I'd have to wait.

The weeks of anticipation were finally over, and I was psyched about previewing *Jaws*. As soon as Kenny came in, we'd get the movie started.

Detective Riggs arrived earlier than expected, around eleven-thirty. I was in the lobby when he pulled up in his unmarked Buick Century, its copper brown exterior glistening in the sun. As he exited the car and walked toward me, I recalled the day of the murder when he had tried to catch me off guard. I had been close to trembling. I was glad to see him now.

"You got my curiosity going, Detective Riggs," I said, as we headed through the lobby toward the office. I stopped and returned to double-check that the lobby entrance doors were locked. This was now my habit, especially with the new uncertainty about who had killed Bullock. "Just to be safe," I said, giving the doors a shake. I led Riggs up the stairs to my office. Instead of sitting behind the desk, I placed two chairs in front of the desk and offered him one. I took the other.

"I need to trust you to keep something under your hat until late tomorrow. Can't be repeated," Riggs said.

"Of course—without question," I said, pleased that he trusted me.

"Turns out we've released Milton. Did it this morning, quietly," Riggs said, as if he had read me right and could move on to the business at hand.

"Great," I said, excitedly. "Spence told me Milton didn't do it."

"Spence?"

"Mr. Reeves. From the start. He knows Milton's parents. If you can believe it, Milton's *granddad* worked for him years ago when Spence had a farm."

Riggs raised his eyebrows and said, "There's something about that man."

"No kidding. And you won't believe what he did last night. He took me over to where he found Mr. Bullock's body. He went into those juniper bushes, grabbed a leaf of poison ivy, and chewed on it."

"What?"

"Thought he was going nuts. Said he does it every year, early, when the stuff first appears. After that, he gets immune to it. A trick his daddy taught him."

"Is he just not allergic to it?" Riggs said. He straightened his back and seemed to get a jolt of energy.

"Not the way he tells it. Anyway, I didn't see where Spence was heading at first, and then I understood. Whoever killed Mr. Bullock may—"

"—have poison ivy rashes by now." Riggs finished my sentence.

"Exactly."

Riggs said nothing.

"And Spence says people who have had it before, get rashes soon after exposure. Otherwise, it can take longer to break out."

He still kept silent.

"Does Milton have any rashes?" I asked, risking that he might bristle at this kind of question.

Riggs eyed me in that no-nonsense way I was now used to.

"No, I will tell you he does not." He was about to say more but paused again.

"Ah, do you have any rashes?" I asked, hoping this wouldn't irritate him.

"No—but I had the gloves—and my jacket protected me." He seemed to be okay with the question.

"How about Detective Dupree?"

He didn't answer, pretending that he didn't know, it

seemed. I didn't push it.

"But guess who does?" I said.

"Hicks, Samantha Hicks, right?" Riggs said, as if he had good reason to suppose it.

"How did you know?" I asked.

Again, he ignored my question and said, "When did you notice it?"

I said, "Last night, while she was working. It sent chills through me."

"Chills?"

I told Riggs what had happened, and when I'd finished, he said, "Interesting. All very interesting."

CHAPTER THIRTY-EIGHT

I didn't want to keep asking Riggs questions I had no business asking. He seemed to be deciding what more he could disclose. After pulling on his chin for a moment, he said,

"I can tell you we've been giving Samantha Hicks a closer look. Don't know what we can do with this poison ivy detail. Let's just say it fits. She's the main reason I contacted you."

The door opened at the bottom of the stairs, and we heard,

"Nate. You up there?" It was Spence.

"Come on up," I said so Spence could hear.

I turned to Riggs. "I'm assuming you'll tell Spence about Milton?"

"I suspect he already knows. And I want to ask him the same questions I have for you."

Spence's tall frame filled the office doorway. He had on his Stetson, but when he saw Riggs, he removed it and gave a small bow of his head.

"Detective Riggs."

"Mr. Reeves."

Riggs stood up and offered Spence his chair. Spence settled into it, while I moved around to my desk chair, Riggs taking the seat I'd been sitting in.

"Mr. Reeves, I want to mention a few confidential facts about this case that I've discussed with Mr. Burton. And I have questions for you both."

"Honored, Detective Riggs."

"I told Detective Riggs about what happened last night with Samantha. And about the poison ivy idea."

Spence's eyes appeared to sparkle.

"You chewed that stuff?" Riggs said, narrowing his eyes.

"Yes, sir."

"You're a brave man."

"Naw."

"It's got me thinking," Riggs said. "I'll grant you that. I suppose you know about Milton Spicer's release?"

Spence paused for a moment, a sly smile announcing that yes indeed this was something he knew. "Know Hector and Lilly Spicer well. From way back. Hector tells me his son panicked. On account of his pulling the knife on Mr. Bullock. Of course that little blade wouldn't have made the cut Mr. Bullock died from."

"Ah, right," Riggs said.

"And he had an alibi, his girlfriend, who he wasn't supposed to be with.

"Correct."

"He didn't want her to get in no trouble, so he kept it secret—till he couldn't keep it secret."

"That's about the size of it."

"And Milton's clean of rashes."

"Correct, again, now that you mention it," Riggs said. He spread his hands outward in defeat.

Spence continued, "Milton *is* in hot water with Mr. and Mrs. Spicer, however."

"That's a fact," Riggs said. Then he shifted directions. "Okay, let me ask. Is there anything about how Mr. Bullock treated Samantha that would have given her reason to do him harm, to kill him?"

Spence and I exchanged glances. I volunteered first and said, "Well, during that evening Horace was killed, I saw him brush up against her breasts with his arm—when he reached over to check the cash drawer. She could tell he did it on purpose, and she didn't like it. I could see that."

"Naturally," Riggs said. "But is that all?"

"Horace probably took liberties with her at other times, like he did with some other female employees. This is what I've been hearing from Mindy Hawkins, one of our concession workers."

Riggs nodded like this wasn't new information.

Spence said, "Don't know Samantha like Nate here does. But is she what we see? Not in my estimating."

Riggs said, "Did she ever tell you why she moved to Durham?"

"Never asked. Not that she would have told me anything."

"How about the guy who gives her rides? Jesse Hooker."

I said, "He's never once come inside. He stands out by his pickup and smokes."

"Camels, right?" Riggs said.

"They Camels," Spence said. "I've picked up a mess of them."

I said, "There's something Carrie Jenkins told me. He's a drug dealer."

Riggs seemed unsurprised by this information too, as if he already knew it, and moved on to another question.

"How close are Jesse and Samantha? Boyfriend, girl-friend?"

"No one knows. He's half her size. He reminds me of those guys at the end of *Easy Rider*," I added.

"Rednecks who killed Wyatt and Billy?" Riggs said.

"Exactly," I said. This surprised me. Not only had he seen the movie, but he had also remembered the names of characters played by Peter Fonda and Dennis Hopper.

"Know the type," Spence said.

Riggs seemed to relax as if he might consider telling us more of his thinking. I felt almost like this was a meeting of friends. He started a sentence and stopped, as if he needed to remind himself that he had professional obligations. We sat, expectantly. He must have sensed our keen interest in knowing more.

"I can tell you that most of our leads are turning up dead ends. The situation is not what it might have appeared. That's all I can say. We'll keep pulling the threads until we figure it out."

He stood up and added, "Gentlemen, thanks for your time."

Spence said, "Reminds me of when I went through basic training with the 10th."

"Basic training? When was this?" Riggs asked, looking puzzled.

Spence ignored the question as if he wanted to avoid weakening the memory.

"Remember that first day, when we were lined up, the sergeant yelled at us real good. He said *For the next eight weeks, I am your mama, I'm your daddy, I'm your uncle, and I'm your aunt. Any questions?*"

Spence had changed to a harsh Southern accent, recreating the voice of the sergeant. He glanced at us, shifting out of his state of reverie.

"Detective Riggs, to answer your question. Nineteen fourteen it was, and, yes, it was basic training for a Buffalo regiment. The tenth, the *famous* tenth.

Riggs glanced at me. He seemed to need my corroboration.

I said. "Just listen."

Riggs sat back, still doubtful.

Spence continued, clearing his throat and retrieving his far-off look,

"See, we were tough hombres. We wanted to serve, but we weren't fond of taking no orders. I figure that the sergeant—whose name was Quantrell by the way, a strange name, which is why I remember it—needed to show us who was boss. Well, one of our guys made a snicker. Quantrell heard it, whipped his head toward the fool fellah who snickered and said, *Oh, so you think it's funny, uh? Come here, boy.*"

Spence again seemed real proud of his Southern accent. He examined us like he wanted to see how impressed we were. Our smiles confirmed it.

"The guy, he was from *De*-troit, swaggered up right in front of Quantrell, who then hauled off and knocked the guy to the ground with one surprise haymaker. A bunch of other officers, who had been watching, gathered around this guy and stomped on him. They stomped him and stomped him some more. And then they backed off while the guy just moaned and groaned, curled up in the dirt. *All right, get rid of that piece of garbage*, Quantrell said.

"They picked him up, pitched him into the back of a wagon, and carted him away. And Quantrell, he aimed his badass eyes at us, like he was starting afresh, and said, *Are there any more snickerers out there?* We stood there, straight as posts—and *quiet*."

Spence paused, and Riggs thought he was finished because he said, "That's some story, Mr. Reeves. But—"

But Spence just started talking again, but losing his far-off look, "This is what I mean. I found out a long time later—because we never again saw the guy they beat up—when I was helping with training myself, that this guy, well, had been in cahoots with Quantrell. He wasn't being stomped on. They just made it *look* like it. They was just blowing smoke, wanting us new guys to know they *wouldn't* take *no* mess."

"Ahh, of course," Riggs and I both said, shaking our heads as we digested the end of the story.

Riggs continued, "That's an amazing bit of personal history, Mr. Reeves. Truly. Another time I'd like to hear more." He checked his watch. "Right now, I need to get going."

Someone opened the stairway door, and we heard, "Da-dum, da-dum, da-dum."

It was Hogan imitating the theme of one of the recent commercials for *Jaws* as he came up the stairs.

Hogan shouted, "Showtime."

"Kenny's not here yet," I called out.

"Screw Kenny's lazy ass," Hogan said, as he stuck his head past the office doorway. "Oh, shoot, Detective Riggs. Didn't realize you were here."

"Mr. Hogan," Riggs said.

After a moment of embarrassed silence, Hogan said, "Anyway, it's ready to *roll*, and I'm not waiting for Kenny."

"Roll over Beethoven," I said.

"My hearts beating a rhythm," Hogan added.

"My temperature's rising," Spence said.

We looked at Riggs, who said,

"Tell *Tchaikovsky* the news."

CHAPTER THIRTY-NINE

Kenny's Fairlane lurched into the parking lot and skidded to a halt in the parking place. Kenny leaped out, slammed the door in the same motion, and hotfooted it to the lobby. He looked like he'd just woken up and thrown on the clothes from the previous day. Perspiration swelled under each arm.

"Kenny, you look like crap," Hogan said, holding the door open for him.

"Up yours, Phil."

"Gotta run," Riggs said, checking his watch again.

"How about catching the first few minutes?" I said.

"Thanks, but—"

"You won't regret it," I insisted, scooping ice for a Coke that I knew Kenny would want. Fizz from carbonation showering my hand as I filled a cup with Coke.

Riggs hesitated.

"I'll take that to be a yes? Great," I said. "You'll be one of the first to see any part of the movie."

"You win," he said. "But just a few minutes."

I called out to Hogan, "Phil, let me pop us some fresh corn. Never watched a movie without popcorn, and I'm not going to start now." Sometimes, I thought it was all about the popcorn.

Riggs once again checked his watch.

"Don't worry, Detective Riggs. It will take three minutes,

tops," I said. "Gotta have popcorn."

I gave Kenny the Coke and raced to the popcorn machine. I turned on the heat and measured out the kernels and seasoning. As it heated, I moved back to the counter.

"Now let me guess what you all want. Kenny, I know." I snatched up a box of Goobers and tossed it his way.

"Peanuts and Coke, like my daddy liked it," Kenny said, giving the box a rattle.

"Phil—that'll be Snickers and Dr Pepper? Am I right?"

"Always."

I sent a Snickers through the air, filled a cup with ice, and topped it with foaming Dr Pepper.

"Phil, complete the orders while I finish up the popcorn?"

Hogan came around the counter and said,

"Spence, you're older than dirt. You're next. Snickers and a grape drink?"

Spence grinned. "*Co*-rrect."

The oil steamed, hissed, and the kernels began popping.

"Detective Riggs. Easy. Kit Kat, and, let's see, Sprite," Hogan said and slapped the counter.

Riggs had a beaten look. He said, "Give 'em to me."

"How about me?" I called out over the now rapid-fire clatter of the corn popping.

"Junior Mints and a Coke," Hogan said.

"Nailed me."

"Nate," said Kenny. "Can you deep-fry that Snickers for Phil?"

The popped corn overflowed from the kettle onto the

warming deck. The familiar, steamy aroma saturated the air. Never got tired of that smell. I could eat popcorn until I almost died from it, until I resembled Templeton, the gluttonous rat in the Disney version of *Charlotte's Web*.

Soon we were heading toward the theater, with drinks, popcorn, and candy at the ready. Hogan rested his popcorn and drink on a lobby bench. He ripped open the wrapper to his Snickers and headed toward the projection booth to start the movie.

We found seats and got comfortable. Riggs took an aisle seat because he wouldn't stay long.

All of us were keyed up. I certainly was. There had been so much buildup for the movie. And so much had happened—Bullock's murder, the tension over the investigation, Milton's arrest, Samantha's behavior. For me, my becoming manager, Mrs. Roe's passing, the frequent daydreams about Carrie, all mingling together as I anticipated this movie. It seemed like I had been traveling down a wild river on a ramshackle canoe. Having made it through one section of rapids after another, I now found myself in a patch of calm water where I could enjoy the scenery for a while. I was ready for some plain old entertainment, a good *harmless* scare.

The *Universal Studios* logo appeared on the screen as Hogan slipped into a seat, and then it went black as if a lid had closed shut on us. A low, vibrating sound began as bold white letters announced:

A ZANUCK/BROWN
Production
which faded to,

ROY SCHEIDER ROBERT SHAW
RICHARD DREYFUSS

The music increased tempo, became louder, and shifted to the spine-chilling theme we had heard in so many commercials.

I realized that the calm water was hardly what we were to experience. Instead, I revisited a different feeling when, on the Swamp Fox roller coaster at Myrtle Beach, the cars had swung free at the top of the first rise, now a short second away from free fall.

Then the title,

JAWS

CHAPTER FORTY

Whatever Riggs's other plans were, they didn't happen. He left his seat a few times during the first hour and stood by the exit, but he sat back down each time and stayed to the end. As soon as the final credits began their roll, he turned to me and said,

"Scared the hell out of me."

He bolted out the nearest exit.

Kenny rose and clapped in a slow, measured way, his hands raised high, staring at the screen as if in homage. Spence also came to his feet, stretched, and gave a nod of approval. Hogan brushed popcorn off his shirt and headed out toward the booth to stop the projector. He said, "A storm's gonna hit. That fool thing made me spill my Dr Pepper."

About a third of the way into the movie, we all had jumped, even Spence. I mean, out of our seats jumped. It happened when the shark expert Hooper was surprised by a severed head. Hooper was in scuba gear, examining a hole in the underside of a sunken boat. He was directing his flashlight at the hole made by the shark. The head rolled into view. I yelled, and everyone else did too. Spence, maybe not.

I yelled one other time, when we actually saw the shark for the first time, about halfway into the movie. This when a group of three men were in a fishing boat hunting the shark. One of the men, Brodie, the police chief of the town that was being terrorized by the shark, was shoveling bloody fish bait over the side. He had his guard down because the hunt had been going for some time without luck. The shark, jaws open, rose out of the ocean, a few feet away from Brodie's hand—that was when we yelled—and then sunk back out of view. He saw it and jerked backward, stunned. Then he back-stepped his way into the cabin where Quint, the boat captain, was and said, "You're going to need a bigger boat." What a great line. We had burst out laughing, releasing the tension. Robert Shaw was the actor who played Quint. He was perfect for the role, as was Roy Scheider, who played Brodie.

Kenny stopped clapping but continued to stare at the screen. Whenever he saw a movie, he studied the credits. I'd got into the habit too, although they had much less meaning for me. Spence left for the lobby.

The movie wasn't what I had expected. I figured the scares would be ordinary and predictable. The shark might be fake-looking, because of the photo I'd seen in *Time* magazine. Well, not like *Godzilla* or *King Kong*, but the effects wouldn't last past the credits. This was different. I guess there were some tricks simply designed to make you jump. But even they were clever—no simple wondering whether something was around a corner. The scares penetrated, sometimes cold and deep, sometimes a whiplash, jolting. More like *Psycho*. And, as I'd heard early reviewers predict, it changed the way I thought about the ocean.

The credits ended.

"Come on, Kenny," I said. "Let's talk in the lobby. What did you think?"

Kenny turned and followed me.

"I'm in awe, Nate."

"It scared me, but it was funny too," I said.

"It gripped me by the throat from start to finish," Kenny said. "Got into my bloodstream. It was—physical."

"I'm worried," I said, Phil's warning from a moment ago echoing in my head. "We're not ready for what's going to happen, Kenny. I mean we'll run out of ice by five on Saturday."

We had a lot of scrambling to do.

Kenny was focused on the movie. He continued, "I need to see it again. Remember, early on, Brodie is sitting on the beach chair scanning the water, anxious. For everyone else, it's ordinary life at the beach. Remember, people walking by in both directions, blocking Brodie's view? Each time, he moves his head to look past them, the only one worried. That makes it more tense, right? And we feel it too."

"Yeah," I said, remembering it clearly. "He sees the black bathing cap of that old man—but another false alarm. Then that scream. Only the girl—scared by her boyfriend."

Kenny asked, "Did you notice what the camera did when Brodie realizes that the shark is out there and that kid is being attacked?"

"What the camera did?" I said. "No, I wasn't thinking about the camera."

"The vertigo effect. You know, from Hitchcock," Kenny said. "The background moved up, but Brodie's face stayed the same size."

"Yeah, yeah, now I remember. How did you notice that?"

"Well, I don't know, but I did," Kenny said. "Made Brodie's reactions more intense."

"And it made me feel weird," I said.

"Dizzy," Kenny said. "Spielberg had the camera move out, probably on a dolly or something, while zooming in with the lens—so it kept Brodie's face the same size. Dolly out, zoom in. That's what does it."

"I need to see it again too," I said.

"And, another thing, Nate. Do you realize that we never saw the shark until they were on the boat?"

"But it feels like we did."

"Never saw it until that last half," Kenny said.

"You're right," I said.

"Do you know Hitchcock's definition of surprise?" Kenny asked. He didn't wait for me to respond. "When the bomb under the table *doesn't* explode."

Spence came out of the restroom.

"What did you think?" I asked.

"I jumped twice, yelled once. Laughed too. We've got a monster on our hands, sure enough."

"Yeah, it was funny," Kenny said. "Like when Hooper crumpled the Styrofoam cup." Hooper had done this in a fake show of strength in response to Quint's crushing of a beer can.

I said, "*And*, when those two guys on the pier think they'll catch the shark with the hunk of meat. I was scared for them, but I kind of *laughed* too." The men had naively underestimated the power of the shark. It snatched the meat, which they had attached to the pier with a hook and chain, and ripped away the end of the pier, dragging it into the sea along with one of the men. The man swam back to the dock, but the shark turned around and headed toward him. As his partner urged him to swim faster and faster— and as the shark theme music crescendoed—he just managed to make it out of the water in time. Both men rested on their knees to catch their breath. One said, "Can we go home now?" That's when I laughed.

Kenny said, "Notice, we never see the shark here either. *And*, how about when Hooper and Quint compare scars— that was funny too—a perfect setup for Quint's description of his surviving the sinking of the Indianapolis. What a contrast."

"That was intense," I said. "You could imagine what it must have been like to be fighting off the sharks while waiting to be rescued. That's something I didn't know anything about."

"Few people do," Spence said. He changed the subject and continued, "I'm thinking about the cleaning."

"Kenny and I will pitch in, Spence. With Ricardo too, it'll be a four-man job." Spence was smart to start thinking about how we would be dealing with this movie.

Spence scratched his scalp for a moment, looked up at the ceiling, and headed to the supply closet.

"Did you recognize who played the mayor?" Kenny asked, still absorbed in the movie.

"No, he was good, though. I mean I hated him."

"The father in *The Graduate*. Murray Hamilton."

"Oh." I had yet to see *The Graduate.* I wanted *to be* a graduate.

Hogan appeared from the entrance to the projectionist booth, a dark patch on one of his thighs from where the Dr Pepper had spilled. He said,

"Boys and girls, ladies and gentlemen—we're going to need a bigger theater."

CHAPTER FORTY-ONE

Thursday night we had light attendance. But there was a charge in the air. It reminded me of one summer when I was a kid before my mom took sick. We had taken a vacation on the South Carolina coast. An approaching hurricane cut it short. The day we left, hours ahead of the storm, I remember looking out over the ocean. The swells were gray, full, and capped with white. The air had a different feel to it, almost explosive. A developing wall of clouds stretched across the skyline like a huge, bulging strip of gray canvas. "Let's get the heck out of Dodge," my dad had said.

I welcomed the slow night. By the second show, I saw Detective Dupree parked in an unmarked car, at least fifty yards away but in a direct line of sight of the theater entrance. What was he up to? I wondered whether he and Riggs were even more concerned about Samantha and Jesse Hooker than they'd let on. Maybe it was about drugs because they now knew Hooker was a dealer. Also, high school kids were rumored to be selling pot across the street, and Dupree would be looking out for this too. For all I knew, Owen was involved. Would he get caught? Did I wish this on him? I wasn't sure.

After the first show, Samantha approached me to get some fives for the cash drawer. She still wore a long-sleeved blouse covering her forearms, but there were a few rashes visible through applications of Calamine lotion. She gave me twenties to exchange. When I returned from the office with the fives, I counted them out in front of her, considering what questions I might ask her. I wanted to understand her better. What was she thinking? Why was she so unfriendly around us? I began with small talk.

"It'll be wild tomorrow," I said. She ignored the comment.

I added, "I'll go by the bank early morning for extra change." Again, nothing. I tried a direct question.

"Samantha, I'm curious. Did you have to deal with sellout crowds where you worked before? Where was it, down in Georgia?"

"Sometimes," she replied after a long moment. I waited for elaboration. None came.

"How many screens did you have?" She gave me a look suggesting I'd asked her a big favor. She said nothing.

I tried another angle.

"About what happened with Owen. He was rude. Sorry about that."

"I don't care a rat's ass what he thinks."

She slid off her chair, causing it to crack and carom off the bottom of the cashier counter. She snatched her Coke and headed past me, forcing me to stand aside. I'd poked the hornet's nest, and from what I heard, they didn't need a good reason to sting.

"I'll watch the window," I said, as she marched toward the restroom. She had me feeling that she was boss and I was the employee. I stayed clear of her for the rest of the evening.

Outside, I spotted the slumped-down silhouette of Detective Dupree in the front seat of his car. It felt good to know he was out there.

Owen's van eased its way past the lobby entrance. Him again. Was he trying to patch things up with Carrie? I wanted him to take a permanent vacation. It occurred to me that he might be intending to sell some pot. Dupree might see him. Should I warn him? I made a quick exit and went over to where he had parked. As I came to the open driver's side window, he was removing something from the glove compartment. I noticed a stash of small plastic bags, filled with what I took to be marijuana. He really was dealing the stuff. How could he be so reckless? So plain stupid. He held a joint, which looked freshly rolled.

"Shit! Don't do that, man!" he said, flinching.

"Sorry, didn't mean to sneak up on you."

"What do *you* want?"

"Listen, listen, just wanted to warn you," I said, almost deciding to let him hang. "Be careful with that pot. We have a cop around here tonight."

"Worry about how many popcorn boxes you need, and I'll worry about me. Stop dipping into my Kool-aid," Owen said. His eyes were wide and scared, and he fumbled the glove compartment shut.

"Have it your way," I said. "Remind me not to attend your funeral."

I returned to the theater but kept an eye on outside. Owen left the van and went over to the far side of the parking area and across the street. Was he going to meet someone for a deal? As much as I could tell, he was empty-handed. He was probably calling it off.

Dupree got out of his car and followed Owen from a distance. This was trouble. As much as I disliked Owen, now that I realized that he might get arrested, I didn't want it to happen. Dupree would probably search the van. And Carrie might get linked with drug dealing too. What could I do? I couldn't warn him. Could I remove his stash and hide it? If I moved quickly. I grabbed two empty popcorn boxes and ran outside to his van.

I tried the side doors. All locked. I tried the rear hatch door. It swung upward. I paused, my chest heaving with anxiety as if this moment in time would decide the direction my life would take. But what if Carrie was questioned and somehow became connected with what he was doing? Did I hold her fate in my hands too? I checked whether Dupree and Owen were returning. They were still heading away. *Do it.*

I climbed in and over the rear section of the van, the glow of the marquee revealing most of the interior. Owen had removed all the backseats. Several crates hugged the left side. I moved over to the front seat and reached over to the glove compartment, opening it after fumbling for the latch. With a few quick grabs, I filled the popcorn boxes with the packages, about twenty in all. I slid open the ashtray. It contained wrapping papers and a half-smoked joint. I pressed the ashtray down and yanked it out, pinching my thumb.

"Damn it," I said, under my breath. A trickle of blood formed, but I ignored it. I emptied all the contents into one of the boxes and then tossed the ashtray into one of the crates. I looked around for any other evidence and exited through the side sliding door, closing it quietly, but leaving a smear of blood on the handle. Would this matter? My heart, already beating fast, now thumped against my chest. Holding both boxes in one arm, I snatched my tie with the other and used it to wipe the blood. Come on. Move. *Move.* I checked for Dupree and Owen. They were heading back. I raced to the rear of the van and brought the hatch down, the resulting thud seeming to announce my presence.

"Damn it," I hissed again.

I needed to get rid of the pot. Crossing the parking lot back to the theater was risky. Dupree might see me. I didn't want to explain why I was carrying the boxes. I had an idea. Kenny's Fairlane was several cars down, further away from the marquee light. Kenny kept it unlocked, mainly because no one would ever steal it. He used the back of the car as a personal dumpster. The legroom space was taken up with layer upon layer of candy and hamburger wrappers, newspapers, magazines and who knows what else. Hunching down, I made my way to his car and half-opened one of the side doors. I wedged the popcorn boxes under at least a foot of trash, evening out the top to disguise any disturbance. I eased the door with my shoulder until I heard it click shut.

I looked over to the other side of the main road where Dupree and Owen stood next to each other, pausing for an opening in the traffic. I ran further down the parking lot, away from the theater lights. I crossed over to the side of the theater, making it easy to return inside unnoticed. The cut on my hand no longer bled. I removed my tie and stuffed it in my pocket.

Dupree led Owen across the parking lot toward the van. Soon he was exploring the van's front and back, as Owen waited, his head bowed. Dupree appeared to give up his search and spent a few minutes in a one-way conversation directed at Owen and then disappeared into the parking lot and back to his car. That was close. I thought about how I might easily have just let him suffer.

Owen came into the lobby. His cheeks were flushed, and a sheen of sweat layered his upper lip and forehead. As he caught me looking at him, he took his forearm and wiped away the sweat with two quick swipes. He looked like he was trying to figure out what had happened. He moved to where Carrie stood behind the concession counter, but she shifted to the other side of the counter, ignoring him. Maybe he suspected she'd seen who had taken his stash. I quickly intervened.

I said, "Owen, we need to talk. Let's go to my office."

Owen froze and looked at me as if he were a high school student caught without a hall pass.

"Owen, just do it," Carrie said.

"Ah, sure," Owen said, with an unfamiliar display of surrender.

He followed me. "I need to thank you for warning me. I was going to tell the guy some other time. That cop, the one you were talking about I guess, was following me all the way. I almost shit in my pants."

"I'm sure he knows horse manure when he smells it."

"Very funny."

"You lucked out, big time."

"Yes, well. Ah, did you take—"

I cut him off as we entered the office.

"Listen. Sit down and shut up. What you do is your business. And I have nothing against pot. But not around the theater."

"For sure, man."

"I wonder. Next time, *I will* turn you in. I promise you," I said, meaning every word. And before he could say anymore, I added, "And I'd appreciate it if you'd leave Carrie alone during working hours."

He studied me with a suspicious expression, trying to figure me out. I continued,

"Anyway, Owen. Why would you throw your life down the drain over some pot? I'd kill to have the chance to be starting college."

He said, "I didn't think—"

"Start thinking," I almost shouted. "Don't you get how dumb this is?"

But Owen, I guessed, had just one thing on his mind. Did I have the missing pot? I pretended ignorance, letting him twist in the wind, until I figured out what to do. I didn't feel bad about it either.

"I need to get back downstairs," I said.

Owen headed out to the van, probably desperate to find an explanation from Carrie about his missing pot. It looked like she had already left, wanting to avoid Owen, I assumed.

I saw Samantha over by the far lobby exit.

"Waiting on your ride?" I tried to be friendly.

"That little chickenshit's late," she said, as she pushed out the exit door. I saw Dupree, still in his car. Was he waiting to follow her when she left? I found ways to seem busy in the lobby and concession area so I could keep watching her.

With her Coke in one hand and a cigarette in the other, she alternated a deep inhaling and exhaling of smoke with a long suck on the straw from her drink as she waited. The smoke gained something from its stay in her lungs, something extra nasty. She finished the first cigarette, smoking it right down to the filter, flicking it into the bushes, close to where Bullock's body had been found. With an efficient sequence of actions with one hand, she shook another cigarette halfway from its packet, pulled it out with her lips, and lit it with her Bic lighter. Her initial inhale about burned the cigarette a third the way down, the smoke settling in her lungs for a good several seconds. She sucked down more Coke and blasted out smoke through her nostrils. Jesse Hooker would suffer, I knew that much.

Jesse had been up to something. Earlier, I'd seen him talking with a dark-skinned Black man, who, I swear, could have stepped off the set of a Blaxploitation flick. He wore a pinkish outfit with bell-bottom slacks and a wide-labeled jacket, crowning the sartorial effect with a white leather hat, cocked to the side. Long, straightened hair splayed out along his shoulders. A mustache drooped down on both sides of his face, Fu Manchu style. It was hard to tell his age, but he moved slow and smooth, ultracool. Superfly in the flesh.

They'd driven off in Hooker's pickup. A Black guy driving off with a redneck displaying a Confederate decal on his back window. It was a crazy thing to see.

Hooker showed up towards the end of cigarette number three, his pickup bouncing over the entrance curb and braking right in front of Samantha. The Black guy was in the passenger seat. They exchanged a few words and a hand slap. He exited the pickup and shuffled away into the darkness of the parking lot.

Samantha watched all of this with a furious expression on her face. Hooker glanced her way, and his small frame shrunk even smaller. I thought he might drive off without her. I would have. She barreled around to the passenger side and squeezed herself into the front seat. Hooker gunned his engine and sped away.

Sure enough, Dupree followed them. I was glad to see them go and glad to know Dupree had them tailed, though they seemed to have the jump on him.

What a strange end to the day. Owen would have been arrested for possession and drug dealing if I hadn't warned him and then crawled into his van to take the pot. What if Carrie had been implicated?

Things had happened between Carrie and me—exactly what I didn't know. My fantasies took shaky flight and then came down to earth. Come on. Did I have a real chance? Nope, not in my circumstances, not with someone like her.

And yet her breaking up with Owen made it less than pure fantasy. Didn't it? Yeah, right. In a few months, she'd be at the University of Chicago. After my brief appearance in her life, her time at the Yorktowne Theater would be a memory filed away, a topic for a college essay on Southern American culture.

CHAPTER FORTY-TWO

A line of over fifty people had already formed by the ticket window when I arrived at the theater the next day. My heart jackhammered. It was only noon, over four hours before we would start selling tickets.

I wedged myself through the line to get to the lobby entrance door.

"When can we buy tickets?" someone yelled.

"Four-thirty," I replied as I unlocked the entrance. Would we be able to handle this? I wasn't sure, and this uncertainty put me in a panic. I entered, re-locked the door, and found myself pacing back and forth.

"Get a grip on yourself," I hissed out loud.

I phoned Kenny.

"Kenny, Kenny."

"Who's this?"

"What do you mean, who's this? Wake up and get your butt over here. I'm serious. There's already a crowd."

"Really?"

"Yes, really!"

"Holy shit."

"Move it. Double time." I hung up.

After hauling out two sets of stanchion posts and ropes, I asked the people in line to move back as I cordoned off space in front of the window with one set. With the other set, I created a path directed toward the rear of the theater building where there would be much more space for the line to expand. The crowd cooperated, taking the edge off my worry. But I had to admit that I was making it up as I went along, half pretending I knew what I was doing. For once, I missed having Bullock's years of experience in the theater business.

I made two signs. One said "Box Office opens at 4:30" in big letters, taping it from the inside of the cashier window sign. The second said, "No Advance Tickets. Tickets Go on Sale One Hour before Shows Start."

"Have you seen it yet?" asked a guy who looked college age. He wore a faded, tie-dyed tee shirt with a peace sign on the front. A bandana across his forehead kept his shoulder-length hair in place.

"Yeah, have you seen it?" asked another guy who resembled a skinny version of Jim Morrison of the Doors.

"We previewed it yesterday. It was great. Fantastic."

"Scary?"

"You bet."

I talked with a few more people, sharing my observations about the movie. Kenny's *Fairlane* tore into the parking lot, the bottom of the chassis scraping the pavement. I thought about the pot. I needed to remove it from his car, but figured I could deal with it later that evening after dark. Kenny parked in one of the reserved spaces, exited, and stared at the line. He mouthed the word, "Dayum."

My thinking exactly. But I regretted my panicked call because I'd never seen Kenny so unfit for serving the public. I considered asking him to return home to take a shower and find cleaner clothes.

"Nate, this is mind-blowing. I'm getting a cold sweat."

"It's not so bad, so far," I said.

"You sure?"

"They're well-behaved. But, Kenny, you need to go back home and make yourself presentable. I can handle this for a while. I panicked over the phone. I felt I was flying blind."

He hesitated.

"Damn it, Kenny," I continued. "I mean it. Go home and get yourself put together. Sorry to have you scramble out of bed."

"I know, I know, I look like the Gill-man. I'm so dirty I'm leaving tracks."

I'd seen *The Creature from the Black Lagoon*. Viewed with the 3D glasses too. He did conjure up the amphibious Gill-man.

"All three dimensions of him, Kenny, to be honest," I said.

"Four dimensions. Stink like a swamp. I'll go home and try it again."

"Shower and fresh clothes, Kenny," I said with emphasis. He was right. He could gag a maggot.

"Aye, aye, ayatollah."

"Sorry I yelled at you."

"I'm good. Right now I'm as welcome as an outhouse breeze."

He returned to his car and drove off.

I noticed Detective Riggs peering through the lobby

glass. I let him in and closed the doors, pretending not to hear someone call out, "Can you sell us some drinks?"

"Couldn't get through. Just got that recorded message about starting times. So, I came by," Riggs said.

"It's been nonstop calls since I got here. That's why we have the message. Never seen anything like this."

"Intimidating," Riggs said. "How are you at crowd control? Maybe we need an officer over here."

"You ain't kidding. We don't open until four-thirty. I mean, look at it. It's around the building."

"Blockbuster, I suspect, is the operative term."

"Exactly."

"But we need to talk," Riggs said.

"Sure."

We went to my office and settled into chairs. We heard Spence's voice,

"Nate, you up there?"

"Yeah, Spence, come on up."

"Mr. Reeves," said Riggs, doffing an imaginary hat before Spence had a chance to remove his.

"We've got ourselves a mess of folks out there," Spence said.

"Damn right, Spence, but have a seat for a second. Detective Riggs was about to fill me in on something important." Spence took the empty chair. He carried a small duffle bag with him, and he placed it on the floor.

Spence said, "Well, that's good—because I've wanting to do the same in your direction. Called over at the police station, and they told me you'd be here. But Detective Riggs, why don't you share what you've got first."

"Okay, I will. Now, we've been made aware of a girl who accused Mr. Burton of assault down in Georgia," Riggs said.

"Sue Ellen Bullock told me about her," I said. "Whatever happened to her?"

"Samantha is what's happened to her," Riggs said.

"What?" I said. Spence seemed unmoved.

"Talked with Mrs. Bullock. She had no memory for her last name, but we tracked it down through my contacts in Atlanta. Turns out she went by the name of Lucille Lamar. We think she and Samantha are one and the same. And she's dangerous, which is why I need to fill you both in on these details."

"Lucille Lamar," said Spence, with a sense of prior familiarity.

Riggs paused, staring at Spence.

I filled the silence and said, "Wouldn't Bullock have recognized her?"

"Porked up," Spence said, as if he were the one telling us the details. "Hair's a wig. And fake glasses. Keeps quiet and changes her accent too."

"I can see it now, Spence. She almost never talks."

"She hated him," said Riggs.

"Wanted to flatten him. Like a freight train," Spence said. "And since Mr. Bullock wouldn't recognize her, she could find the opportunity to do it—"

"Without suspicion, yes," Riggs said. "And it turns out the theater where she worked last, The Regal, was robbed a week after she left. She and Hooker are probably a team."

"Bonnie and Clyde. Well, sort of, without the good looks and charm," I said.

"So it appears," Riggs said. "And this thing with Bullock was likely personal."

"You're not kidding," I said.

"She bided her time," Riggs said.

"Can you arrest her on this?" I asked.

"Ah, we'll bring her in for more questioning. Perhaps we can get a confession. We're working on the hard evidence."

"No weapon?" Spence asked, his eyes bright with anticipation.

"That's a problem. Nothing at the scene. Except a cigarette butt. We're going to try to bring her in this evening. Want to watch her for a while. Hooker too. We still don't know where she lives."

I said, "That's right. She's never given us an actual home address. Just a post office box."

"Figures," Riggs said. "She can work the first show, but that'll be it. We want to pick up Hooker too. We don't know where he lives either."

"I understand, but, excuse me a second, I need to find another cashier. This is *the* worst timing."

Fear swept over me. On this of all nights, losing our main cashier was a disaster. At least we'd have Samantha for the first show, but how could we handle the second two shows?

I tried calling our part-time cashier, but there was no answer.

CHAPTER FORTY-THREE

I tried calling a few more times but no luck. Spence distracted me by reaching into his duffle bag and taking out two plastic bags. One contained a cigarette butt, and the other, an envelope. He fished out a piece of paper too.

"What's all this, Spence?" I asked, half putting the phone down.

"The butt is a *Camel*, like the one you found, Detective Riggs, near them juniper bushes. It's Hooker's," Spence said. "The envelope, it's addressed to a one, Lucille Lamar. Post office box address downtown. Haven't opened it. You might want to do that. And this here piece of paper says where she's staying."

We both exchanged glances and stared at Spence

"Mr. Reeves, where did you get these?" Riggs said, clearly amazed by what Spence had produced.

"I took them from that little snake's pickup."

"Spence," I said, almost yelling. "How did you pull this off?"

"Gentlemen, let me tell you a story." He would answer our questions in his own way and at his own pace. Spence was in a different region of time and space.

"See, Spence Reeves ain't the name given me."

Spence paused and stared past us both, unseeing, deep in memory.

"I don't say *that* name," he continued, almost angry. "It

won't me, and won't who I *imagined* I would be. About the time I decided I'd be a Buffalo Soldier, I'd already decided I would be a Reeves instead."

We settled back in our chairs. I'd have to wait to make more calls.

"Why Reeves you might ask? I'll tell you why. Well, you don't know this but maybe the best lawman in the outlaw West was a man named Bass Reeves. Born a slave in Arkansas, but ended up working over thirty years as a US Marshal in Oklahoma Indian territory. Before Bass hung up his guns, as an old man, they say he brought in over three thousand outlaws."

Spence's eyes, dreamy but intense, kept focused on a point in space, willing us to go back in time and enter into the historical record, as if a diorama of sepia-tinged images projected from his pupils, an opening to the past.

"Most of these desperadoes, he tracked down, caught, and brought in alive. Bass could shoot the rifle and the pistol, a legend who lived up to the legend. He tangled with the real dangerous gunslingers, the mean desperados. Fact, he killed fourteen, they say, even though he claimed never to have been wounded bad himself. But killing wasn't his way. When he killed, it was self-defense."

"Spence, people should know more about this guy," I said, regretting my interruption.

Spence paused again and seemed to shift out of his dream state. He shook himself, and his eyes bore down on me, then at Riggs. His demeanor suggested he wanted to make sure we didn't have any doubts about what he was relating. Then he continued,

"Detective work, that made him most prized by the federal judges. I'd hear such stories about Reeves when I was a little boy. I met a man who had known Reeves. Learned all I could. I wanted to be just like Bass Reeves. After turning ten in 1910, that's when I started using the name. Chose 'Spence' for my first name, because there will never be another Bass Reeves. I liked the name. Went good with Reeves."

Spence paused again. I had questions. I'm sure Riggs did. But we let him keep going.

"My daddy, he humored me. Never knew my mother. Soon, Spence Reeves was who I was. Later, the Army didn't care. Didn't have no birth certificate, anyway. At fifteen I was big and tall. All that mattered to the recruiters. Found out afterwards that Bass died in 1910. Makes you think, though I don't believe in reincarnation. Now, you're wondering what this has to do with Jesse Hooker and Lucille Lamar?"

We nodded.

"See, Bass Reeves was a master of disguise. He studied each situation hard and came up with a plan, oftentimes pretending to be someone else—if that's what it took to round people up. Bass preferred being his own snazzy self, with two Colt pistols, butts looking at you, for the quicker draw. But he might be a farmer, a tramp, gunslinger—even an outlaw—whatever it took to bring 'em in. Course, this was one case where being a Black man was an advantage. Always under-*es*-timated."

He stopped and gave each of us stares. "Figured it out yet?"

"Ah, no," I said, shaking my head. "Honestly, Spence, I have no idea where you're heading. No idea whatsoever." I had long ago realized that leaps of imagination for me were ordinary thoughts for Spence.

"Detective Riggs?"

"Not a clue."

Spence reached into his bag again, and this time pulled out something wrapped in a towel. He unfolded it to reveal a black wig and two strips of hair.

"Spencer Damn Reeves. Superfly! Of course!" I blurted out.

"Superfly?" Riggs said.

"Yeah, you, *you* were the guy talking with Jesse Hooker last night. I mean, you looked like a Harlem drug dealer. Spence, you got in that pickup with Hooker?"

"As you say it, Nate."

"Would someone explain this to me," Riggs pleaded.

"I've been watching the goings-on around here," Spence said. "Been hearing things. Jesse Hooker, he had all the signs of a small-time drug dealer. Looks like a coke head too. Seen enough of it in my time, though I've never touched the stuff myself. Anyway, been pondering things, and I decided I would get the skinny on Hooker and Samantha— well, Looocille. Found me this getup and got to talking with Jesse. I told him I didn't want to meet around the theater. Neither did he, so we took a ride. Found me the chance to take one these cigarette butts and slip that letter into my coat pocket."

"Damn," Riggs said, shaking his head.

"Amazing, Spence," I added.

"How about the address?" Riggs asked. "How did you get that?"

"Turns out Jesse liked the idea of doing business in the colored side of town, Haiti, we call it. Before too long, I got his confidence."

"Weren't you scared?" I asked.

"Of that bony thing? Had me a weapon. And I got him wanting something from me. He could see from my threads I was doing well."

"The address?" Riggs pressed the issue.

"Told him I needed a sample of his stuff. He's dumb as a pine cone. We stopped by the place. I stayed in his pickup and watched."

"How did you figure she lived there too?" Riggs asked.

"Easy. He told me his girlfriend was working at the theater. Anyway, he came out with a sample. I told him I'd get back with him tonight. Meet him behind that warehouse near the theater, eight o'clock. Oh, and here's the sample."

Spence produced yet another plastic bag, this one containing a section of what looked like tin foil, folded over a few times.

"Here you go, Detective."

"Don't know what to say, Mr. Reeves," Riggs said. Neither did I. I felt goosebumps.

"I had me some fun. Done more stranger things."

"I'd like to hear about them. Truly would," Riggs said.

"But, gentlemen, you and I need to part company. Spence, you say eight, at that warehouse across the way?" Riggs pointed in the direction of the warehouse.

"Yep," Spence said.

I said, "And if you both don't mind, I'm going to try again to find me a cashier."

"Got things to do too," Spence said. He folded back the cloth over the disguise and returned it to the duffle bag. He and Riggs left the office together.

"Superfly," I said. "Catch you on the flip side."

We all felt revved up and supercharged. I know I did.

CHAPTER FORTY-FOUR

By four o'clock, except for Samantha, everyone scheduled to work had shown up—and early like I'd asked. Kenny had returned and cleaned up. The line stretched to the end of the building and doubled back around.

Both popcorn machines were popping at full tilt, and we had already filled extra popcorn boxes in advance of the first show. The lobby was thick with the aroma that would leave most customers helpless. The candy was replenished in neat rows, from Milk Duds, Reese Cups, and Raisinets to Junior Mints, Dots, and Kit Kats. I had checked the *Coke*, Sprite, and Dr Pepper syrup and carbonation canisters. The blades in the grape and orange drink machines were turning, the butter vats were topped up and bubbling, and the ice machines were sending hunks of crushed ice into the ice chests.

Carrie helped with the popping and whatever else was needed. We exchanged looks, causing my imagination to go wild.

Samantha had never been late, and I figured this meant she wouldn't show, leaving me relieved and worried both. Who knew what she was capable of doing—even with Dupree, Riggs, and others being on guard? I didn't want any of us in her crosshairs. Hooker was a wild card too. Maybe she wouldn't show up at all, if she suspected her cover had been discovered?

But I tried again to get through to another cashier. Still no luck. *Damn.* It would be *me* doing tickets. Kenny was error-prone with money. Kaywood Turrentine had warned me about this. He would forget whether someone gave him a twenty. We might be short a hundred or more for this reason alone.

Wait a second, I thought. I went up to Carrie and said, "Carrie, you're doing tickets."

"Nate, I've never done it," she whispered, intensely.

"It's easy. I'll show you. We've got plenty of time."

"But…" She glanced toward the long line and back at me.

"You'll be great at it. Trust me. You'll like it too."

"Where's Samantha?"

"Samantha's not coming in. You're it."

"How about Kenny?"

"I need him to keep a watch on the projector and other things." In a low voice I added, "Honestly, he's not good with giving change."

She looked scared, her eyes wider, showing more white around the stunning blue.

"Listen to me," I said. "It's easy. I'll start, and you can watch me. Then, you take over."

"But—"

"I promise you. It will be fun."

Carrie reflected for a second, took another look at the line, and said, "Show me." Her natural confidence was in full gear.

I'd finished showing her the basics when Owen

appeared, standing right in front of the ticket window. Carrie gave him a murderous stare.

"Listen," Owen said, after Billy Gossett had let him in, "I'm just here to apologize to everyone. I've been a butt hole. I know it. And, I wanted to see all this. It's crazy man, crazy."

He looked sincere. And I had another idea. I could use him.

"Owen, you owe me one, right?" I led him over to the side, near the water fountain.

"For real."

"I need you to work concessions tonight," I said.

He checked the long line outside and said, "Are you kidding?"

"Samantha didn't show. I've got Carrie doing tickets."

"Is this an offer I can't refuse?"

"You'll pick it up easy."

He thought for a moment, looked at the line again, and said with a sly smile, "Do you know what happened to my stash?"

I returned the smile and said, "I might be able to help you on that."

"I'm in."

"Great!"

I slapped him on the shoulder and brought him over to Mindy for a quick training. I hoped she wouldn't hold this against me.

Cheers swept up and down the line as the news spread that we had started selling tickets.

"Funkadelic," someone yelled.

I wrote on an index card the ticket number where we would need to stop selling and placed it in front of Carrie. Carrie took over after I'd handled about forty people. Her instincts were good. A one-trial learner. Her clear, smart voice did half the trick. And she kept her cool.

People found their seats first and came back for concessions, creating half a dozen long lines. The popcorn machines worked at a nonstop pace. Candy depleted faster than it could be restocked. We hadn't considered how much hungrier and thirstier people would be because of the wait. This was lunch and dinner for some.

Owen took easily to doing concessions. We didn't use cash registers for concessions, and so employees added the various combinations in their heads. But he was good at it, and soon he was having fun. He turned on his natural charm, especially with the girls.

Riggs and Dupree came by around five-thirty and talked near the theater entrance. I noticed they'd found parking across the street in the Midas Muffler lot. Dupree returned to his car while Riggs entered the lobby and waved to get my attention. He threaded his way to the front of the concession line where I was helping. He held up two fingers.

"Two minutes. Give me two minutes. Something you need to know for tonight," he said. I apologized to the couple I was about to serve and met him over by the office stairs.

"We lost them, Hicks and Hooker both," Riggs said.

"Really?"

"Samantha won't be showing up tonight."

"I figured as much. She's late, something she's never done before."

"Tried to call. Couldn't get through."

"Yeah, sorry about that. Constant calls."

"How did they get away?" I asked, hesitantly, not wanting to overstep what I could ask.

Riggs seemed unbothered by my question and said, "They changed cars. Her Impala was abandoned at a Best Western on the Interstate. Nobody saw her. Hooker's pickup either. Her apartment is cleaned out. We figure she may have been planning to rob the theater again tonight, probably with Hooker, and leave town. Must have realized we were onto them."

"Will you catch them?" I said, pleased he was sharing these details and intensely interested in these details too. And now that Carrie had taken over the cashier's job and that even Owen had come through, I was glad that Samantha hadn't shown up.

"Yeah, we'll get 'em. I'm glad they took off. If they'd tried something here again, someone might have gotten hurt. No, this is better. Confirms our suspicions. State Police are on it. We'll be watching over this place tonight even so. Wanted to tell you that too."

"You can help with concessions," I said. I was only half kidding because I needed to get back to work. I wanted everyone served and seated by the time the movie started.

"We'll just keep out your way," Riggs said, laughing. "Can I make some calls from your office?"

"Sure." I handed over my keys, indicating the one to the office.

"I recognize it."

"Use line three. The other two are always busy," I said as I headed back to the concession counter.

"I've noticed," Riggs said.

Mindy Hawkins stuck her head in the doorway and said in a panicked voice,

"Mr. Burton, we're out of Goobers!"

CHAPTER FORTY-FIVE

That took care of Samantha. Then again, would she return to the theater? Not if she was spooked. But assuming anything would be a mistake. With Hooker thrown into the equation, who knew what this perversion of Bonnie and Clyde might produce. But I had little time to digest what Riggs had told me.

I checked with Carrie. She and Kenny huddled together. Kenny used a black marker to make a "Five O'clock Show Sold Out" sign.

"Kenny, what do you think? Let's start selling for the seven-twenty show?"

"Makes sense."

"That was thrilling," Carrie said, her eyes radiating excitement.

"I knew you'd like it," I said. "I wouldn't steer you wrong." I was relieved, though. As smart and as capable as Carrie was, handling that crowd without any previous experience would have terrified almost anyone. But as soon as she had sized up the task, she had jumped into it without fear.

Billy Gossett came running toward me from the main theater.

"Mr. Burton, I need help with seating. We oversold."

"Did I make a mistake?" Carrie said.

"Probably some people couldn't find seats together. We

didn't oversell. Billy, let's see what we can do." Actually, I wasn't sure. Maybe we did make a mistake. Did I figure the tickets numbers wrong?

There were at least five clusters of people, mostly kids, looking for seats. I went up to the first group, five high school girls.

"Hey, listen, guys, there're seats for everybody. There won't be five together though. Why don't you pair up? Billy, you can find at least two together."

"Yeah, over there. Three." Billy pointed at a group of three empty seats. I called out to the people next to the seats whether they were taken. No, they weren't.

"Why don't you three take those seats?" Billy said.

"Great," I said. "I'll help these kids."

I whispered in his ear,

"Just keep your cool. It'll work out. Some folks will get frustrated. You're a natural at this."

By the time Hogan started the projector at five twenty, we'd found seats for everyone. We kept the house lights on through the ten minutes of previews, as some customers filtered back from getting concessions.

The lobby was clear when the movie started. It was strange to see it empty now, with the press of the crowd outside waiting for the next show. There'd been so much madhouse clatter and excitement, and, now, suddenly quiet, except for the sound of the previews, just audible through the theater entrance doors. I had the weird sense that we were exotic aquarium creatures being observed by a curious public.

Popcorn kernels, most crushed flat, covered the carpet. Billy and the two new kids set about sweeping them up. Mindy, with Owen eager to follow her lead, restocked the candy. All seemed forgiven between them. And Mindy seemed a different kid. She took charge of showing Owen the ropes. I figured she wanted to show that the trust I had given her was deserved. I was impressed.

Ice was a problem. We were almost out, and our two machines couldn't keep up. We'd survive that night, but not tomorrow, with additional afternoon shows and customers likely to be more thirsty. Kenny and I would have to think this through. The Riverview could help us out. We could purchase extra sacks of crushed ice. Warm soft drinks were unacceptable.

We had plenty of popcorn kernels, but twice Mindy told me that actual popped corn ran out. I instructed everyone to keep popping it, even between shows, and to start filling and stacking boxes. It wouldn't be as fresh as we typically served it, and wouldn't be as warm, but it would have to do.

I checked my watch. Exactly five-thirty, just when the movie would start. I wanted to experience this moment. I entered the theater as the Universal Films logo was disappearing into blackness for a few seconds. The white letters appeared announcing a "Zanuck/Brown Production" and then the low-register sound of the foreboding theme music,

Excitement spread through the audience. This was going to be fantastic. The scene shifted to an ocean floor from the perspective of something moving through undulating growths of seaweed and small sea creatures.

The title appeared in bold, white letters.

JAWS

The music quickened and peaked. Another current of excitement spread through the audience, accompanied by strange grunts. The music went quiet, and the scene changed to a beach party of high school students smoking and drinking around a fire. A boy blew on a harmonica, another strummed a guitar, a couple kissed. The effect was hardly calming though. The audience surely knew this happy, carefree sequence was a prelude to something terrifying. Although I had already seen it, somehow I felt the tension all the more because now I shared it with this large crowd.

Then, appearing on screen,

Directed

by

Steven Spielberg

I looked around and noticed that most people had either forgotten about their candy and popcorn or were nervously shoveling it into their mouths. This was good. I wanted to keep watching, but I had many tasks to do.

I asked Billy to set up the stanchion ropes so that people exiting the theater when the movie ended would be directed to the left exit of the lobby, away from the waiting crowd. I took most of the cash from the first show to the office safe to count later, leaving enough bills to make change for the next show. Owen struggled with a leaking carbonation cable, but before I had a chance to show him how to fix it, he'd managed it on his own.

Owen said, "I'm feeling *très* efficacious."

I came back with, "And you're not even wearing an assistant manager pin." I was beginning to half like him.

A loud, collective scream erupted from the theater, shaking the building's foundations—as if eight hundred people had reared back in their seats as one. Was this the head roll scene? Seconds later, a young girl burst out of the main theater and vomited in a compact projectile. I remembered the reactions to the early viewings of the movie described in *Time* magazine.

Riggs had just exited from the manager's office door and was nearest to her.

"Are you okay?" he said, as he rushed up to her.

She glanced at him and scurried back into the theater.

Billy was close by and said, "Just like in the preview! I'll get something to clean it up."

Hogan emerged from the projection booth door. He was laughing.

"All right, what did you do?" I said.

"Turned up the volume right before that head appeared."

"A girl vomited right on the carpet," I said.

"That's good. She'll want to see it again."

"Back for another bite," I said.

"A second helping. And bring her friends too," Hogan said.

As he headed out, Riggs said, "Thanks for letting me use

your phone. Call me if you need me. Or, talk to Detective Dupree. He'll be around."

Sometime later, we heard another eruption of screams. I peered through the window of an exit door. Brodie had seen the shark. But this was followed by laughter when Brodie said they would need a "bigger boat."

What a great line, I thought again.

At six forty-five we let the second crowd into the lobby. Like the first group, they were hungry and thirsty, and they formed lines at the concession area. We had long ago sold out for the second show, and we had the final line formed outside for the last, nine-fifteen show. Carrie now seemed supremely confident when I stuck my head in the ticket booth.

"Great job, Carrie."

"It's a gas. Sure beats concessions." Her eyes, sparkling blue, showed her pleasure too.

I said. "Did you see what happened? A girl ran out of the movie and threw up on the rug."

"Really?"

"And she rushed back in. Never seen anything like it."

We heard the packed theater roar in unison.

"I think the shark just blew up," I said.

CHAPTER FORTY-SIX

We handled the next show and the start of the last show without problems. But Saturday and Sunday continued to worry me. It seemed like day one of the D-Day invasion. We'd established a beachhead, but making it inland would be a long slog. Five sellouts each day, and the weekend lines might be longer.

I made quick calls to other theaters and asked for help. Kaywood Turrentine at the Riverview and Jimmy Reynolds at the Center agreed on the spot and said they'd haul over extra crushed ice, our main need, sometime late Saturday morning.

After we closed down the concession counter, Owen approached me and said, "Thanks again for last night. You saved my ass, man. I see that. And you didn't have to do it."

"Well, you saved mine tonight. You're a natural. There's a career waiting for you in concessions."

"It was a blast."

But he had something else on his mind. The stash. He gave me an expectant, almost pleading look. I motioned him over toward the lobby exit.

"Yeah, I have it, sort of."

"What do you mean, 'sort of'?" His face whitened, giving me a cheap thrill.

"I know where it is. It's hidden and safe," I reassured him quickly.

"Great. Do you realize how much it cost me?" He wanted this stuff bad.

"You know what I think, Owen. I don't want it around here. I swear I'll turn you in."

"I get it. I get it," he said with an innocent expression.

"I bet you want to know how I *got* it, right?" I said.

"Yeah, I mean, I locked the van."

"Not the back, you didn't. Climbed in and right over the engine block. Stuffed it all in two popcorn boxes, you know, the ones you like to make fun of. Thirty seconds and I was out the side door."

"Okay, okay, Tarzan—but *what* did you *do* with them?"

"Take that back."

"Sorry, sorry."

"You won't believe where they are."

"Just tell me."

"In the back of Kenny's Fairlane."

"What? All this time? Is that safe?" Owen said, looking anxious, his eyes darting about.

"Don't pee in your pants. They're under layers of trash. Kenny's car hasn't had anyone in the back seat for ten years. I'm not kidding. I'll show you. It's parked down the slope."

We exited the lobby together. I glanced around to make sure no one was watching, and we headed to where Kenny's car was parked among the mass of other cars.

"Wouldn't he notice?" Owen said, still unconvinced.

"You'll see. Trust me."

I squeezed into the space between Kenny's Fairlane and

the next car and hunched down. Owen followed my lead. I grabbed the handle of the rear door.

I said, "Hold your breath. The smell would kill a skunk."

I heard something. Further down the lot was the approaching shadow of someone walking our way.

"Get down, get down," I hissed.

We waited for several seconds as the figure passed by. It was Spence. Sometimes, he'd go outside to get some air.

"It's all right. It's just Spence," I said.

Owen said, "That's a bad hat he wears. He looks like Smokey the Bear."

"You knew he was a Buffalo Soldier, didn't you?"

"Buffalo Soldier? What's a Buffalo Soldier?"

"Owen, for someone who thinks he knows a lot, you don't know much."

"Why should I know that? Anyway, open it."

"Never mind," I said. But I was recalling what Spence had told me. His cavalry regiment took part in a campaign against Indian tribes in the 1870s. It was these Indians, Cheyennes, or was it Apaches, who came up with the name of Buffalo Soldier, on account of how fierce those Black soldiers fought, or so one legend went, Spence said. The style of hat came later, during the 1890s, when a group of Buffalo Soldiers patrolled places like Yosemite. Sort of early forest rangers. They got into the habit of pinching their hats to help shed the rain.

"Open it, come on, man," Owen said.

I could understand him being worried, under the circumstances, but what a pothead he'd turned out to be, every bit of one. I opened the car door as wide as I could without hitting the adjacent car.

"Jeez, you're right. Putrid," Owen said, contorting his face. This was the version of his face I wanted to remember him by.

There was just enough light to make out the layers of trash.

"See what I mean?" I said.

"Yeah, this is like a modern-day Olduvai Gorge. You could study ten years of Southern culture, layer by layer."

"Good point. Like rings on a southern pine," I said. I might really get to like him, despite myself, Butch Cassidy to his Sundance Kid.

"So, where're the boxes?" Owen said.

I held my breath, took both hands, and made a wedge about where I remembered stuffing the boxes.

"There's one!" Owen said.

"Grab it. The other one's deeper. Come on, quick," I said.

Owen pulled out both boxes.

"Outstanding." Owen inspected the boxes, grinning wide, without a hint of self-consciousness. Aside from being flattened by the weight of the upper layers of trash, the top of one slightly splayed open, both boxes were intact.

"Owen, take your precious cargo and clear out of here. I don't want it anywhere near this theater."

"Capisce."

"Beat it," I said.

He needed no encouragement.

CHAPTER FORTY-SEVEN

Where was Carrie? I wanted to thank her again for filling in for Samantha. I heard her voice, and Spence's too, coming from the cleaning room. I entered the room and Carrie looked up at me, her eyes shining with excitement.

Spence said, "Want to get a start on two. Get it knocked out quick."

I said, "We'll all help out with the main theater later."

"I can help too," Carrie offered. Spence glanced at me. She continued.

"I have the Volvo tonight."

"Great," Spence and I blurted out in unison.

Screams and then laughter came from the main theater.

Spence said, "Since I've got me another helper, how about her and me get started now, show Carrie the ropes?"

"Good plan. Get this tenderfoot ready for the main event. I need to finish the deposit bags."

Carrie followed Spence, almost skipping. Spence had a bounce in his step too.

Kenny soon joined me in the office after he'd shut down the projector in theater two. With the haul of cash, we filled four deposit bags rather than the usual two. *Jaws* was close to over by the time we finished. We went down to the lobby to prop open the exit doors and watch the crowd leave.

Hogan must have been thinking like us because he came out from the door leading up to the projection booth just as we entered the lobby.

"Gonna watch?" I said.

"Sure enough am. This is off the hook," Hogan answered. Like me, he wanted to see the reactions of the crowd up close.

"Party hardy," said Kenny.

"Out of sight," said Hogan.

"Radical," said Kenny.

"Wicked," said Hogan.

"Ah, Phil, can you stick around and help with the cleanup?" I said, having no rejoinder.

"I'm all in."

A cheer erupted from the theater. I peered through one of the exit door windows. People clapped and continued to cheer as the pieces of shark flesh filtered down through the ocean water. And when Brodie saw Hooper surface, alive and safe, people cheered once again.

We propped open each exit door, and the crowd streamed out, full of enthusiastic chatter.

Hogan and I exchanged satisfied looks. We had all pulled through. Even the crowds were accommodating. Kenny looked like he needed another shower, but I was grateful to have him as an assistant. I looked forward to what we could do together with midnight shows after *Jaws* had completed its run.

And what a movie we had on our hands. The poster, the theme music, the characters whose lives we cared about, the blend of terror and humor—the shark—everything. Critics might argue that there was no great trick in frightening moviegoers, but this hardly summed up what

Spielberg had accomplished. I figured the movie's effects would reverberate beyond the immediate initial experience. An instant classic, inspiring multiple viewings, a quantum leap forward in what we would expect for summer entertainment. Heck, I wasn't sure I even wanted to try out a water bed, much less take a swim in the ocean.

I thought about Bullock and felt a slight pang of sorrow. But it was fleeting. I found it increasingly hard to discover that his murder had led to *anything* but good outcomes—for the theater and those associated with the theater. Even Sue Ellen was better off for it. Was it bad luck to think this way about anyone's death? That's the path my thoughts had taken. I knocked on a doorway's wooden frame.

Spence and Carrie were making their way over from theater two.

"Mr. Reeves has been telling me about his time with the Buffalo Soldiers. It's amazing, simply amazing."

"Carrie listened it out of me," Spence said.

"My dad's area is American history. He's written about Teddy Roosevelt. Do you realize Mr. Reeves knew men who fought with the Rough Riders in Cuba? They saved Roosevelt from getting defeated in the Battle of San Juan Hill. My dad's going to love hearing about this."

"A true fact, Nate," Spence said. "I got that from Sergeant Berry of the 10th, *his*self. Berry was the first one to place the flag on the second hill they took, Kettle Hill. Those aren't the known facts but are *the* facts."

"Spence, this should be in the history books," I said.

"My dad can do something about that," Carrie said with

a fierce sense of justice in her voice. She looked so good I hurt inside.

We remained quiet for a few moments. Carrie, with another turn of emotion, said,

"Mr. Reeves, you—you contain *multitudes*. I mean it."

I agreed. A fitting description for Spence Reeves. The word caused a deep echo in my soul.

CHAPTER FORTY-EIGHT

Spence and Carrie tossed the waste into a barrel while Kenny followed with a broom down each row. I did the mopping. When the barrel filled up, Phil emptied it into the dumpster behind the theater while we started on a fresh barrel. We made quick progress, and soon Spence split off from us to get a head start on the restrooms. Carrie volunteered to help there too. I turned to vacuuming the carpets. Kenny and Phil took off early.

After finishing the carpets, I went up to the office for the deposit bags, which I placed in an old gym bag. It had a broken zipper, and so I couldn't close it up, but it was a good enough way of hiding what was inside. *Don't give a thief an opportunity to steal*, another Korean phrase my mom had been fond of using.

When I got back down to the lobby, Spence had cut off the theater lights. He and Carrie were already outside and standing together. I joined them. It was close to one o'clock, the theater now dark and empty, except for a single light above the cashier window.

The wind had picked up. Off to the south, a storm gathered. Spence placed a hand over his hat to stop a gust of the wind from carrying it away. Swirls of dry earth, dust, and trash kicked up and funneled near where we were standing. A car rocketed by on the main road, strangely in a hurry for so late at night. Maybe the driver wanted to beat the storm home. I heard the metal frame of the marquee creak as the wind whipped against it.

The only cars in the parking lot were my Dodge, Carrie's Volvo near the marquee, and Spence's Buick, way down to the left, the closest space he had found. Dupree, I presumed, had taken off at least an hour earlier. With the theater lights turned off, the cars resembled three boats in anchor on a dark patch of water. This sense was so strong that I half wondered whether I would sink through the asphalt if I stepped onto it. A memory came to me of my dad describing the landing of the Marine Corps at Inchon during the Korean War. This had been at night too.

Another gust of wind surprised us, sending Spence's hat across the asphalt before he could grab it. Carrie was the first to react and ran to retrieve it before the wind caught it again. She faced us both and instead of handing Spence his hat placed it on her head.

She gave the hat a slight tilt and said with a cowboy accent, "Name's Carrie, Carrie Jenkins."

Spence and I stood there stunned by her transformation. He spoke first, trying out his own cowboy accent, "Sure glad you showed up, Jenkins. Got us a heap of cattle to rustle up 'cause of this here storm."

I said, "Let's head 'em up, move 'em out."

Carrie gave the hat back and said, "The jig is up. Without your hat, I'm just a city-slicker."

We all laughed. None of us seemed eager to leave despite the coming storm and the late hour. I had been wanting to talk to Spence about Samantha, and I decided to bring Carrie into our small circle of those having inside knowledge.

"Detective Riggs told you about Samantha, right?" I asked Spence.

Spence gave me a glance suggesting he realized I was giving him a green light to talk about it in front of Carrie. "Appears she got a rattled," he said.

"They'll get her," I added.

"Guess so," he said, going along.

"You don't think she would have shown up again? That would have been stupid, wouldn't it?"

"Reckon so."

Carrie looked back and forth at both of us, trying to follow what it all meant.

"We need to catch you up on things," I said.

Spence and I took turns filling in the details. I described how Samantha was hired and how we only became suspicious of her after noticing the poison ivy rash.

"So, while we were reacting to the shark bite, you were thinking more about whether she had killed Mr. Bullock," Carrie said.

"Exactly."

Spence said, "But knowing this only suggested she could have, *might* have done it. It didn't explain why she *would* have done it."

Spence gave an account of his ride with Jesse Hooker.

"I saw him. I saw him. So you were the guy with the Fu Manchu wearing that pink suit?" Carrie said in disbelief. "But how? I mean *how* did you engineer that with him knowing?"

Spence took a few steps and recreated the stroll he had used while in character and gave us a satisfied grin.

"You are looking at the master of disguise. I kid you not," I said.

Carrie examined Spence as if she was getting to know him for the first time.

As she kept shaking her head in wonder, I explained what happened with Mr. Bullock in Georgia and Detective Riggs finding that Samantha was actually the woman who had accused Bullock of assault.

"There's the motive, the reason for hating him," Carrie said.

"Detective Riggs thinks she and Jesse Hooker have done a string of robberies," I said.

"Why would they stick around?" Carrie asked. "Why wouldn't they just vanish?"

I said, "I think they were seduced by how much money they could get after the first night of *Jaws*."

"But then, like you said, Mr. Reeves, they got spooked," Carrie said.

"They flew the coop," I said.

"Chickened out," Spence added with a grin, Carrie joining him with a drop-dead gorgeous smile.

"She must have really hated Mr. Bullock," Carrie said.

"But she took her time to get him," Spence said. "Which is often how it happens. When it's ripe. Reminds me of something I heard Jackie Robinson did, not too long after he got his chance to play in the majors."

"Jackie Robinson?" I said.

"Yes, Jackie."

The wind blew Carrie's hair across her face, and she used a hand to clear it from her eyes. She gave me a puzzled look, still unfamiliar with Spence's roundabout way of making a point with a story. Just hold on, you'll see, my returning expression tried to communicate.

"Well, Jackie, he knew he would get a lot of abuse when he first started in the professional leagues—being the first Black man. But he'd have to take it. Ignore it."

"I read about that, Spence," I said.

"A right fielder named Enos Slaughter was one of the players who didn't like Jackie being in the league," Spence continued. "One day, Slaughter—this was early on—was at bat and Jackie, he was playing first base. Slaughter hit a grounder, and as he crossed first base, he spiked Jackie's foot."

Spence stomped his right foot.

"He did it deliberate, on purpose. It hurt, and it bled, but what did Jackie do? Pretended like it was nothing."

The urge for payback welled up in me. Carrie's face had the fire of injustice stamped on it too.

Carrie said, "How could he just take it?"

"Jackie was an educated man. Graduate of *U-C-L-A*," Spence said, elongating the letters.

"But might that have made him even more angry?" I said.

"Didn't say he won't angry. This is what he did. Or, what he *didn't* do. He said to Slaughter, quiet like, 'I'll remember that.' About two years later I think it was, at least that long. The teams were playing each other again. Slaughter was at bat, but this time Jackie was playing second base. Slaughter hit a ball past the infield and tried to stretch a single into a double. Jackie took the throw from the outfielder and tagged Slaughter in the mouth, *accidentally on purpose*, and knocked out six of his teeth."

"Yes!" I said.

"Just what he deserved," Carrie said.

Spence continued, "And know what Jackie said?"

"What?" Carrie and I both said together.

"He said, he said, 'I told you I'd remember it.'"

We laughed.

"Looks like Samantha got her revenge too," I reflected.

"In her own good time," Carrie said.

"Another thing," Spence said, "Slaughter told this story—it was a radio interview—years later. That's why I know it's likely true. He felt bad about what he'd done. He'd changed along with the times. He grew up down the road in Roxboro, by the way."

Lightning flashed, so thick and bright it seemed to remain in the sky as if it left a shell of hot steel, still full of electric charge and climbing to the top of the heavens. In outline, I saw storm clouds, churning and steamrolling in our direction. We'd been so wrapped up in Spence's story we hadn't noticed their quick advance.

"We'd better get moving," I said. I hoped I could make the deposit before the storm hit."

Spence said, "Don't look too good, does it, by the looks

of it."

"I've never seen lightning like that," I said.

"Neither have I," Carrie said.

"Didn't grow up a farm, did you?" Spence said.

"No, but I know we're in for something potent," Carrie said.

The thunder from the lightning suddenly shattered the air. Carrie and I flinched.

"Agreed," I said.

A black cat came from around the marquee and streaked past us and across the road.

"Did you see that?" I said.

"Sure did," Spence said.

Carrie said, "That can't be a good sign."

"A black cat is good luck in Korea," I said, remembering that my Mom would say this whenever we started believing silly superstitions.

The mass of advancing storm clouds seemed darker still and frightening in power. I imagined one of those long-legged Martian creatures from *The War of the Worlds* appearing at the head of these clouds, ready to obliterate everything in its path.

"Let's git a going," Spence said.

"Yeah, let's split," I agreed.

"Wait, wait," Carrie said. She stretched her body and gave Spence a peck on his cheek. Then she turned to me and pressed her lips to mine, rocking all five of my senses, every cell in my body.

"Thanks, you guys," Carrie said.

Another scary bolt of lightning lit up the sky. All of us moved fast, even Spence. I got to my Dart first, just as another blast of thunder reached us.

"Jeesus," I said out loud, but I watched to make sure Carrie was safe inside her Volvo. I was so wired from Carrie's unexpected kiss that I wondered whether a lightning strike would affect me. I tossed the gym bag across to the passenger seat and threw myself into the front seat. I cranked the engine and could see Spence's Electra shake and rumble to a start as well, with a few plumes of burnt oil, buffeted by the wind. Carrie got her Volvo going too.

For a few moments we all remained poised, ready to leave, our engines idling. Spence move closer to the exit and stopped, continuing to chug away. He hit his horn and waved us ahead. He wouldn't be leaving until we left first.

We exchanged waves and nods. Carrie led the way, and I followed. Her lips seemed to have made a permanent imprint on mine, joined with an unfading taste and fragrance. I had all the signs of running a high fever, but I'd never felt in better health.

CHAPTER FORTY-NINE

My life had turned on a fulcrum. Before the kiss and after it. Tomorrow couldn't come soon enough, my anticipation of seeing Carrie again, maybe kissing again, so intense.

I entered the mall's parking deck in a form of trance, barely aware that I had a task to complete, and possibly a dangerous one.

The parking deck was mostly dark and empty except for two cars parked close together near the entrance to the mall's second deck, likely belonging to the nightly cleaning crew. Still under Carrie's spell, I was ready to get this last manager's task done for the day.

The bank deposit box, lit by a small overhead light, was just to the right of the mall's second-floor main entrance. A bridgeway stretched from the deck to the entrance. Four metal poles were set a few yards apart to prevent vehicles from driving onto it.

I drove to where the poles stood and parked at a slight angle so that the headlights gave the deposit box area the most light. Another terrifying flash of lightning, followed a few seconds later by a blast of thunder, shook me from my dream state.

The rain would soon come down hard and heavy, but I hoped to drop the bags in the deposit box before this happened. I kept the engine running, removed the spare deposit key from the glove compartment, grabbed the gym bag, and exited the car.

I ran across the bridgeway toward the deposit box as large drops of rain polka-dotted my clothes. Another fork of lightning and a simultaneous detonation of thunder froze me for a second. It felt like a direct hit on the bridgeway, and I covered my head with my free arm. This was stupid. The deposit could wait. I started back to the car, but my sudden movement caused me to slip on the rain-slick concrete. Two deposit bags fell out of the gym bag and slid across the concrete.

"Damn!"

The rain began in full force, enveloping me. I reached back toward the deposit bags but got little traction, and I fell to the concrete, striking a knee. The deposit key fell from my hand and skidded to the edge of a drain.

"Damn!" I yelled again.

Water thickened near the drain. I reached for the key, but too late. It disappeared down the drain. I couldn't believe what was happening. I rubbed my knee to relieve the sharp, throbbing stabs of pain. I was wet through.

The lights on the deck and the deposit box flickered and went out, the walkway now partially lit by my car headlights. I had to shield the rain from my eyes. The deposit bags were dark shapes spread a few feet apart.

Two bright lights appeared to my left—car lights, their beams made thick by reflection off the rain. They were from one of the parked cars I had seen earlier, now advancing right up to the poles. This was trouble. I grabbed each rain-soaked deposit bag and stuffed them back into the gym bag, thinking I'd make a run for it. But someone exited the car and moved in front of its headlights, creating a squat, rounded silhouette. Another flash of lightning briefly illuminated who it was. Samantha. I froze, shaken by what I saw.

She bent to a crouch and raised her arms to chest height. She had a gun pointed at me.

"Don't shoot!" I yelled.

I extended the gym bag in Samantha's direction, causing several of the deposit bags again to scatter across the concrete. I desperately hoped the money was all she wanted. She lowered the gun, and I jerked my body to the left and sprinted away from the headlight beams, shielding myself in a shadowed area behind a trash barrel.

The rain continued to come down hard. This would help too. Samantha's vision had to be as blurred as my own. I risked looking around the other side of the trash barrel. Samantha had moved toward the deposit bags and was no longer pointing the gun directly my way. Good, she might take the bags and go.

Behind and above me to my right, I heard a voice, clear despite the noise from the rain.

"This is the police. Drop the gun!" I knew the voice. It was Riggs. He was standing at the edge of the roof and aiming his own gun at Samantha.

"Drop it!" Riggs shouted.

Another violent combination of lightning and thunder shook the air. The lightning hit something toward the back of the roof, but the force of it caused Riggs to drop his gun.

It fell to the concrete. I prayed Riggs had not been hit.

I kept quiet, protected by the barrel and ready to dart away at the first opportunity. She moved toward the nearest bag and picked it up as if to confirm what it was. With one hand, she placed each deposit bag in the gym bag, keeping the gun partially aimed in my direction. Still no movement or sound from the roof, and again I feared Riggs had been hit by the lightning. I readied myself to run, but Samantha had a good angle on me. I was uncertain how hidden I was and how good she was at handling a gun. I hoped she'd just take off with the money.

I saw more car lights cut a reflecting path across the mall's entrance. The car's horn sounded several times. Samantha turned toward the sound as the car came to a stop right next to Samantha's. The horn's sound was deep, and I thought I recognized it. It was Spence. He had followed me.

The driver's side door opened, and a moment later, the passenger's side door opened too. This seemed to confuse Samantha, because she raised her gun toward the car, but moved her aim from one side to the other, indecisively. Then she took a shot. I heard a cracking sound, the shattering of a car window. Was Spence hit? I couldn't tell.

I was about to charge at Samantha, surprise her from behind, and try to knock the gun out of her hand. But I hesitated when I saw the outline of Spence's distinctive frame and hat on the passenger side of his car. He must have slipped out the other side. I heard a weird yell, the one I had heard months before, distinct and penetrating, despite the sounds made by the storm. Something flew through the air, just as Samantha took a second shot. She clutched her chest, her gun falling to the concrete. She remained standing for a moment, and then her arms fell to her sides. She went limp and fell backward.

I ran to where she lay. Spence's sickle had struck her right in the center of her chest, probably piercing her heart. Her arms shook. She seemed to be trying to lift them, to gather strength, her chest heaving for air. The car lights reflected in her eyes. She stared up at me, unseeing, her eyelids fluttering.

Spence was now standing next to me. Rain spilled over the brim of his Stetson. He kicked her gun off to the side.

"She's a goner," he said.

"No kidding, poor creature," I said.

"Whoohee, she was a mean thing. Won't right in the head."

"I'm glad you showed up, Spence. I swear she would have killed me. How did you do that?"

He ignored my question. "Let's ride this out in my buggy. I'll call the police on my CB."

But I wasn't thinking about Samantha anymore. "Spence, Detective Riggs is up on the roof. I think he might be hurt, maybe struck by lightning."

"He's up there?"

"Yeah. We've got to get up there."

"Better we call an ambulance on my CB first. Let's go."

We moved fast over to the Buick. Spence slid inside and flipped the switch on his CB. He found a good channel and said, "Somebody get an ambulance out to the mall. Second deck, main entrance. We have an officer down. Make it fast. He's on the roof."

After several repetitions because of the static, he got a clear reply.

"We're on it. Second deck, main entrance, over."

"Double time it, over," Spence said.

The rain picked up again.

Spence looked at me and said, "Let's move."

We rushed past Samantha's body and to the edge of the building.

"Lift me," I said.

Spence cupped his hands together where I placed a foot. He hoisted me up to his shoulders and then raised me higher with his long arms.

"Can't reach, Spence," I yelled.

Spence seemed to grunt with pain, but he twisted his body and lifted me even higher. I just managed to grab the roof's edge with my right hand.

"I got it Spence. Got it."

I pulled myself up and over.

The dark shape of Riggs stretched out several feet in front of me.

I shouted, "Spence, get on your CB, again. Tell them to hurry it up."

Spence hustled back to his Buick.

"Detective Riggs," I called out. He lay face down in an inch of water.

"Detective Riggs. It's me, Nate Burton."

He didn't respond. I knelt and turned him over. I felt his chest. Was he breathing? I placed myself so that my back protected him from the rain and started alternately pushing on his chest and blowing air into his lungs. There was a smell of something burned. The lightning must have hit him. "Detective Riggs! Breathe." He coughed forcefully and gasped for breath.

"That's it. Breathe, man. Breathe, breathe."

He coughed again, this time spitting out water that he must have swallowed. I pulled him up to a sitting position.

"That's it, that's it. Are you okay?"

He said nothing.

"Lightning hit you," I said. I wanted to hear him say something.

"Detective Riggs. Are you okay?"

He needed to get to the hospital. I put my arm around his shoulder to give him warmth and to protect him further from the rain. Fortunately, the rain had eased.

He looked at me and mumbled, "What happened? Where's Samantha?"

"Detective Riggs, you're made of tough stuff. You're going to be fine."

"Lightning?" I don't think he knew what had happened. It didn't appear to be a direct hit. The lightning may have arced over from the metal door of the roof entrance.

"Yeah, and Samantha, she's dead. Spence got her. With his sickle," I said. "You should have seen it."

"Mr. Reeves?"

"With his sickle. From about thirty feet. You can see."

The rain had let up even more. I helped Riggs up, and we both surveyed the bridgeway where Samantha lay, outlined by the car lights.

Coughing out the words, Riggs said, "That's the damnedest thing I've ever seen." He staggered and crumpled down to one knee.

"You need a doctor."

A siren wailed in the distance. I hoped it was the ambulance.

"A little dizzy. I'll be fine," Riggs said. I thought he might be in shock, or something close to it.

Spence emerged from his Buick and looked up at us. I gave him a thumbs-up, though I was still worried about Riggs.

CHAPTER FIFTY

"This way," I said to Riggs.

We exited through the roof access door, its encasement battered and charred from where the lightning had probably struck. We made our way down the stairs to another door opening near the mall entrance. I kept his arm around my shoulders, holding his wrist firm with one hand and the other grabbing his side.

"How did you get up there?" I asked.

"Security guard let me in. Parked in the lower deck."

"But how did you know?"

"A hunch."

"You're shaking," I said.

"My legs are rubber."

I was relieved to see an ambulance was already past the main ramp and heading to the bridgeway. We pushed through the mall entrance door.

"Firebolt got you good," said Spence, who stood waiting for us, water still dripping from his Stetson.

"Apparently."

"You were fried. Can smell it," Spence said, as he took Riggs's other arm, placing it over his shoulders.

I saw Riggs's gun off to the side. I stooped and picked it up.

"Here's your gun," I said, inserting it in his shoulder holster for him.

"Thanks, I remember now," Riggs said. "I was taking shelter in that access entrance, and I saw something, the lights from the cars."

Riggs was not looking good. His steps faltered again.

"Still light-headed," he said.

"You need a doctor," I said. I also noticed something about Spence, a swelling of red on his left side, smeared by the rain. He stumbled.

"Spence, did you get shot?"

"Grazed my side. Just an oil leak."

"I don't know, Spence. That's a lot of blood."

Two paramedics scrambled out of the ambulance and ran toward us. One veered off toward Samantha.

"She's dead," I yelled to them. "This man was struck by lightning. And he's been shot. They need your help."

"I'm okay," Riggs said. He was looking at Samantha, turning in her direction, as if he wanted to start doing his job. His eyes seemed unfocused.

Spence then sank to the ground and held his head.

"Get them to a hospital, quick," I shouted. The situation had taken a scary turn.

One paramedic lifted Spence by the shoulder and the other stopped heading toward Samantha and came over to help Riggs. Soon, both Spence and Riggs were placed on stretchers in the ambulance.

I called out to Spence, "I'll take care of your Buick. And your sickle." I wasn't sure he'd heard me. He already had an oxygen mask over his face. His eyes were closed.

"Detective Riggs, I'll come by the hospital later."

He didn't respond.

"Can you please get them to the hospital—and fast," I shouted at one of the men.

He hesitated, glancing over at Samantha for a second. There was another siren in the distance, maybe two.

"Right, let's go," he said to the other man, who was already moving toward the driver side of the ambulance.

He slammed the doors tight, and they hauled off, lights flashing and siren blaring. I prayed to myself that they both would be okay.

The rain picked up again. A second surge was about to hit and so I figured I'd wait in my car for more help to arrive. I first collected the gym bag—I wouldn't be making the deposit tonight.

I took another quick look at Samantha. Her hair had changed. It was wet and stringy from the rain—and dark. This was her natural hair. Yes, like Spence had said, she'd been wearing a wig at the theater. Her eyes, motionless, showed no life, all the hate gone from her. I felt a rush of pity for her. Spence's sickle, thrusting up from the center of her chest, reminded me of the killing of the vampire in the Christopher Lee movie version of *Dracula*.

Another lightning strike hit nearby as I ran to my car. I tossed the bag onto the passenger side and jumped in by the time the thunder arrived. The rain again came down in swirling gusts.

I wanted to go to the hospital to check on Riggs and Spence. Riggs had appeared fine at first but looked bad now. Spence, he must have lost more blood than he'd let on.

Like Riggs, he hadn't responded to the last thing I had said to him.

Then the rear side door opened.

CHAPTER FIFTY-ONE

My heart slammed against my chest. A man wearing a baseball cap flung himself into the back seat. It was Samantha's friend, Jesse Hooker. He held a gun.

"You just keep still, real calm like, hands on that wheel—and I won't have to shoot you." He pressed the gun against my neck.

"Okay, okay," I said with as steady a voice as I could manage. My body shook and the pounding of my heart made a whooshing sound in my ears.

The lights of an ambulance flashed off to the side as it entered the parking deck. I heard the distant shriek of another siren too. Police? Should I jump out of the car and run? No, that would be too risky.

"You want the money?" I said. "Go ahead take it. It's right here in the bag." I stammered out the words, praying he wouldn't shoot.

"You shut your damn mouth and listen up. Cut the lights. Don't try nothing stupid." I smelled beer and cigarettes on his breath.

I hesitated. He yelled in my ear, "I said cut the damn lights." The gun press harder into my neck. *Do what he says, you idiot.* I fumbled for headlight controls, found them, and turned off the lights. I had an image of a bullet ripping through my neck, shattering my spine—bone, flesh, and blood.

"Watch out with that gun. I'll do what you say!"

"Drive real slow over to that side exit, the one yonder," he hissed. "Come on. Come on. Move it."

I released the brake, shifted into drive, and gave the car a little gas. I turned the steering wheel sharply to avoid the poles.

"I can't see," I said. "Let me turn on the wipers."

"Go ahead, but keep moving. Head for the ramp."

I turned the wipers on, but it was still hard to see. I slowed.

"Step on it," Hooker said, the gun still jammed against my neck.

"Okay, okay. *Okay*. I'm trying not to wreck this thing."

I pressed the pedal, and the car sailed over the top of the ramp, gliding to the left and scraping the side of the concrete. I flinched, anxious that the gun might fire accidentally, relieved when it didn't. The gun slipped away from my neck as Hooker caught his balance.

The front bumper slammed against the road at the bottom of the ramp, tossing us both up into the air.

"Watch what you're doing, fool!"

"You told me to step on it," I said. "And I can't see!"

"Turn them lights on and shut up. Keep going."

I felt for the light switch and turned the lights back on. Again, I felt the gun against my neck. It was small, but it felt like a twelve-gauge shotgun.

The rain picked up even more, but with the lights on, I managed to steer toward the main road, which was a straight shot. Through the rearview mirror, I made out the distant, blurry shape of a second vehicle, probably a police car. It sped across the parking deck to the bridgeway, still lit by the headlights of the cars. But I wouldn't be getting any help. I was on my own with this crazy, drunk bastard.

I plowed through a sheet of water collected at the intersection of the main road.

"Go left," Hooker said.

I turned, trying to avoid swerving off the road.

"You're Jesse, right?" I said. Now that we were on a straight section of the main road, the driving was easier. I altered my accent to one slightly more Southern. He removed the gun from my neck, relieving some of the tension and fear I felt.

"You worry about the damn road."

The window glass had fogged up. I veered to the right, hitting gravel.

"Watch where you're going!"

"I need to open the fresh air vent. Look, it's fogging up."

"Do it."

I opened the vent and put the fan on full blast. The windshield began to clear. "See, that's better," I said.

"You talk too much. Keep going," Jesse said, but he seemed less angry. I focused on the road as the wipers did their best to clear the windshield. The wind hurled small branches and debris across our path. We were in a more rural area now, and the canopy of tall pines on either side of the road whipped about. I thought of the scene in *Psycho* when Marion Crane, the woman played by Janet Leigh, encounters a heavy rainstorm as she escapes with the stolen money. Unfortunately for her, she was forced to make a stop—at the Bates Motel—the place of her infamous murder by Norman Bates. Where were we heading? I had to be ready to act if I got the opportunity. I had a sudden image of my dead body resting on a slab in the morgue. I didn't plan on having my life get snuffed out by this lunatic.

Neither of us spoke for half a minute while I focused on the curving centerline of the road. The rain eased up a bit.

"Are you some kind of chink?" Hooker asked.

"Well, my mom was Korean."

"*Ko*-rea, I knew it. I knew it. I told Lucille you were a chink. She didn't believe me."

"You're a smart guy, Jesse," I said, hiding my resentment. So he used her real name. They must have known each other for a while.

I had to do something. When we got far enough away, he might kill me. I felt more and more sure of it. Could I drive off the road? I didn't have my seat belt on, but neither did he. I liked my chances. If I slowed, I could turn sharply, and then dive out and run like hell.

"That bitch was crazy. I wasn't going to get myself killed by lightning."

"That's what I mean. I thought you were smart. You were in the car?"

"Damn right I was."

The flattery seemed to be working. I laid it on thicker. "I figured you for someone who paddles his own canoe. Smarter than me too. And Detective Riggs, he got hit on the roof."

"He got hit? I knew it. I thought that was him," Hooker said with a laugh and lifting his face. Glancing at the rearview mirror, I saw the skin peel away from his jumbled teeth, reminding me of the *Jaws* poster.

"Yeah, Jesse. Don't know if it was a direct hit though. I think it jumped from the roof entrance. But he was fried for sure." I stayed friendly, like we were buddies.

"He was dumb to be up on that roof," said Hooker.

"How did you get mixed up with Lucille?" I asked. He didn't reply. "She was the one who killed Bullock, right? I didn't take you for someone who would kill somebody."

"Who are you? Jesus Christ?" Hooker said, as if I had accused him of something.

"I didn't mean anything," I quickly added.

"Anyway, yeah, she hated him. I just wanted the money. Like tonight."

"Listen, Jesse. You want the money. I don't blame you. There's a lot. A cool five grand and change. Right here."

"Five? That's what she said it would be."

"Sure is, Jesse."

"Sweet."

"It don't matter to me if you take it. Insurance will cover it. You can use it more than they can. Do you know they never gave me a raise? Can you believe that? The assholes."

"Figures. The little guy always gets the shaft," Hooker said angrily, almost sounding like he identified with me. Maybe he'd let me live.

"You know it, I know it. Take the car and the money and go. Just let me out. I can deal with this storm."

He said nothing. A double blast of lightning and thunder detonated. The rain thickened.

"I can't see where I'm going, man. We need to stop," I said.

"Keep going," he yelled.

"Where are we going?"

"Shut up."

The road ahead was flooded over with water where there was a creek or river. The water had to be deep. As far as I could tell, it was moving fast, right over a small bridge. We would be swept away, and so I slowed.

"Move it," Hooker screamed in my ear.

"The bridge. It's flooded."

"I said, move it!"

This was the break I needed. Could he see how flooded the creek was? We'd stall and likely be swept across the road into the creek. Then I might be able to get away from him. If he would just stop pointing that gun at me. My nerves were stretched to their limit as every bump created the real chance of its accidental firing. We were heading for a rough jolt.

I braced myself, keeping my arms stiff against the steering wheel as we sped right into the water. The car jerked to a stop.

Hooker lost his grip on the seat. I shifted my head as his body lunged forward. His face and neck banged against the passenger seat headrest and whiplashed backward. The gun flew out of his hand and fell to the front passenger seat. He tried to scramble over the front seat, but I slammed my elbow across his nose, knocking him back. I grabbed the gun, spun around, and aimed it at him.

"Freeze," I screamed, shaking with anger. "I swear I'll shoot you right in that stupid face of yours, you goddamned, sneaky son of a bitch!"

"Don't shoot, don't shoot!"

He realized I meant it. I was furious over a lot of things. Bullock's murder, Samantha's shooting Spence, and also the fact that this sorry ass redneck had been willing to shoot me too—with his smelly breath and brain wired like the Civil War never happened.

He held up both hands. The car lifted off the road and began to spin.

"Please don't shoot, man. I didn't kill your boss. That crazy bitch did it." Blood flowed from his nose.

The car floated with surprising speed right over the edge of where the bridge must have been. With the gun in my hand, I struggled to keep a steady aim on Hooker. He seized the headrest to steady himself. Water was at the level of the windows and coming up through the floorboards. The reflected light from the headlights against the water and the instrument panel a created strange, greenish illumination inside. For the moment, we seemed protected. But we were in serious trouble.

The car continued its uneven spin. I anchored myself with one arm pressed to the dashboard. The creek was now a deep, fast-moving river. Water outside rose past the windows and spurted into the car through any openings, the level rising up to my knees. I needed to get out of this car and fast.

Hooker panicked. He ignored my gun and fumbled with the door handle as he pushed against the door. The water pressure from the outside was already too great and the door wouldn't budge.

"It won't open, it won't open." He kept pushing.

I didn't need the gun. I tossed it aside. While he struggled with the door, I moved to my side window and rolled it down, ignoring the rush of water this created. This would be the only way to escape.

"What are you doing? Are you crazy?" Hooker yelled.

I ignored him and took in a deep breath of air.

"Help me, man, help me," Hooker screamed. "I cain't swim good."

Water swallowed up his terrified, bony face.

That was his problem.

CHAPTER FIFTY-TWO

The filthy, mud-filled water enveloped me as well, but I forced my eyes open, ignoring the sting. The headlights reflecting in the water and the green glow of the instrument panel created enough light to show Jesse choking and gagging. I readied myself to go out the window, but the car made a sudden, downward tilt, slamming against the creek bottom and throwing me against the opposite passenger door. I was lucky. I might have been crushed as I went out the window. The car now seemed wedged in a bank of mud, despite the strong current of floodwater.

I could just make out the dark shape of Hooker as he thrashed his arms about desperately. I already needed air, and I knew I had little time to get out through the other window. With the inside now full of water, I thought the door would open. I felt for the door handle, yanked it hard, and pushed against the door with my shoulder, bracing my feet on the steering column. The door opened a few inches, and the current caught it, swinging it open.

My lungs burned. I readied myself to push out before the door might swing shut. Hooker was no longer moving, but his body floated toward me. Instinctively, I wrapped my legs around his shoulders and directed both us out the door. We both spun and twisted in the dark water.

I swam upward. Something scraped across my shoulder, stunning me for a moment. I held my grip on Hooker. He felt heavy and my lungs seemed to explode with each thrust of my limbs.

Another object grazed my cheek. I saw a flash of light. Lightning. The surface was close. With a few more strokes, I broke the surface and took in deep gulps of air.

I looped an arm under Hooker's shoulders, keeping his head above water. Ahead I saw the outline of a bridge, and I swam with the current in its direction. I grabbed the concrete and pulled us both around and away from the current to a shallow stretch of water and onto a patch of grass.

Hooker coughed up water and gasped for air. He was a resilient little weasel. I wasn't sure if it made me happy to see him breathing, except that I had gone to so much trouble to save him. I removed his shirt, pulled his arms together, and used the shirt to tie them tight. He struggled and coughed. For some reason, he remained quiet. But he couldn't do much damage with his arms tied. And he couldn't run far if he tried—even if he regained his strength.

I dragged him along down a road that ran parallel to the creek. I don't think he quite knew where he was and what had happened. But I didn't trust him. I figured he'd try something if he got the opportunity.

There was a pickup truck off to the side of the road with its lights on. The driver seemed about ready to pull out, but I stepped out in front of the headlights. I kept a grip on one of Hooker's arms. The driver rolled down the window a crack.

I said, "My car got washed into the creek. We need help.

He almost drowned."

"What's with his arms like that?"

"He tried to rob me. I can explain. I need something to tie him up better."

"Rob you?" I didn't think the guy trusted me. Why should he? We were an odd sight. Maybe we'd try to rob *him*.

"It's a long story. Got any rope?"

Hooker ripped his arms away from me. He'd been faking it. He shot down the road about twenty yards and tripped over his feet. His face struck the asphalt.

I approached him cautiously like I would a wounded animal. There was a fresh gash on his cheek. The makeshift binding had come loose, and his arms were free. He leaped up and pulled something out of his jeans. It was a small switchblade. He shook it open and thrust the blade in my direction, the steel catching the headlight beams from the truck.

"I ain't going to no jail," he said.

I backed away again, keeping a focus on the knife as I sized him up. He made another thrust, but it was unsteady and weak. As one knee seemed to buckle, I seized the wrist holding the knife and directed it away from me. I knelt and brought his forearm hard against the top of my thigh. I heard a snap. He shrieked in pain, and the knife fell to the ground. I kicked him in the nose, right where I hit him earlier with my elbow. He fell backward and lay still.

"You asked for it, you ungrateful piece of garbage," I said. I picked up the knife and hurled it as far as I could.

The driver had exited his truck and ran toward me. He must have seen it all, and I think it convinced him that I'd been telling the truth. He carried a stretch of wire and handed it to me.

"Looks like you really do need this," he said.

"Thanks. He's psycho," I said.

The man pressed down on the back of Hooker's neck as I took the wire and tied Hooker's arms together at his back with one end. I tied the other end around his ankles. He screamed in pain.

"My arm's broke in two. I ain't gonna run."

"I might just toss you back in that river. Start saying your prayers." I was still plenty mad at him.

I turned to the man and said, "Can we put him in the back of your truck?"

"Sure."

We took Hooker by each shoulder and dragged him over to the truck. The man let down the back of the truck, and we slid Hooker in. The rain had almost stopped.

"My arm's in two pieces, man. My nose is broke," Jesse moaned.

"Complain to the police. They'll get you a doctor," I said, as we slammed the back of the truck shut.

"Nate Burton," I said to the man.

"Gus Hawley," he replied. We shook hands.

I said, "Can you take me to the mall? I guarantee there will be cops there. That's where he tried to rob me. I was making the theater deposit. I'm the manager of the Yorktowne Theater."

As he took in all I had said, I got my first clear look at him, and I was glad he now trusted me. He looked strong and in shape.

"*Jaws* is playing there, right?"

"You got it."

"I was planning on seeing it with my boy tomorrow."

"Take me to the mall, and you've got passes for tomorrow. Your pick of seats."

"Dang, Bobby's gonna love it. Let's go."

We shook hands again. I jumped into the front passenger seat. He gunned the engine, and we headed toward the mall.

CHAPTER FIFTY-THREE

I counted five police cars and two ambulances surrounding the bank entrance, all with lights flashing. Two TV vans had also arrived. The eerie form of Samantha lay with Spence's sickle still lodged upright in her chest. It was a bizarre, grisly scene reminding me of the last part of *Chinatown*, when Faye Dunaway's dead body spills from her car as Jack Nicholson opens the driver's side door. We had played the movie for most of the previous summer. Less than half an hour had passed since Hooker had forced me to drive away with him, a gun pressed against my neck, but it seemed a light year. I was glad to see Detective Dupree standing near one of the police cars, his mouth to a radio receiver. This would make things go much smoother.

I said, "Wait here a second, Mr. Hawley. I'll get the police to deal with this guy. I recognize one of them."

"He's not going anywhere," Hawley said.

I glanced at Hooker. He lay curled up in one corner, his eyes squinting and focused on me.

"Everything hurts," he said.

"If you hadn't tried to kill me twice, I'd feel sorry for you."

And, anyway, my face stung from a cut, my eyes ached from fighting the foul creek water, and my lungs hurt from being stretched to their limit.

"I won't gonna kill you," he groaned.

"Yeah, right." I walked away.

As I got close to the crime tape, an officer came over and stopped me from going any further.

"Hey, Detective Dupree, over here, over here," I called out.

I waved, and he looked over my way and recognized me. He put his hand on the shoulder of one of the officers, said a few words, and strode toward me.

"What in tarnation? Did someone drag you through a wet briar patch?"

"You've got that about right."

"They tell me both Bernie and your friend Reeves are in the hospital. That must be Reeve's car, the one with the bullet hole in the window. And this poor, crazy woman has what looks like a spear *a*-lodged in her chest. I mean, what exactly transpired here?"

"I can explain it all. But do you know whether Detective Riggs and Mr. Reeves are okay?

"I'd like to know too. I'll be getting word shortly."

"I'm real concerned, because Detective Riggs got hit by lightning, and Spence took a bullet in the side."

"Don't like the sound of neither. Now, how about you fill me in."

"I will, but can you come over to that guy's truck first? We've got Jesse Hooker tied up in the back."

"What? Hooker? Let me see."

Hawley was standing by his truck, gawking at all the activity.

I said, pointing at Hooker, "That lowlife pulled a gun on

me first and then kidnapped me. We ended up underwater in a flooded creek. Had to tie him up with Mr. Hawley's wire. Otherwise, he'd have tried to do me in again. His arm's busted."

After Dupree gave Hawley a polite nod, he directed a flashlight into the back the truck revealing Hooker's curled up shape.

"He looks like a caught possum," Dupree said. Hooker moaned, his eyes reflecting back the flashlight beam.

"Well, the rascal did try to play dead a while ago," I said.

Dupree introduced himself to Mr. Hawley and called for help. Two officers came over.

"You fellahs, if you don't mind, keep him company for a while. I need to get statements from these two gentlemen. Looks like this one needs medical attention," Dupree said, pointing toward me.

"It can wait," I said, although I hurt all over.

Mr. Hawley gave Dupree a summary of how I how had stopped him and asked for help. As soon as Dupree got Hawley's number and address, Hawley was eager to leave.

"Which show tomorrow?" I asked him.

"Second?"

"Got it. Just ask for me. Starts at three-fifteen, but come early so I can find you good seats."

He thanked me and took off for home.

"So," Dupree said, flipping to the next page in his notepad with a flourish. "Fill me in. What in holy hell happened? How is it that you ended up miles away from here in that creek—and now here with this, miscreant, Jesse

Hooker? He looks like a mutt with rabies. I ain't Albert Einstein, so take it slow."

He didn't ask many questions. Mostly, he punctuated my account with a variety of colorful expletives. By this time, the area had been photographed and gone over. TV reporters continued to press for statements. I avoided them. A van spirited Samantha away to a place I hoped I wouldn't visit anytime soon. They'd probably find out more about her from Hooker, who by now had been taken away by the two officers watching him. Not sure there was much more to know.

"And by the way," Dupree said. "I had an interesting exchange with a couple who saw your shark movie tonight—right after the second show let out. I was keeping a watch in the parking lot area, you know, for most of the evening. The man was bawling like a baby. His wife was comforting him. I went over to make sure they were okay. The guy was at least in his 50s, and you don't see that happen."

"Why was he upset?"

"Turns out he was a Navy vet whose ship sunk during the last part of World War II. Many of his buddies were killed by sharks as they waited to be picked up by other ships. It was a nasty business. He was one of the few lucky ones to survive."

"Wow. Poor guy. There is a scene in the movie where Quint, the guy who leads the shark hunt, remembers the sinking of the Indianapolis and all the sailors who were killed by sharks. He was one of the survivors. This event actually happened. It was horrible."

Dupree said, "Never heard of it."

"Me neither. Ah, so he didn't like the movie?" I asked, hoping this wouldn't be a general reaction.

"No, no. His wife said it was good for him. Cathartic. He'd never really talked about what had happened during the sinking. He'd kept it bottled in."

"It was maybe the most powerful scene in the movie—now that I think about it."

"Anyway," Dupree said emphatically. "It's more than just a mindless scare movie. It's special."

It was almost five o'clock, and I was bone-tired and sore. Maybe a paramedic could have checked me out, but I wanted to stop by the hospital. Someone could look me over there if I needed it. I asked Dupree if I might drive Spence's car.

"Under the circumstances, I'm going to look the other way," he said.

"Take good care of Spence's sickle."

"Roger, that. And, son, make sure you get that scrape on your face checked out at the hospital. And your eyes too."

"Good idea," I said.

I chugged off in the Electra.

CHAPTER FIFTY-FOUR

I found Riggs wearing a hospital gown and sitting in a chair next to Spence's bed. A plasma bag hung on one side, and a tube fed into Spence's arm. Spence was in worse shape than Riggs, probably because he'd lost so much blood, especially for a man his age.

Dupree had called ahead, and so they'd been expecting me. He'd also given Riggs a brief rundown of what had happened, but I filled them in on more details.

"I envy you and Spence," Riggs said. "Both of you have had interesting rides with Jesse Hooker—and lived to tell the tale."

"I'm no Spence Reeves," I said. "And I'm no good at tossing spears."

"Now that I'd like to have seen," Riggs said.

"It was a miracle throw," I said. "And, Spence, I saw that curveball you threw her first, opening the driver's door and coming out the other."

Spence grinned and said, "I reckon that was a nifty move. Had to make it count. Leastwise she might have killed me and you both."

Spence stopped. He seemed out of energy.

"Mr. Reeves, you need to rest. The nurse doesn't want you talking," Riggs said with a serious look on his face.

I put a hand on Spence's shoulder and said, "Spence, you keep quiet."

Spence said, his energy fading, "Well, won't only me tossed it, as I see it. The man who made it, he helped. Though, maybe I did most of the tossing." He smiled and laughed again, even more weakly. I sensed the presence of another man, straddling a century and two continents. I swear I felt him next to us. Spence's eyes closed, and he drifted off into sleep. I studied his face. Fresh swirls of silver stubble spread across his cheeks. He now looked every one of those eighty-plus years.

"I've got the biggest lump in my throat," I said.

"Me too. Let's leave him be," Riggs said in a whisper.

"Yeah," I agreed. Riggs turned off the fluorescent light spanning the back of the hospital bed.

Riggs said, "I love this job."

"But you about died back there."

"And that's one reason I love it. I told you I'd been a lawyer. Always wanted to be one. Like my dad was. What I didn't know was that I'd hate it. I'll tell you why in a moment."

We left Spence's room, quietly closing his door.

Riggs said, "One of Spence's daughters has been contacted. She's on her way."

"There'll be a mess of his family crawling all over this place soon."

"Let's go to my room," Riggs said, "I'm supposed to be in bed too. They're probably looking for me. My nurse will give me hell. My wife too when she gets here. Had to see Mr. Reeves."

"Yeah," I said.

Riggs and I hightailed it to his room.

Near his room was a nurse with a worried expression on her face, and standing with his back to us, a tall, silver-haired man with a doctor's white coat.

"Uh-oh," said Riggs.

The nurse noticed Riggs, and the doctor spun around. I recognized him. It was Dr. Halderman, his tanned face crumpled up with irritation, his eyes looking daggers at us.

"There he is," said the nurse. "I told him not to move, Dr. Halderman."

"Gird your loins," Riggs said under his breath. Then he called out, "This is all my fault. Nurse Withers told me to stay put. My fault, my fault. I needed to see my friend, Mr. Reeves, who came in with me in the ambulance—"

"Mr. Riggs, I can't have you going against my orders," snapped Halderman.

"I know. It won't happen again," Riggs said apologetically.

"Good."

The nurse took Riggs by the arm and led him to his room. She said, "You just keep calm, Mr. Riggs. We don't want you getting excited. Someone will give you another EKG soon."

Halderman must have been on call for the night and, as a heart doctor, was the specialist taking care of Riggs. Once Riggs was back in his room, Halderman wrote something in an open chart at the nurse's station. Gathering enough courage, I approached him.

I said, "Mr. Reeves helped save Detective Riggs's life a few hours ago. I was there. That's why he left his bed, to thank him."

He kept writing and without turning said,

"He needs to stay in his bed."

"I understand, Dr. Halderman," I said. I waited for a few seconds, trying to think of what I could add. His pager rang. He examined it and bolted down the hallway without giving me another look, just like when I tore his ticket stub a few days earlier.

The nurse left to attend to something else, and this allowed me an opportunity to slip into Riggs's room. He was already in his bed with a sheet covering him.

"Don't be put off by his style, Nate. He knows what he's doing. It was stupid of me to leave the bed. I do feel a little woozy."

"Yeah, maybe you deserved it. But I don't have to like him. He gives me a strange feeling, I don't know, like I need to give a sieg heil."

"The fact is, I wouldn't be putting one foot after the other if you hadn't got up on that roof and got me breathing again."

"Well, the fact is if you hadn't been *up* on that roof, *I* wouldn't be breathing. Samantha, or I should say, Lucille, would have probably shot me before Spence tossed that spear. I've got to know. How did you figure she and Jesse Hooker would show up at the mall?"

"I'm not sure I thought it likely. Mr. Reeves told me he'd look out for you when you left, but the more I considered it, the more I just got this strong feeling. I doubled back from home. There was a lot of money in those deposit bags."

"That reminds me. I need to find out where my Dart ended up. Those bags are still in my front seat."

Riggs said, "Lonnie Dupree will be working on that."

"How did you get on that roof?" I asked.

"I came up the back way, after the security guy let me in. Almost left the roof when the storm got close, but a little earlier I had seen an extra car pull up. I wanted to keep a watch on it."

I said, "I guess it was clever to make it look like they'd left town."

Riggs said, "And they changed cars. Probably stolen."

"You went to a lot of trouble over a feeling. I'm glad you did."

"I suppose there's a rough justice in all that's happened."

"Yeah."

"You must be beat. And five shows tomorrow, right? And Mr. Reeves won't be working for a while."

"I need to get some sleep. I'm hoping Milton Spicer can help out for a few weeks. I'll make it worth his while."

Riggs said, "Before you leave, see my jacket on over there. Look in the inside pocket. There're some brochures for you."

I examined Riggs's jacket, still damp from the rain. Three brochures jutted out of the inside pocket, for DePaul, Northwestern, and the University of Chicago.

Riggs said, "My son requested them when he was deciding where to apply two years ago. He's at Carolina, a sophomore now. I thought you might use them. Was going to give them to you earlier."

"I really appreciate this, Detective Riggs." I felt a flood of emotions. To have him looking out for me like this—the kind of thing my dad would have done if he were around. I gave him a long hug.

"These are some of the schools I've been thinking about." How had he figured this out?

"Don't sell yourself short."

Riggs stared up at the ceiling for a moment and then turned to me. He said,

"I was going to tell you why I quit being a lawyer."

"I've been wanting to know."

"You see, one day, early on in the law firm where I worked, I was sitting at my desk with a pile of briefs. I dropped my pencil on the floor. I stared at it. And stared at it. But I couldn't pick it up. I was that depressed. Law, fine for my dad, wasn't for me. But I knew that every time I'd met a detective, I wished I was doing what he was doing. I switched careers. Haven't looked back."

He gave me another steady look. He continued,

"And you might need a letter of recommendation for one of those institutions of higher learning. You've got one from me if you need it. From the very first I figured you for the 'a' team, not the 'b' team."

"I don't know what to say, Detective Riggs," I stuttered.

"Hey, hand me that cup of water."

There was a hospital cup just beyond Riggs's easy reach. I handed it to him, and he finished its contents in one gulp. We were thinking the same thing, the funny scene in *Jaws* when Hooper crushes a Styrofoam cup with exaggerated bravado in response to Quint's crushing a beer can. We stared into each other's eyes with mock intensity. Hooper to my Quint, he crushed the cup.

"Now get out of here before we get into more trouble. We'll talk about it later. I mean it, git," Riggs said.

I did as I was told and almost knocked Nurse Withers over as I exited the room. I apologized and kept moving.

Before leaving the hospital, I wanted to check in on Spence one more time. I returned to the corridor where his room was and peered through the small window of the corridor entrance door. A group of people stood near his room. One was Halderman, along with a nurse, having a conversation with Ricardo and his mom. I wondered whether this was why Halderman sped away so quickly. I hesitated. I didn't want to insert myself into a family situation. Nor did I want to aggravate Halderman yet another time. He might go at me with cleavers. No one seemed distressed, and so I figured Spence must be fine. Dead-tired and relieved that Spence seemed okay, I decided to leave.

I noticed a water fountain and took a few gulps. I hadn't realized how thirsty I was.

Halderman came through the door. We locked stares. I assumed he'd just continue on his way, but he came up to me. My first instinct was to apologize again.

"Dr. Halderman, I'm sorry about earlier. Can I ask how Mr. Reeves is doing?"

His face turned surprisingly reflective.

"Mr. Reeves has the body of a man of fifty. He'll be fine. Buffalo soldiers are a tough breed."

"That's for sure," I said, sensing a genuine warmth coming from Halderman.

"He told me how they got their name," Halderman continued. "One of the early Buffalo Soldiers single-handedly fought off about seventy Cheyenne warriors. All he had was a pistol. By the time help arrived, he'd killed thirteen of those warriors, and been shot and stabbed. He lived to tell the tale. Turned out that word got about among the Cheyenne of a new kind of soldier, who, like a cornered buffalo, kept fighting despite repeated wounds. Mr. Reeves is in the same mold."

I shuddered all over. I hadn't heard this story.

His pager went off.

"One more thing," Halderman said, as he examined the pager. "I plan on using those passes you gave me, for that shark movie. Perhaps, then, we can be properly introduced."

He raced down the corridor.

I'll be damned, I thought.

I needed to get home for some rest. Mrs. Roe's house was no more than a twenty-minute walk from the hospital. I headed home on foot.

CHAPTER FIFTY-FIVE

As I came up the driveway, I detected movement through the kitchen window. A face peered out at me. But then its features seemed to scramble together. It was the window glass, distorted by age, catching the first light of the morning sun, just lifting across the horizon.

Byron must have heard my feet hitting the back steps because he made a ruckus. A scratching behind the ears calmed him down. Marion Lester had already been over to let him out and feed him. I poured myself a glass of orange juice as Keats appeared and wove his shoulders back and forth against my legs. I found a fresh apple and began eating it for a quick breakfast.

My attention was drawn to the unfinished jigsaw puzzle, untouched since Mrs. Roe had passed away. As I worked my way around the apple, I studied the puzzle for the first time with the goal of finishing it. A piece of solid blue caught my attention, its shape suggesting it might fit near the upper corner. It did, giving me a small pleasure.

But what I needed to do was take a shower and set the alarm for three hours of sleep. I was feeling the full effects of all that had happened during the day. I'd never felt so worn out, so spent.

I tossed the apple core in the kitchen trash and noticed a letter with "Nate" written on it, placed to the counter next to the sink. I open it and unfolded a note it contained.

Dear Nate,

I saw on the TV about the long lines at the theater for the new movie. I know you must have had a trying day.

I have some very good news for you. I have recently had the opportunity to sit down with her attorney to go over Hillary's will. Within the last couple of months, Hillary made some changes. Originally, as she had no immediate relatives, she planned on leaving all of her estate to the local Humane Society. However, she had altered it in one significant way and in one small way. You will be pleased to know that she has left you $30,000 in an educational trust toward paying for a college of your choice.

We can discuss all this very soon of course. It will take a while for the estate to go through probate. I am very happy for you. I know Hillary would be gratified to know that she could give your life a boost in this way.

Marion

One more thing, I almost forgot. The other change made has to do with a piece of jewelry. Hillary also left you a small ring—the one she usually wore—the one that gave her a "certain power."

A rush of feelings welled up in me as I read the letter. Mrs. Roe's recognizing my learning problem had already realigned my beliefs about what I could do, and now she was giving me a clear path toward a college education. And the ring too. A new sense of the course my future would take filled me gratitude.

The doorbell chimed.

Byron came to attention, directing both ears toward the front door. Was this Marion? No. I could make out a smaller, thinner shape through the door's panes of frosted glass. I turned the porch light on and opened the door.

It was Carrie.

"Nate, I'm so—"

"Carrie."

I stood, frozen, for a moment. She seemed to freeze as well. Then, suddenly, she rushed forward and threw her arms around me tight. So surprised by what was happening, I remained rigid, awkward, unable to return to her embrace, overwhelmed by her sudden presence.

"I heard the sirens. And then the news on the radio at home. It mentioned a robbery at the mall." Her curls pressed against my face bringing with them the smell of rain mixed with her soapy, sweet scent.

Carrie released her arms and took a step back and said, "I drove to the mall, and they told me that you were visiting Spence and Detective Riggs at Duke Hospital. By the time I got there you had left. Detective Riggs gave me your address."

"I'm fine. You didn't need to." I was thrilled, in fact.

"Your cheek. There's a scrape," Carrie said, her face filled with concern. "Didn't they look at it?" She placed her right hand on my chin, shifting to adjust the angle for more light. "This needs better cleaning."

"Really, it's fine," I said. But she insisted, and I liked the attention. I led her to the kitchen, Byron trailing behind us, excited over having a visitor. I searched the cabinets and found Mrs. Roe's first aid kit.

Carrie tore open a packet of gauze from the kit, moistened a section, dabbed at the wound, and then applied a touch of iodine to it. As she did this, I answered her eager questions about how I'd received the wound and what had happened at the mall. Some details she already knew through Dupree and Riggs. Some others I left out for another day. All the while, I couldn't quite believe she was there.

"So you didn't get to see Spence," I said.

"No, they told me he was sleeping. He was with family too."

"He'd lost a lot of blood. He's strong though," I said.

"Yeah. I'm so glad he followed you. And, Nate, do you realize Spence can barely read or write?"

"Really?" I was astounded. And how had I missed it? Ricardo must have helped him with the paperwork for his rental property. Of course.

"I overheard a nurse saying this to Detective Riggs. She had asked Spence to sign a form, but she had to read most of it to him. He signed it with something closer to an 'X' than his full name. What's wrong. You're tearing up, Nate."

"I mean, this is the United States of America," I said, with no embarrassment over my tears. "This, this country robbed him. What would Spence have become if he'd been born at a later time? A general, a professor? An archaeologist searching for the grave of an ancient African king? Anything he damn wanted to be."

"Dreams deferred," Carrie said. "They dry up like a raisin in the sun."

"And yet, you know, Spence wouldn't want our pity," I said, quickly composing myself. "He's not a bitter man, nor one unfulfilled, at least as far as I can read him. He once told me that a man's life was mostly clay in his own hands—though he put a lot of emphasis on *mostly*. I'm so proud of him."

"Me too. He's a man for the ages." Carrie's eyes widened with energy. Her eyes had teared up too. The alignment of our feelings stirred me to my core.

The book of Frost's poems was on the counter where I'd left it a few days earlier, and it caught Carrie's notice. She picked it up and thumbed through a few pages, her face lighting up when she came across the familiar favorite. I wanted to kiss her.

She said, "Ah, two roads."

"You know that one well," I said, laughing.

But she seemed more focused on the poem, scanning it, even though she knew it by heart. About halfway through, she began reading it out loud.

"Because it was grassy and wanted wear;
Though as for that the passing there
Had worn them really about the same.
And both that morning equally lay
In leaves no step had trodden black."

She stopped and looked up at me. We seemed to be thinking alike.

"Really about the same," Carrie repeated the line.

"Yes," I said. "Really about the same."

"We have it wrong." Carrie recited the rest of the poem, her voice excited.

> *"Oh, I kept the first for another day!*
> *Yet knowing how way leads on to way,*
> *I doubted if I should ever come back.*
> *I shall be telling this with a sigh*
> *Somewhere ages and ages hence:*
> *Two roads diverged in a wood, and I—*
> *I took the road less traveled by*
> *And that has made all the difference."*

I said, "Of course. Why didn't we see it? Frost is not saying to take the road less traveled by."

Carrie added, "His main point is a different twist, very different."

"Both roads were much same," I said.

"They equally lay. Equally."

"And why the 'signing'? Because—"

"Because you will probably never come back."

We exchanged intense looks of revelation. I drank in the pleasure of agreement. Did Carrie also feel the same chills that I did? It seemed so.

I would have to make good choices. Mrs. Roe's recognizing my learning problem had indeed realigned my beliefs about what I could do. What would I do with this knowledge—now that she had also given me financial resources? Riggs had taken charge of his life, and this had made him happy. The brochures he had given me signaled me to take charge as well. I would find a way to follow Carrie to the University of Chicago, or a place close by. I was sure I could do it. But, now, looking straight into Carrie's bright, welcoming eyes, I decided there was one choice I could make then and there—and I did.

ACKNOWLEDGMENTS

Vaida Thompson, Stephen Thielke, Josh Gressel, Delbert Ault, and Mark Alicke read early drafts and gave very helpful feedback. Particular thanks to Ken Wetherington and Monica Kern who offered especially detailed comments. To all these folks, I am very grateful. I also received excellent editorial suggestions from Andrew Shaffer, Robin Baskette, and Laurie Boris. Maria Novillo Saravia of BEAUTeBOOK designed a fitting cover and helped with the nuts and bolts of getting the book ready for publication. My daughters, Rosanna and Caroline, as well as my brother, Eric, read an early version and gave me the needed encouragement to finish it. My sister, Helen, and my brother-in-law, Arch, provided astute advice as I developed the story idea. Lastly, my wife, Sung Hee, was a constant cheerleader and a constructive, patient commenter throughout.

ABOUT THE AUTHOR

Richard H. Smith is a social psychologist and freelance writer. He is the author of *The Joy of Pain: Schadenfreude and the Dark Side of Human Nature.*

Made in the USA
Middletown, DE
19 June 2020